The Safety of Deeper Water

A Novel

Tim Poland

Vandalia Press

MORGANTOWN 2008

Vandalia Press, Morgantown 26506

© 2008 by West Virginia University Press. All rights reserved.

First edition published 2008 by West Virginia University Press.

Vandalia Press is an imprint of West Virginia University Press.

Printed in the United States of America.

15 14 13 12 11 10 09 08   1 2 3 4 5 6 7 8 9

Library of Congress Cataloguing-in-Publication Data
Poland, Tim.
  The safety of deeper water : a novel / Tim Poland.
      p. cm.
  ISBN 978-1-933202-32-7 (pbk. : alk. paper)
  1. Women fishers--Fiction. 2. Prisoners' spouses--Fiction. 3. Fly fishing-
-Fiction. 4.   Appalachian Region, Southern--Fiction. 5.   Mountain life--
Fiction. 6. Domestic fiction. I. Title.
  PS3566.O419S34 2009
  813'.54--dc22
Library of Congress Control Number: 2008941275

Cover Design: by Than Saffel / Vandalia Press.
Cover Image: Photograph by James Lady / http://stillwaterstudio.us
Interior layout by Rachel Rosolina / Vandalia Press

This novel is a work of fiction. All characters and events are of the author's imagination. Any resemblance to actual people is entirely coincidental. The prologue of this novel, "A Fish Like That," first appeared, in a different form, under the title "Escapee" in *The Beloit Fiction Journal* and subsequently as the title story of *Escapee* (America House, 2001).

Mixed Sources
Product group from well-managed forests and recycled wood or fiber
www.fsc.org Cert no. BV-COC-070702
FSC   © 1996 Forest Stewardship Council

The Safety of Deeper Water

for my mother and father
and
to the memory of Scott Christianson (1955–2004)

Acknowledgments

I owe a debt of gratitude to those who gave so selflessly of their time to read early versions of this novel and offer invaluable guidance: K. Gorcheva-Newberry, Donald Seacreast, Lisa Faith Phillips, and Gerri Glass. This work could never have been completed without the tireless efforts of Rosemary Fithian-Guruswamy, who scheduled my teaching life to allow time for my writing life as well. And my sincere thanks to the editors at West Virginia University Press, who reached down the throat of one book and helped me pull out a better one.

A Fish Like That

One of the first things Sandy did after it was all over and she had the house to herself was to open his tackle box. She thought she would be lonely, miss him, and that touching the contents of the box might ignite a contact with him. Manslaughter. He'd been sentenced to five years in the Bland County Correctional Facility for manslaughter. Five years would roll out long and slow if she waited for him. She would touch something. Something of his, of him. Something to keep the connection unbroken, if there had ever been a connection at all. Something to maintain her contact with his certainty, his plan. Fishing had been his only peaceful pleasure, had been since boyhood. When fishing, he came as close as he ever would to serenity. The tackle box seemed a likely place to start.

Hooks, leaders and small pliers, pellets of split-shot, a spool of line, red and white bobbers of different sizes and shapes, a bottle opener, a stringer, and assorted lures. All neatly arranged in compartments on hinged trays that rose out of the box as the lid opened. She stroked the contents smoothly, tentatively, cautious not to snag a finger on a hook. These were his things, but nothing electric had yet fired in her fingertips. She lightly tapped a purple, rubber worm, skewered with hooks, and remembered a story he had told of seeing someone eat one of these worms on a dare. Sure enough, he had seen it with his own eyes. Was that a fish story, and if true, had that someone taken the hooks out first? She remembered, too, how surprised she had been when she first realized that his fishing stories didn't really bore her as she thought they should. She actually listened to them sometimes.

Despite the careful course her hands followed through the tackle box, she pricked a finger on a shiny, plastic minnow, gaudy and insidious, thickly trimmed with pendants of hooks. She sucked a droplet of blood from her fingertip and dropped the lure back into the box, pronouncing that one simply too vicious, a glistening, garish traitor to the living fish its design aimed to seduce.

"Dardevle," she said, quietly reading the odd spelling of the worn writing on another lure.

Clean and precise, red and white bands on one side, silver on the other, shaped like the business end of a small spoon, with a single pendant of three hooks. She liked this one, its cool smoothness, and rubbed its surface between her thumb and forefinger, then spun it, soothed by the fluctuating silver and red and white.

"Take the hooks off, and this would make a nice earring," she said to herself.

Shoved into a corner in the bottom of the tackle box, a tiny plastic case. The flies she bought to go with the inexpensive fly rod and reel she gave him for a birthday present once. It seemed a good idea at the time. He had never had a fly rod, and when she rented a copy of *A River Runs Through It*, he said he liked the fishing scenes. The characters were a bit preachy and teachy for his taste, he said, but they seemed like real folks and the fishing was good. He said he would cut off his left nut to catch a trout like the one Brad Pitt got at the end, right before he got killed.

She always wondered at the oath of mutilating testicles as a show of sincerity. Cut off his left nut. And why the left one? What made that one, in particular, so special, so appropriate for sacrifice?

"Fish like that, be worth dying for," he had said.

But he had never fished with her gift. He tried casting with the long, willowy rod in the backyard but got the line tangled around his neck and shoulders.

"Too much trouble. Too much work. But thanks anyway, babe," he had said, embarrassed to have to relearn something he thought he already knew. Besides, what he claimed he liked most about fishing was just sitting on the bank, relaxed, watching his bobber, knocking back a few beers. Too much work, fly fishing. He jammed the box of flies into the bottom of his tackle box and set the fly rig in the back of his closet and never touched them again.

It had been a good idea, worth a try, but the tackle box had failed. No spark of contact had flared. He remained fully absent. She could try other things that were his. She might come back to the tackle box later.

Her breath blew steam lightly across a hot cup of herbal tea she carried gingerly down the hallway to their bedroom. Before they arrested him, she had never slept a night without him since their marriage. She thought of that as she sat on the bed and carefully placed the cup of tea on the nightstand. She ran her hand over rumpled sheets and knew she wouldn't cry. She had cried at first, almost an involuntary, electrical reaction. But she had finished with it weeks ago, quickly spent with crying for two men, one a husband to be locked away from her in a prison for five years, the other, red-haired and dead with his forehead split open on a lacquered bar top.

She pressed her face down onto the mattress and breathed deeply through the bedding. Nothing. After a few sips of the hot tea, she stepped into his closet and gathered an armful of his abandoned clothing into a deep embrace, rammed her face into the folds, inhaled profoundly. Nothing. Her foot bumped something that rattled and fell to the floor. The fly rig, disassembled and untouched since the only time he ever tried it. Exhaling, she scooped up the pieces of rod, the thin reel still attached to the butt, and walked back to the bed. She laid the fly rig on the bed beside her and slurped more of her tea. As she sipped, she looked down at her fingertips gliding lightly along the rod and reel, tracing the circle of the reel, pinching the line guides, stroking the cool graphite, and she felt it. A tingle, a subtle charge running up her arm from her fingers, a touch of electricity flowing out of the one thing of his he had hardly touched at all.

She finished her tea and sniffed the air of their bedroom. Two years together here and now nothing. Had the change come quickly or had this absence been lurking all along? How could he have lived here with her for two years and left behind no scent? Stale odor of his cigarettes, clothing, work boots, knick-knacks, fishing rods, the tackle box, but no palpable, animal track of his presence. It was her house now. The things he left behind—things she searched, touched, stroked—merely in storage.

* * *

"I don't know how much more of this shit I can take," he said, after she asked how he was, touched his hand, and passed him two rolls of quarters and two cartons of cigarettes across the table. Kissing was not allowed.

Every Sunday for six months now she had made the thirty-mile drive to Bland County for visiting day. She felt a guilty gratitude for his place of incarceration being conveniently located so close to home. A pleasant drive through ancient mountains and valleys to see him. She would have enjoyed the drive, whether to visit him or not. And somehow it fit, seemed appropriate, that he would do his time here, in the county of his birth, only a few miles from where he had grown up, so close to the streams he had fished as a boy. On her first Sunday visit he had told her that, as a child, whenever he passed the prison, he had shivered with a fear that one day he would be forced to live behind the tall cyclone fencing, under the spools of razor-wire, the searchlights, the guard towers. Now, here he sat. Come full circle.

"Hell of a homecoming," he had said.

She glanced quickly at the guards weaving slowly among the long tables in the visiting room. Everything was barred or bolted down. Nothing moved freely except the guards. She set her hands lightly on his hands that still clutched the rolled coins and cigarettes, this new prison currency he now traded in, needed. She struggled to understand it and often shuddered to imagine the possible methods of exchange.

His hands remained fixed and clenched, unresponsive, as she traced the ridges of his knuckles, touching fresh bruises she found there.

"What is it, Vernon? What's wrong?"

He tilted his head to the side and looked at her as if she'd spoken in a foreign language. "You fucking kidding me? What's wrong? What's wrong is I'm in this goddamn place, and everything else is out there. You're out there. Everything. It isn't supposed to be like this."

His face glared back at her dark and rigid, his eyes cold and flat, resentful. An undeniable quiver rippled down her spine into a knot in the small of her back when she realized that this was his face, a new face, different and permanent, not a temporary aberration or trick of the light. When had the change occurred? Had it been sudden or gradual? Had she simply failed to notice? She remembered that during her first visits she had thought it almost sweet, even courageous, how he had tried so hard to be optimistic, upbeat. Tough it out. Tow the line and with luck and good time, he could be out on parole in two and a half, three years, he had said. Things could obviously be better, but they could survive this, he had said. She would still be there, waiting for him, he had said. Of course, she had said.

His new face revealed itself, hard, desperate, and reptilian. He seemed to stare through her, and she wondered if she showed a different face to him through his new eyes.

"What's happened?

"Prison's what happened, goddamn it."

"I'm sure it must be awful."

"You don't know shit. Never will know shit. Can't know shit about the inside unless you're on the inside."

She wondered about his new face and now this new voice, full of prison, as she crossed the parking lot, dropped her purse in the car, and looked into the back seat to check her fishing gear. She hadn't told him that for the last three months she had combined her prison visits with fishing trips to nearby streams where the trout fishing was said to be good. Streams he had fished many times and told her about. She hadn't told him that she had learned to use his fly rod, had practiced casting in the yard behind their house. She hadn't told him that she had first started doing it as an attempt to be nearer to him somehow, to duplicate his life with her own, to complete his life, to use the unused parts, to keep his plan intact while he was locked up. She had even tried to wear his clothes, his gear, sinking her legs into an old pair of waders he occasionally used, but they were simply too big. Her feet could find no footing, flapping loosely in the enormous boots. To tell him would have been cruel, she thought, too much for an imprisoned man who could smash open another man's head on a bar top because that man had tried to buy his wife a drink while he stood across the barroom talking on the telephone. She kept it to herself, fishing in secret. She couldn't tell him that she had dusted off the little plastic case with the flies she had bought him, learned to tie leaders to the fly line and flies to the leader, learned how long to hesitate, drift, before bringing her cast forward, learned how to read the water and to select the proper fly for that water. She couldn't tell him that she had caught and released two small brook trout in the little creek just the other side of the mountain from the prison. She wouldn't tell him that the fishing she had begun as an attempt to sustain a connection with him had become something wholly her own. She liked it. She wore her own new waders now.

* * *

The following Sunday his new face again appeared across from her at the bolted-down table. As she pushed his quarters and cigarettes to him and touched his beaten hands, she thought of the big brook trout she had spied last week lingering in a deep pool under a cutbank and wondered if the same fish would be there this week. She had read that a trout frequently inhabits the same stretch of stream its entire life.

"How are you, Vernon? Any better this week?"

"Just shut up and listen," he said, almost a whisper.

His new face, still cold and fixed, had a new feature. She remembered a word from a high school vocabulary test. *Furtive.* A cold, rigid, furtive face. The word fit.

"And don't look around or make any weird faces. Just sit still and listen, like I'm talking about any old thing."

She kept still and quiet, focused on the odd new face. His eyes followed the movement of the nearest guard.

"I'm getting the fuck out of here."

Her stomach churned and she could feel her sphincter twitch in a tight spasm, but she remained still on the hard, wooden seat.

"You got to get off work on Mondays. Can you do that?"

She nodded too slowly, not speaking. Yes, she could get off. Thanks to a new contract negotiated by the nurses' union, she had staggered schedules and a salary she could get by on while he was here. Yes, she could do it.

"Good. Every Monday we work down in field number three."

She recalled the white barn, marked with a huge black 3 in a circle, set in the middle of a rolling field of timothy. "It's the best spot. A quick run out of the field and disappear into the woods and over the hill. I know that ground like the back of my hand. Used to fish just the other side of that hill when I was a kid."

"But Vernon," she said, and he cut her off, a razor-edged hiss to his whisper.

"No buts. Just listen. All I have to do is wait for a break. For the guards to get distracted. Get out of shotgun range."

"But they could . . ."

"Listen, damn it. It's going to go down. Now, here's where you come in. All you got to do is wait for me with the car."

"Where?"

She eyed a guard walking slowly along the far side of the room.

"Take the forest service road by the little grocery. Follow it a few miles along Dismal Creek till you get to a clearing on the right. There's a National Forest sign says White Pine Horse Camp. There's a little corral there, right by Dismal Creek. Big sign. Can't miss it."

She didn't tell him that she knew the spot, that she'd been fishing there for the last two weeks. His planned getaway rendezvous was the same spot she had seen the big brook trout and after their visit today she would be fishing in that exact same place. She had wondered at first why a creek so lovely, so perfect in its meandering clarity, would be called Dismal. She had thought that perhaps it had been a ruse, a way to disguise the beauty, a name given by a man long ago to discourage outsiders, to keep the creek to himself.

"But Vernon, they could . . ."

"Look. I'm telling you. There's no way I'm going to stick it out here. I have to get out. You just do your part."

Sandy looked at her hands lying flat on his atop the carton of cigarettes. She pulled her hands back, breathed deep and exhaled with a rasp.

"Okay." She heard her own voice speak the word as if it came from the mouth of some other woman. She was still part of his plan, but she no longer felt reassured by that.

"Good. You be there at nine in the morning. Wait until three. If I ain't there by three, I ain't coming that day."

"Okay."

"Just be there every Monday, remember, nine to three, until I get an opening to make my break. Sooner or later, they'll slip up and I'll be gone. Every Monday."

"You'll have to wait a week," she said. "I won't be able to get rescheduled until next Monday."

His new face went flat, blank.

"Well," he said. "Waited this long. Suppose I can handle another week. And then we'll be together. Right, babe?"

"Right," she said, and the image of the big brook trout finning the thick current of the deep pool floated before her.

* * *

She left the car parked by the corral at the edge of the clearing, pointed toward the service road. The clearing unfolded into a grassy apron behind the corral, and she crossed it, moving downstream, and ducked through a stand of rhododendron. After weeks of use, the dense, new-rubber smell of her waders remained strong, gliding up from her thighs to her nose, as she inched across the creek and began to work her way upstream on the far side from the clearing. Her legs were pliant and sure in their new rubber armor, sliding slowly, carefully, along the stony bottom, disturbing little, seeking a firm footing. She scanned the stream's surface, squatting into the riffling water. She rubbed her earring—the

9

red and white Dardevle lure from Vernon's tackle box, now converted to jewelry—plucked a fly from the little plastic case and tied it on.

Her wrist arched deftly as she rolled her line out upstream. She held the rod high and trimmed her line smoothly into a snaking mass, floating in the stream beside her, as she let the fly ride downstream. The current pulled her line until she caught it up, holding the fly in the swirl around the rock where she knew a fish would be waiting. She would then work her way slowly upstream to the deeper pool where the big brook trout would be. She had all day.

Since the escape plan had been set, Sunday visits at the prison had become forced, awkward, neither of them able to pretend to talk of much of anything because the one thing on both their minds was the one thing they could not discuss. She brought his quarters and cigarettes and studied the lines of his new face, the new scars on his hands, and thought of trout waters. She began to check her watch, anxious for the visit to end, anxious to be fishing.

The first Monday she waited at the rendezvous, she did not fish. She kept the car at the ready, pointed out of the clearing, her foot on the accelerator, her ears twitching at any sound that might announce a desperate man, crashing through underbrush and splashing across a stream, armed, angry guards in pursuit. Munching apples, she tried to pass the time reading a recent issue of *Cosmopolitan* she had taken from a waiting lounge at the hospital, an article entitled "Bad Boys and Why We Love Them." The article offered no answers she could use, and she wondered if bad boys were really as "lovable" as the magazine made them out to be. She thought for a brief moment that bad boys who could split open a red-haired man's head in a jealous rage might be better locked away after all. She snapped the magazine shut and threw it in the back seat. She stayed rooted in the driver's seat all day, getting out only to pee behind a thicket, worried that urinating in the open might be taken as a sure sign of guilt by any passerby. She saw no one all day.

The second Monday she sat on the grass in the clearing, alert but relaxed, listening to the gurgling of the creek, and read a copy of *Fly Fisherman* from cover to cover. Escape from a prison farm was no mean feat, and she decided he would come when he came. She began to doubt that he would ever actually be able to make the attempt at all. She might as well make use of her time here. After all, the escape plan afforded her an extra day of fishing each week. Make the most of it.

After a month and a half of Mondays following Sundays along Dismal Creek, waiting for the escape to come, she fell into the rhythm of the waiting, the rhythm of the rushing waters, the rhythm and motion of her cast, her line running out over the rippling surface of the stream, the rhythmic quiver of the tension in her arms as she waited out the completion of her seduction of a trout that would rise to her offering. Waiting there, she became a fly fisher.

By three o'clock she had released three good fish and had been playing tag with the big brook trout in the deep pool for the better part of two hours, trying, resting the water, trying again, still unable to coax him out of his hole, still unable to offer up the right temptation at the right time. But there would be more chances. There would be more Mondays following more Sundays, and the fish would be there waiting. One day she would play him right.

"You just stay right there. See you again next week," she said, out loud, speaking directly to a present companion.

Only as she reeled in her line and stepped out of the stream toward the car did she realize she had not listened once, all day, for the sound of a running man in the surrounding woods.

* * *

On the next Monday, she entered the creek at a point upstream from her usual spot, eased into the shadow of the rhododendron on the far side, and moved gracefully against the current into position to fish the deep pool under the cutbank. Today she was coming right for him.

Her step fell slow and delicate, her own shadow dissolved into that of the rhododendron. He hadn't seen her yet.

She saw him. Flashing on the surface, rolling from the shadows into erratic patches of sunlight leaking through the overhang. He whirled giddy in his deep pool—jubilant, brazen, glutting himself on a rare, heavy hatch.

"There you are. Today," she said, silent, completely to herself. The only sound her body contributed to, the surge of the water around her legs, firm and resilient, set in place in the stream bed, forking the flow.

She fed out line and leader and tied on a fly. The right one. She knew. She could see him feeding.

"Today," she said, almost an audible whisper.

Thumb and forefinger stroked her earring, then dropped to the reel and peeled off line. Her cast was agile, elegant, rolling out upstream, perfectly splitting the close overhang. She held high and trimmed in time with the flow of the current until she placed the fly on the rippling edge of the pool. Pull and release, take and give, rhythmic and regular, she kept the fly at the edge of his pool, inching it out onto the calmer surface against the sucking current, floating well, a dance of simulation. She stood fast, focused, waited at the ready. He fed voraciously, but hers was only one seduction among many. She would have to wait, play him carefully, but he would come. Soon he would rise, come to her.

The angle of light through the rhododendron shifted through the morning as she worked his pool, rested the water, worked his pool again, patient, deliberate, confident. She adjusted and recast when the current jerked her line off target. She flicked false casts over the surface to dry her fly and line when it began to slip under, reeled in and blew on her fly to fluff the hackles.

Another change in the angle of light, and his pool came into high relief, visible to its full depth. She had him in clear focus as he flashed and shot back to the creek bed. Her cast was perfect, silent, natural, and her fly rode effortlessly onto the surface of his pool. She was ready. Her finger locked her line against the rod grip. She had waited weeks for him. Now he was coming. She inhaled. He saw it. She didn't breathe. He rose. She waited. He flashed. She set it.

Too soon. She flinched as she moved to set the hook and missed him. A distant sound, a sharp report, rolling down the mountain through the woods broke her balance. What was it? Gunfire? And now what? So distant yet audible. Voices? The crackle and whoosh of the bodies of men running through thick brush. He was coming.

She gazed vaguely through the woods in the direction of the approaching sounds. He was coming. She had waited weeks for him, and now he was coming. Now, of all times. She was set, ready, and now he was coming. Snapping brush grew louder. Shouting voices became nearly intelligible. The rush of water around her legs was thick and inviting. Now he was coming.

She looked once, long and deep, at the pool, at the big brook trout still flashing joyfully, and lunged from the stream onto the bank. Dragging her unreeled line, she broke down her rod on the run, the tops of her waders flapping against her thighs. Her pulse pounded as she stumbled against the corral and lurched forward to the car. As she ripped the car door open and flung the pieces of her fly rig into the back seat, she shot a glance toward the creek as he broke through the rhododendron and pitched forward into the water. Farther back in the brush she could just make out the intermittent dark blue of the guards' uniforms and hear their shouts. She had waited weeks for him and now he was coming.

"Move it, babe. Goddamn move it," Vernon shouted, as he stumbled across the stream.

She jammed herself into the driver's seat, bulky in her waders, and fired the ignition. A quick look in the rearview mirror revealed him emerging from the creek and bolting into the clearing toward the revving, waiting car. Everything had built to this moment. The planning, the waiting. She must act quickly, decisively. Everything depended on it. Just as he reached the car, panting, soaked and desperate, she snapped the door locks and slammed down on the accelerator, swerving out of the clearing and spraying gravel in the face of the stranded convict.

Filtered through the roar of the engine and the clatter of gravel against the underbelly of the car, she could just hear his frantic voice, screaming.

"What the hell are you doing? Stop. You crazy fucking bitch. Sandy, goddamn it, stop."

At the moment she spun out of the clearing onto the service road, she could just see from the corner of her eye the guards burst from the rhododendron and draw down on the abandoned escapee in the clearing.

Her foot in her waders stayed firmly on the accelerator until she reached the main road. Sliding from the gravel surface onto smoother pavement, she cut her speed a bit as a line of prison vehicles, lights strobing, sirens screaming, turned past her at the little grocery and rocketed down the service road.

Her pulse began to settle as she eased through the curves in the road. It had been a close call. She had barely escaped. She had waited weeks, months for him. Her fly rig rattled in the back seat in rhythm with the vibrations of the moving car. Weeks, months of waiting. She could wait another week. A fish like that was worth waiting for.

"Fish like that, be worth dying for."

1

The Watershed

Some time ago, Inmate #52674 at the Bland County Correctional Facility wrote and mailed the following letter:

Dear Sandy,

You heartless bitch. How could you? All the planning. The waiting. It could have worked. You said you'd be there for me. You promised. You were part of the plan. And then you just left me standing there, likely to get shot. Goddamn it, I'm your husband. Who are you? My wife? The one I love? The one I killed for? Who are you? And what were you doing there? Were you fishing? Is that what I saw? Damn you, you rotten traitor.

Don't suppose you'll be coming to visit me now, right? But you ought to. You owe me. You owe me an explanation.

Your Loving Husband,

Vernon

The letter was duly delivered, but received no response.

* * *

Something moist and warm like breath licks her ear. She swats at it as she would a mosquito or gnat and jerks her head around, searching for its source. Nothing. No one. Nothing but a tickling breeze at her neck and the empty, narrow path leading away into the thick brush. Vernon wouldn't be coming for her now. He wouldn't be released for another five months yet.

Alone on the bank, Sandy Holston turns back to the river. Her rod cocked against her shoulder, she waits for the surging water to recede and settle. She waits and watches. Her free hand roams her fishing vest, patting, pinching, probing, squeezing, casually reviewing each compartment. Fly box, forceps, leader, water bottle, knife, flashlight, an extra scrunchie, a packet of tissues, two tampons, split-shot. Out of habit she fingers the old lure dangling from her left ear lobe. Never had she fished with such clunky gear, but she admired the smooth simplicity of the old lure, one side silver, the other marked by bands of fading red and white, worn from her ritual of rubbing the earring before moving into the water.

A kingfisher strafes the surface of the rushing water, turns into an abrupt upswing, and perches on a sycamore branch, its metallic squawk rattling across the stream. Sandy checks her wristwatch. Another minute or two. The hydroelectric dam upstream should have stopped generating power about a half-hour ago, according to the posted schedule. It should take that long for the decreased water level to arrive this far downstream. Another minute or two, she estimates, and the river will settle down to a flow into which she can wade—wade into that seam between turbulence and placidity, that moment when the fish is distracted by the process of water redefining its nature. A moment of uncertainty and reorientation when big brown trout holding in deep pools will strike fiercely. Sandy waits and watches, eager for the moment when the shifting river will be ready to receive her.

She tightens the green scrunchie around her ponytail, adjusts the bill of her cap, and steps into the current as the river settles into its new flow and the first trout rises.

Walking on land, Sandy Holston is nothing special. Attractive enough by most standards, generally capable, an experienced licensed practical nurse, a thirty-two-year-old woman putting one foot in front of the other along a sidewalk, across a parking lot, down a hallway, up a trail through trees and brush—common. But when she steps into the current of a fishy river, she becomes extraordinary. Graceful, elegant, flawless, in her element, more in tune with the thick, fluid density of water than the routine density of air.

The trout rises again, and her eyes lock on the rippling ring of the rise. The fish is everything. Her gaze never wavers as her body glides into position. She turns her rod to the target and casts the line in a tight loop just to the right of the rise. The tiny yellow and brown fly settles onto the film, and she sets herself just as a fat brown trout shoots from under a submerged tree trunk, rises to the fly, and gulps it.

The trout flashes, the surface explodes; Sandy sets the hook and turns her rod and the fish away from the sunken snag. The fish dives to the bottom, seeking to hide in the depths, and Sandy allows it. Her rod arches high over her head and she lets the trout settle down, run a bit, settle down again, before she draws it in to her.

She pinches the fly from the trout's bony lip. Her wet hands cup the fish and hold it in the current until she can rest it, replenish the oxygen lost in its struggle, before releasing it. The trout is large. Not an absurdly huge trophy like the ones held by gawking fishermen in magazine photos, but a large, healthy, wild fish. Its belly is fat and glows bright yellow, nearly iridescent. The red, blue, and black spots marking its flanks are distinct. Sandy looks into the trout's terrified eyes, knowing it sees something very different from her. Flat fishy eyes, the elemental desire to continue, seeking only survival and escape from the alien form that has come into possession of it through subterfuge. She slides the big brown trout back into the river. A flash of yellow glimmers for a moment beneath the water at her feet before the fish flees into the safety of deeper water.

Sandy wades upstream, tracking the surface as she moves. As she comes around a streamside stand of wild rhododendron at a bend in the river, she hears a voice—a male voice, angry and grunting. Matching the sound of the voice to another noise, a ripping, tearing sound, Sandy knows what she will find before she rounds the bend.

"Goddamn it, my favorite lure."

The man stands on the opposite bank, a deep channel between him and Sandy, flailing with his spinning rod. He has cast across the channel to the far bank, where Sandy now appears, and his lure is caught in the rhododendrons. Cursing, grumbling, he yanks, tugs, and whips in a desperate attempt to disengage his lure from the branches. Each yank and tug further entangles the lure. He calls out when he sees Sandy wade around the bend and arrive alongside the stand of rhododendron.

"Hey, buddy. How 'bout a hand there?"

He stands on the bank in front of a folding lawn chair, a small red and white cooler on the ground beside the chair. His jacket has a camouflage pattern and his head appears to be shaved under his ball cap. One of his legs is wet to the ankle from slipping into the water from the muddy bank while whipping his rod around.

"Hang on there," Sandy says. "You're only making it worse. I'll get it."

"Thanks . . . uh, ma'am," he says.

"No problem," she says.

"Sorry about that. Calling you *buddy*. Don't usually see women out here fishing."

"Me either," says Sandy, as she approaches his tangled lure in the bushes.

She begins to unravel the mess he's made.

"Looks like a treble-hook spinner. A good one," she says.

"Yep. My favorite one. Be damned grateful if you can get it free. They don't make that kind anymore."

"Almost out now."

Sandy reaches to her vest, pulls out her forceps, and inserts them into the branches and leaves surrounding the lure.

"You know, as far as I know, this stretch of river is special regulation. Only supposed to use single-hook lures."

"Hunh?"

"Single-hook lures. That's all you're supposed to use in these waters."

The man scratches under his chin and tilts his head.

"Yeah, but who cares? Fish and game people never check down here."

Sandy nods as she pulls the spinner lure free, still keeping the man's line taut, not yet letting him know his favorite has been saved. She clasps two of the three hooks on the spinner's prong in her forceps and breaks them off.

"There you go," she says.

She throws the man's freed line into the current, and he reels it in quickly. She touches the brim of her cap and continues upstream.

"What happened to the hooks?" he calls out to her. "There's only one left."

"I broke off the other two."

"You what?"

"Don't mention it. Glad to help. Wouldn't want you getting in trouble for breaking regulations."

"Goddamn it. You got no right."

"Single hook, *buddy*."

Sandy sees the next rise about fifty yards upstream, under an overhanging hemlock branch, and glides toward it.

"You goddamn bitch."

The man stomps and screams and flails his rod from the bank. Before Sandy is halfway to her next trout, he hopelessly tangles the lure again, this time in an overhead branch. Sandy hopes he's not a local. If she is going to live down here now, and she is, she'll likely run into him on occasion. A fool like this guy is nothing she can't handle, but it would be a nuisance.

Two hours and four good fish later, the angry man with the mutilated lure is far behind her. The sun has dipped below the ridge of the hillside, and Sandy Holston steps from the river and walks back to her truck. Far upstream the siren at the dam sounds, announcing the impending increase in water level. Willard Lake, the reservoir behind the dam, is bursting with early spring rains and winter run-off, and the turbines in the dam have been generating electricity at near capacity, filling the riverbed with churning, fast water, shutting down just long enough for a few hours of late afternoon fishing.

Sandy is gone by the time the rugged new water level arrives. She has stowed her gear in her truck and is driving north to her old home in Dalton's Ferry to continue packing for the move down here, to Damascus and this river, the Ripshin River, the heart of her new home.

* * *

Sandy wants to get off the phone and return to her packing, but Margie Sutton is her best friend, her only friend, and she can't be rude to her.

"If you're moving to get away from Vernon, then why in the hell don't you really move away?"

Margie's voice sounds like cracking plastic in the receiver. Sandy presses her hand to her forehead.

"I told you," she says.

"Yes, I know, the water thing, whatever that is," Margie says. "But they must have trout streams farther away, in other states."

"A few."

"Well, then. He can't leave the state if he gets paroled."

"He's not getting paroled. He's getting out."

"Well, you don't have to make it so goddamn easy for him to find you. Put some distance between you and that bastard."

Sandy leans her head back, stares at the ceiling, and rubs her neck.

"He's not a bastard, Margie."

Sandy can tell that Margie has turned away from the phone to bark at one of her children.

"Matthew, take that out of your nose this instant."

The volume of her voice increases when Margie turns back to the phone.

"Not a bastard? He's threatened to . . ."

"Margie. Please. I know you mean well, and I appreciate it. But I won't leave the watershed. I can't."

"Watershed. Geez, the way you talk these days, girl."

"I really need to get back to packing. I'll talk to you at work tomorrow."

"I'm always here for you, honey. Bye-bye. Matthew, what did I just tell you?"

Sandy hangs up the phone, brushes a strand of hair from her face, and looks again at the box of letters on her kitchen table. Seven years ago he had become a killer, but he remained faithful, she would give him that. The letters always arrived. The pace of delivery changed over the years, but they always arrived, like the rhythm of a trout rising. And she always read each letter, stored the new ones in chronological order in the box with the others, and never wrote back.

She had tried. Once. Right after she received that first short letter, so full of questions, so full of his bitter hurt, confusion, anger. Vernon's words gouged into the sheet of lined notebook paper, the point of the pen piercing the paper, tearing it at one point. Sandy had run her fingertips over the words, feeling the impressions the pen left in the paper, touching the residue of his bewildered rage. She felt she had to say something, respond in some way. Find some arrangement of words to explain what sent her running out of the clearing. She had sat late into the night at this same kitchen table, the remains of her tea long cold in the bottom of the mug, and stared at the blank page before her, blank but for the only two words she could muster—*Dear Vernon*, scribbled at the top of the page. The pen lay notched in her fingers like a cigarette, waiting, but the page remained blank, refused to accept any attempt at explanation, each possible phrase ringing hollow to her as soon as she imagined it. The gap between what she felt when she ran from the clearing and the words she could assemble to explain it widened inexorably across the blank page. She knew why she ran, could feel it deep in her bones, but she could not speak it, could not write it, not in any way that would possibly soothe Vernon or help him understand. How could she tell him that the fish had become more important than him? She couldn't match the shapes she might scrawl across the blank page with the shapes finning the waters that haunted her now. It had been well after midnight when she crumpled the blank sheet of paper into a ball, tossed it in the trash can, and poured the dregs of her cold tea into the sink. Better left unsaid, she thought. She never tried to write again.

Sandy selects one letter at random, slides it from its envelope, and unfolds it. She scans it carelessly, recognizing and remembering it immediately. *If you had known, really known what this place was like, what this life did to a man, you wouldn't have, couldn't have left me there. And now there's nothing else left for me do.* She folds the letter and returns it to its place in the box. Pushing herself up from the table, she slides the chair back into place, presses her hands to the small of her back, and arches backward in a brief stretch. A worn pair of waders hangs over the back of the one other chair at the table. She reminds herself yet again that she had no choice, considering the circumstances. Nothing else she could have done. And if she had stuck with the plan, the most likely result would have been that she'd end up in prison too. She wasn't the guilty one here.

Over the past few months, knowing this time was approaching, Sandy had simplified and emptied out much of her material life, and there isn't much left to pack up now. She is ready to move. Vernon will be coming for her, that much is certain. After what she'd done, how could he not? She had been married to him for two years before he was sent up. She had been married to him for another year after that before she divorced him and changed her name from Adams back to Holston, still marveling at how easy it had been to divorce a husband in prison for a violent crime. She knows Vernon, how his world has always been divided into simple, clear-cut categories. He would be coming, and he would be justified in so doing. But Sandy has no intention of surrendering to his approach. She was right, too—there was nothing else she could have done. She will elude him as best she can, but when he comes she will meet him head-on. People of conviction, both of them.

Two weeks and one yard sale after she began packing, she is almost finished now. Only a few things yet to tend to before she leaves the day after tomorrow. The kitchen is already packed. She has fed primarily on fast food for the last week and the odor of crude, fried fat lingers stubbornly in her bare kitchen. A spoon, a fork, a small plate, and a single stoneware mug remain on the kitchen counter beside an unsealed cardboard box. Green and sturdy, the mug has a leaping trout etched into its surface. The tea kettle sits on the stove. The trash can is crammed with greasy waxed paper and styrene containers, and several cardboard boxes, sealed with masking tape, are stacked against the kitchen wall. She stuffs the box of Vernon's letters down into the packed trash can and walks into her bedroom.

In the bedroom, Sandy turns to her dresser and begins to open drawers. Other than a single large duffel bag, all her clothing has been stashed in boxes or trash bags. Clothes in the cardboard boxes would go along to her new house; those in the trash bags—mostly the dresses, skirts, and blouses she rarely has occasion to wear these days—would be dropped off at the county clothing bank. From one drawer she removes panties—simple cotton briefs in blue, black, and gray—and drops them one by one into a box. Each pair is scanned to see if it is worn, torn, or frayed enough to be thrown out. Sandy can't remember the last time she bought underwear. All but one pair makes it into the box.

From the next drawer down Sandy removes balled up cotton and wool socks and tosses them into the box on the bed. The drawer is deep, and there are dozens of pairs of socks. The deeper she digs, the more unfamiliar the socks become, and Sandy feels as if she is rifling through the belongings of another woman. Under the main layer of white cotton socks and gray wool socks, the next layer becomes more colorful—bright primary colors, pastels, and patterns. There is even a pair of anklets with frilled cuffs. Sandy wonders if she ever actually wore these as she drops the anklets and most of the colored socks into the trash bag. Beneath the colored socks appear wads of ripped and pilled panty hose that Sandy quickly transfers to the trash bag without a second thought, except for two new pairs still in the packages.

"Never know," she says, and drops them into the box.

The drawer is empty except for a thin box, pushed into the back corner. A gift box, bright red, a glossy red ribbon around it. The ribbon is wrinkled and creased, confirming it had been removed to open the box at one time, then put back in place. She knows immediately what it is and is surprised she has forgotten such a thing and not thrown it out years ago. Sandy lifts the box from the drawer, holding it out from her body, gingerly between thumbs and forefingers, as if it held a small poisonous snake, coiled to strike if unduly roused. She turns the box over and back, examining it, and a half-smile, half-smirk appears around the corners of her mouth. Slowly hooking her finger under a portion of the ribbon, she pulls it off and opens the box. She sets it on the bed and peals the tissue paper back from the red lace bustier and matching thong.

"What must he have been thinking?" she says. "Did he really . . .?"

She remembers exactly when he gave it to her—remembers all too well. The same night. Valentine's Day, for godsakes. Vernon had been happy that night. So happy, she remembers. And he'd been sweet and thoughtful, romantic even. That night was to be the beginning of a new phase of their life, and Vernon wanted to celebrate. He'd finally gotten his contractor's license and already had three good home remodeling jobs lined up. He'd had his white van painted with his company name—Adams Home Construction—and Sandy remembers how tightly he held his arm around her shoulder as he proudly showed her the newly-painted vehicle. Everything was clicking into place. He was a self-employed American man, independent and confident. He would live and work on his own terms, with no one other than himself to answer to. Hard work and drive were all that was needed to succeed. His life was becoming what a man's life was supposed to be, and he would go forth to meet it with a swagger in his step and his wife by his side.

Sandy had felt the firmness of his chest through his sweatshirt as his arm encircled her, pressed her to him. His other arm swept through the cold February air around them, indicating the precisely stenciled letters on the side of the van.

"Looks great, don't it?" he had said.

"Yes, it does," she had said.

"Everything's falling into place now, babe," he had said.

His chest had filled and risen with pride as he looked at his van and clasped his wife to his side. This was why she had said yes when he asked her to marry him, she thought. Vernon was bathed in certainty. The world worked in specific and definite ways. Some things were and some things weren't, and that was that. If things didn't appear to work out accordingly, there was always a specific reason for that, specific blame to be laid, and a specific way to correct the error. He had charted a course for his life and carefully planned how to complete that course. She could count on him.

Impossible as it was for her to imagine now, she had accepted that role then, welcomed it even. She had never had a plan of her own. Never envisioned a course for her life. Just out of high school, she had stumbled into a job as a nurses' aide, and kept on at it, not because she found her work particularly meaningful, but because it seemed as good as anything else she could imagine. In fact, she had imagined nothing else at all. She had gone on and taken her nursing degree at the community college because it made sense. Why not? No reason to waste the nursing experience she already had as an aide.

Vernon had been foreman of a roofing crew doing repairs at the hospital when she met him and he first asked her out. She had been drawn to his stability, determination, and that certainty. He had it all planned out. All that was required now was time and hard work. And it soon became clear that there was a place in his plan for her. He called it *love,* and she thought that as good a word for it as any other. True, he was prone to occasional fits of temper, but they were never, not ever, directed at Sandy. She thought it would be good to be part of a plan, to attach herself to something definite. There would be direction to her life, even if it was his direction and she had merely borrowed it. The thought of this had made her feel oddly secure and good as her husband pressed her closer to his chest that Valentine's Day as they looked at the sharp blue lettering on the side of the white van.

"Now, let's see if there's any Valentine's Day presents inside this here good-looking Adams Home Construction company vehicle," he had said as he released his grip on her and stepped to the van door.

Sandy lifts the bustier from the box with her fingertips and holds it to the lamp light. Her lips purse and her eyebrows pinch as she examines it, pinking light piercing the porous fabric. She turns the sheer garment front to back, back to front, snags a ragged cuticle in the lace netting, and tries to recall how she responded when he gave it to her. The look on his face when she opened the package had been mixed, part playful smile, part leer. She remembers that.

"A little something to jazz up the celebration when we get home later." That's what he had said, and she remembers that, too. She remembers even how the end of the word *jazz* had hissed through his teeth when he spoke.

But her recollection of her own reaction is a blank, as if she hadn't been present on the occasion. As if Vernon had given this thing to another woman, one without ragged cuticles, one not tossing her old clothing into cardboard boxes and trash bags in this room at this particular moment, one who didn't prefer trout fishing to all other human endeavors. What had she said, if anything? How did her face look? What had Vernon seen on her face through his half-leer? Did she smile? Did she laugh? Had she been surprised or shocked? Had she appeared confused, as she now felt? Nothing. Her response then, a complete blank.

Now, she holds merely a silly scrap of skimpy lingerie, its intended purpose an irrelevant remnant of a life she no longer inhabits. She thinks that, all in all, it had been thoughtful of Vernon. She'd heard enough of the other women at work complain about how thoughtless their husbands were, forgetting the little things—birthdays, Valentine's Day, anniversaries—the romantic holidays. Or if they did remember, the best they came up with was a paltry clump of dyed carnations, bought as an afterthought at the supermarket. Vernon always remembered, and that Valentine's Day he'd brought her a huge spray of red roses, a pair of heart-shaped silver earrings, and the red bustier and thong. No, she couldn't fault him on remembering those little occasions, she thinks, as she holds the bustier up to the light, here in this small bedroom they once shared. It had been sweet and thoughtful of him. But she shakes her head now at the thoughtlessness of his thoughtfulness. Typical. Red roses for Valentine's Day. Heart-shaped earrings for Valentine's Day. Cheesy red lingerie for Valentine's Day, Valentine's Night. Thoughtful but unimaginative. He showered her with an armload of clichés, and she wonders if he had, in fact, killed the man at the bar over those clichés.

Vernon had only been away from the bar for ten minutes, maybe, making a couple of phone calls, something about subcontracting another plumber for the job he was starting the following week. The man with thinning red hair and a gray sport jacket, already drunk, had entered the bar right after Vernon slipped out to use the phone. Ten minutes had been more than enough time for the red-haired man to get another drink, scan the crowd at the bar, slide into the open space beside Sandy, lean over her, drape his arm over the back of her stool, and ask her name and if he could buy her a drink. And that's what Vernon would have seen when he returned from the phone. But now she wonders if he saw more than that. If he saw the red-haired man in the gray sport jacket leering at his wife, leering at his wife dressed only in the lacy red bustier and thong, as he was imagining her later that night. If he saw the red-haired man encroaching upon his dream of the self-reliant man meeting his life with confidence, self-assurance, and a scantily-clad and faithful wife with spunky breasts and a perky butt.

"Excuse me," Vernon had said as he attempted to slip back up to the bar beside Sandy.

"Excuse me, buddy," the red-haired man had said, "but I'm talking to the lady here."

What was the red-haired man's name? How could she have forgotten the name of the man who played such a pivotal role in their lives? She'd heard the name so many times during the trial. She could still see him so clearly. Could hear Vernon say, "back off, buddy—this is my wife" as the red-haired man, Vernon's words not registering, lifted his arm from the back of her stool and casually shoved Vernon back. She could see the red-haired man's face so clearly. How his eyes widened when Vernon clutched a wad of thinning hair at the back of his head. How the blood splattered from his nose onto the bar top and Sandy's face and blouse the first time Vernon drove his face into the bar top. How his nose finally lay mashed to the side, how one eye was partially out of its socket, how flat and dull and pulpy his face looked as it lay briefly in the pooling blood on the bar once Vernon stopped slamming his face into it, before his limp body slumped to the floor. She could see the stunned look on Vernon's face as other bar customers struggled to subdue him, and she could feel how the February mist froze on her hair and across her shoulders as the red-haired man's body was shoved into an ambulance and Vernon was shoved into a police cruiser. But the red-haired man's name was gone.

Tilting her head to the side, she looks again at the red bustier, then lays it on the bed and pulls her sweatshirt off, dropping it in a heap beside the lingerie. The air in the room is cool. Sandy's skin tightens into goose bumps, and her nipples stiffen.

"At least try it on. Suppose I owe him that much," she says.

The lace chafes against her skin as she slides it over her head. The hem barely reaches her navel, and the bra stops just above her nipples. The front of the bustier is open to the navel, held together with crisscrossed red ribbon. On each breast is a hole surrounded by a bit of rose-shaped red satin, and Sandy winces as she tugs the bustier into place and one of her erect nipples pops through the opening. The other nipple somehow manages to stay under the lace. Perhaps a flaw in the manufacturing or a flaw in her breasts, she thinks. Standing before the mirror on the back of her dresser, Sandy looks at herself in red lace bustier, worn blue jeans, and fleece house slippers, her hair loosely pulled back in a ponytail. Her naked torso chafes under the lace, and she squirms slightly, trying to find if there is any position she could assume that would make this lingerie comfortable. She shrugs her shoulders, shakes her head, then laughs, as she imagines herself wearing the bustier while fishing. The short laugh turns into a scoffing giggle as she sees herself in waders, cap, fishing vest, and bustier, standing midstream, rolling out a tight-looped cast to a tricky brown trout holding at the fall line of an overhanging hemlock tree. When she imagines the weight of the canvas straps of her vest pressing rough lace into raw nipples, she snorts, pulls the bustier off, and flings it and the thong into one of the trash bags.

"What *are* men thinking?" She slips back into her sweatshirt, pulls open the remaining two drawers, and begins to pack wool sweaters in one of the cardboard boxes.

The sweaters are the last of it. She has left a change of underwear and her work clothes out for tomorrow. Other than that, she thinks she is ready to go. Nothing of Vernon remains. She took the last of his things to his parents' house over five years ago, right after the divorce was final. She'd piled his belongings, clothes and tools mostly, and his fishing rods and tackle box, in his van and parked it in his parents' carport. She hadn't intended to say anything to them, just leave the van and go. Margie had followed her and waited in her mini-van at the curb. She wasn't surprised when his mother didn't even turn to look at her from her chair at the kitchen table, though Sandy was clearly visible through the screen door, only a few feet away. Vernon's mother still blamed her for the downfall of her "boy." Sandy had been surprised when Vernon's father stepped through the screen door and caught her gently by the arm as she walked down the driveway toward Margie.

His graying hair was disheveled, and the sadness in his eyes had a depth she hadn't noticed before.

"I'm just so sorry 'bout all this. All of it," he had said, squeezed her arm gently, and turned back up the driveway to his house, his wife, and his son's van.

Sandy steps over a stray box in the kitchen and turns on the flame under the tea kettle. While the water comes to a boil, she takes her waders from the back of the chair and lays them out on the counter. There is a pinhole leak in the knee of one leg, which Sandy found and marked earlier. A small duffle, in which she keeps her fishing gear, always in order and ready to go, sits by the armchair in the bare living room. From this she removes some patching tape and a tube of sealant. By the time the tea kettle begins to rumble, she has stuck a small piece of patch tape over the hole, meticulously covered it with sealant, and hung the waders back on the chair to dry.

Sandy carries the green mug into the living room, dipping the tea bag in the steaming water, and settles into the armchair. She digs around in the cushion under her, pulls up the remote, and clicks on the television. Leno has just begun his monologue. She rarely watches television, but from time to time she finds it mildly relaxing to have a cup of herbal tea before bed and watch Leno mug into the camera, rub his hands together, and read his lampoons of current events from the cue cards. She never watches long enough for the show's guests to appear. Just the monologue and maybe one of Jay's bits. "Jaywalking" is funny enough, but finally it all seems a bit mean to her, ridiculing the intellectual shortcomings of the boob-on-the-street. More than anything, she thinks that she's just a little fascinated by Leno's chin, the way it juts out there, so brazen and unapologetic.

Sandy has drunk half her tea as Leno begins to wind down, mixing in references to the evening's guests with a few wisecracks about them. Suddenly she shifts in her chair, sits up straight, and grabs the remote, clicking off Leno mid-quip. She is overcome with an uncomfortable sensation, a disturbing sense of uniform linkage to a vast mass of people, all watching Leno at exactly that moment, all hearing the same voice and the same words at the same time. She feels as if she's under attack. Rising from the armchair, she shakes off the sensation, and walks through the kitchen and steps outside her back door.

Most of the other little houses in her neighborhood have gone dark, residents trying to get a few hours of sleep before another day of work. A light here and there, the shimmering silver glow through curtains, indicating another television set, perhaps another of that mass connected to Leno or maybe Letterman. Sandy reaches back inside the kitchen and switches off the porch light so she can see more stars. Her new house on Willard Road outside Damascus is much the same as this one. A small rectangle, a few rooms, nondescript. But the new house is outside the little town she's moving to, further away from the lights of settlement and closer to the billions of stars she will soon be able to see so many more of when she steps outside her house at night.

She breathes the night air deep into her lungs, sips from her mug, and tilts her head back to see what stars are available in this place on this night. The racket of chirping crickets washes over her, and she gazes out over the roof of the dark house behind hers. In the night under the stars, Sandy feels something not yet defined, waiting for her out there, somewhere behind the night, behind the mountains to the south and the waters rushing down their slopes.

* * *

The fish died easily tonight. A weak lot, he thinks. The killing was easy. A couple of minutes, the flip of the switch, the sweep of the wand. A simple act, with the right equipment, to electrocute a few thousand stupid fish trapped in concrete hatchery pens.

He hears something moving slowly over the dead leaves carpeting the forest floor up the hillside. Possum, he thinks. Bending to half his height, he waddles into the cave and drags the big pack frame in behind him. Inside the small, oval hollow of the cave he can crawl about easily and sit cross-legged with nearly a foot of space above his head. By the light of a small flashlight, he slides the pack into an enormous nylon duffle bag and zips it shut. The hip boots make a sucking sound as they slide from his legs, and he sets them to the side. From a smaller duffel, containing spare batteries and an extra flashlight, he removes a worn pair of deck shoes and closes the bag. The two duffle bags are stacked neatly against the cave wall. He wriggles his feet into the deck shoes and leans back, sitting, pressing his back into the cool damp of the cave wall. Binoculars dangle by a strap from his neck. He switches off the small flashlight, and the cave collapses into pure dark around him.

He gropes for the pulse of the mountain encasing him, listens, and waits to exhale the weight of tonight's killing. This was not his first attack. The first time had been small-scale, sloppy, erratic, a mess, with bodies popping from the pens, flopping on the ground, occasionally mashed beneath his boots. After that experience he made the necessary adjustments and had now become a precise and efficient killer. The power settings were exact and correct, and he transacted wholesale slaughter quickly. The pitiful hatchery trout jolted from the shock and rolled up on their pallid silver sides, dead in the water. They had to die. Too many of them, and they didn't belong here. The killing was good, decent, righteous, but still, the density of such a concentration of death pressed on him, clung to him like a coating of heavy oil. He had killed so many tonight, more than before. They would suspect something deliberate now. He would have to be careful. But it had to be done.

The mountain breathes around him, into him. He sets his head back against the cave wall and listens to the pulse, the rush of underground springs in the earth behind him. Crickets and cicadas hum in the forest outside the cave, and subterranean water pumps through the ground around him. He hears it all, cohered into a seamless murmur inside his ears, and he loves it all. He exhales a long, raspy plume of hot air into the cool cave. He did what must be done, and he was right to do so.

"They don't belong here," he whispers into the live rock.

* * *

Sandy would have preferred to work quietly through her last shift at the hospital and slip away unnoticed, but Margie was having none of that. When Sandy returned to her wing following her afternoon break and everyone who gathered at the nurses' station shouted "surprise," she groaned, rolled her eyes, and glared good-naturedly at Margie.

"If you think, after all these years, I'm going to let you pull one of your vanishing acts," Margie said, "well, honey, you got another thing coming."

Margie's thoughtfulness nearly wore her out sometimes, but Sandy could only love her the more for it. She knows that Margie is the closest thing she has to a real friend, as close as Sandy will let anyone get these days. And despite her craving for solitude, despite Margie's nagging, she admits to herself that she'd be adrift in the world without this one friend.

The little going away party had been relatively tolerable for Sandy, as those things go. Margie and the other nurses knew there'd be no "girls' night out" with Sandy, no pitchers of margaritas at a local bar, no hours of gossip over melting drinks and clogged ashtrays, no male strippers. They knew that to do anything to commemorate Sandy's departure, they'd have to keep it simple and catch her by surprise. A white sheet cake from the local Food Lion, with "Good Luck Sandy" written in blue icing around a small plastic figure of a fisherman implanted in the cake. Sandy said nothing about the fact that this miniature angler was using a spinning rod, but Margie saw her looking at it just the same.

"Yeah, I know, but Food Lion was fresh out of fly fishing decorations."

Sandy smiled at Margie and gave her a light, playful shove.

There were a few cards. No flowers. No balloons. No gag gifts, only a single gift they had all chipped in on—a mahogany fly box with "Sandy Holston" engraved on a brass plate on the top. Margie's work, for sure. The nurses working on Sandy's wing were there, smiling, occasionally sliding an arm around her shoulder and wishing her well, stepping away from the party from time to time to attend to patients as necessary. Even a couple of the doctors and a few nurses from other wings in the hospital popped in for a moment as they could. Not that many people, really. Sandy wasn't particularly well known to many on the staff, just the ones who knew her before "the change," as Margie called it. From before Vernon went to prison and Sandy began fishing. From before Sandy melted away into the world of trout streams and fly rods and began wearing fishing lures for earrings. To those who thought about her at all she was distant, a figure of some mystery.

"Cold as a fish and a seriously strange woman, that one," an orderly had said once.

To the rest of the staff, unknown, just as Sandy liked it. Except for Margie. Margie was her friend and would stay her friend, whether Sandy liked it or not.

* * *

After the party breaks up and Sandy endures the final good-byes of acquaintances and coworkers, she and Margie walk to her truck in the parking lot. Sandy opens the cab and sets her cards and gift on the passenger seat. She turns to Margie, who stands behind her, a large purse hanging from one elbow, cradling the long tray with the remains of Sandy's cake in her arms.

"I should just kill you for that," Sandy says.

"Fine," Margie says, "but could you take this damn cake from me before you do? I'm about to drop it."

Sandy takes the sheet cake, covered with wrinkled aluminum foil, and sets it on the hood of her truck. She pulls the scrunchie from her ponytail and shakes her hair out across her shoulders.

"Why don't you take the cake home to the boys? I can't eat it all, and I'm sure as hell not going to take it with me tomorrow."

"Thanks. The little maniacs will love it. After all this sugar, I'll have to scrape them off the damn walls with a putty knife."

Sandy smiles and looks at her friend.

"Thank you. For all this. I'll miss you."

"I know that's a lie," Margie says, smiling, "but thanks for saying it anyway."

"And the fly box. I know it was you who thought of that. It's beautiful. Thank you."

Margie digs a cigarette out of her purse and lights it.

"You sure you don't need help tomorrow?" she asks. "I could call in sick."

"No. Nothing to it. I'm not taking that much. The new place is sort of furnished, and I can load everything else in the back of my truck. I'm ready to go, but thanks."

"You crazy bitch, you won't tell me your new address. Won't tell me where you're going. Nothing. Why so much mystery?"

"That should be obvious."

"I know that, but shit girl?"

Sandy pushes her fingers up through her hair, pulls it tight, and tugs the scrunchie around a fresh ponytail.

"I'll call you."

"Look. I know Vernon's getting out this fall. Really, I understand all that. But why so extreme? You're not even leaving me, anyone, a forwarding address. You're just going to disappear?"

"Sort of. Margie, it'll be simpler this way. The less you know, the better."

"Not like I'm going to tell the son of a bitch where you are."

Margie stomps her cigarette out and digs in her huge purse for another.

"Let me have one of those," Sandy says.

"Since when do you smoke?"

"I don't. Just seemed like a good time for one."

Margie sets her purse on the pavement and snaps her lighter. Sandy cups her hands around the flame and leans her cigarette into it. She lets most of the smoke float out of her mouth, inhaling only a tiny portion of it, and coughs.

"I know you wouldn't mean to tell him anything," Sandy says, "but you don't know what might happen. It's just safer this way. You know, after he goes to his parents house, to see his dad and mom . . ."

"That old bitch," Margie says.

"Yeah. But after that, if he starts looking for me, the first place he's going to start looking is you."

"Great. And I won't know shit. So he'll kill me because I don't have what he wants. Thanks, old friend."

Sandy pauses, the cigarette in her fingers frozen halfway to her mouth, a strand of smoke trailing up into the breeze. She had never considered this possibility.

"Relax. I'm just razzing you. He's not going to do anything to me. And even if he tries, I've got my little .25. Had it ever since the asshole left us. Just in case."

On the rare occasions that Margie even mentioned her ex-husband, she always referred to him as the "asshole," except in front of her children, and even that was not a hard and fast rule.

"It's just that . . ." Margie's voice trails off. She looks at the pavement and exhales a plume of smoke.

"What?"

"It's just that this is all so . . . so . . . complete. You're here. We're friends. Then you're just gone. Completely gone. Like you died or something."

"Not completely gone. Just not here. I'll stay in touch. I'll call once I get the phone hooked up."

"The phone. Right," Margie says and smirks. "Or, here's an idea. You could get a cell phone like everyone else in the goddamn world. It's almost the twenty-first century, girl. Catch up."

"Don't start with that again," Sandy says.

Margie flicks her second cigarette away and leans against the bed of Sandy's pickup.

"Sorry to whine. I just don't really get it all. You could take out a restraining order against him. Put the police on the look-out. God knows you've got enough proof in those goddamn letters of his."

"I threw them out last night."

"About time."

"Really, Margie, I don't think he'd do anything to me. It's all talk. He's hurting. Poor guy still loves me."

"'Poor guy'?" Margie says. "Uh, that 'poor guy' killed a man."

"I know, but he won't kill me. I just don't want to be around here when he gets out. It'd be too complicated."

"So, if you're going to get away, why don't you really get away? Other side of the country or something? You're an experienced nurse. You can get a job anywhere."

"I told you. The . . ."

"I know. I know. The *waterhead*."

"Watershed."

"I guess that's what I don't understand more than anything else. Just don't get it."

Sandy drops her cigarette to the ground and crushes it out with her foot. She leans against the truck beside Margie, their hips just barely touching, and gazes off in the direction of a ridge of mountains, distant and invisible from this hospital parking lot.

"Hard to explain. It's something kind of new for me, too. I've changed since Vernon went away. Since I started fishing."

"Big understatement, girl."

"It's like . . . like I can't just live any place where I can get a house and a job. It has to be this place. Not right here, this town, but somewhere in this area."

Sandy sweeps her arm widely before her.

"The watershed. What is it? The Roy Rogers watershed?" Margie says, grinning.

"Rogers Ridge," Sandy says, smiling briefly. "I feel like I couldn't be alive if I wasn't at least near it."

"Well, if Vernon finds you, no matter what you think, you may not be alive at all, near your precious watershed or anywhere else."

"At least I have a chance. I can handle Vernon. But I couldn't handle not having this."

She waves her arm before her again.

"Honey, you are truly one strange woman."

Sandy nods and rests a hand on Margie's shoulder. Margie reaches across to Sandy's hand and squeezes it.

"You know," Margie says, "maybe I'm just a little jealous."

"Of what?"

"That you can change your life like this. Take off, whether you're running from Vernon or not."

"I'm not running from him. Just keeping away. Keeping a bit out of the line of fire. Keeping things simple."

"Okay, but still, to go, to find a new place, a new way to live. I might envy that. Or maybe I'm a little jealous of feeling that strongly about something—anything, other than my kids—the way you do about this *watershed*."

Sandy pushes away from the side of her truck. Margie wraps her arms around Sandy and squeezes her. Sandy is uncomfortable, embarrassed, being held so tightly, is having trouble breathing, in fact, but returns her friend's embrace, allows it to run its course.

"Be careful," Margie says, as Sandy climbs into her truck and fires the ignition.

"I will. You, too."

"Call me," Margie says above the hum of the engine.

"I will," Sandy says.

"Promise? If you don't, I'll be hunting you down right along with Vernon."

"I promise."

* * *

Some time ago, Inmate #52674 at the Bland County Correctional Facility wrote and mailed the following letter:

Dear Sandy,

They gave me an extra year. I hope you're happy. Are you happy? Do you even care? I suppose not. It's been four months, three months since I got out of solitary, and still not a word from you. You owe me, bitch. And do you know what makes me most angry out of all this? You looked happy. You looked happy standing there with that damned fly rod in your hand.

I've killed before. I can do it again. It's not that hard to do, not if you're mad enough. You're next, Sandy.

Your loving husband,

Vernon

The letter was duly delivered, but received no response.

* * *

J.D. Callander stares down into a concrete hatchery pen choked with the floating carcasses of a thousand dead trout and thinks, not again. Once, he could write off as a fluke. Such a thing could happen. Such fish die from time to time. But now it had happened twice, and so many more fish dead this time. No fluke, this was a deliberate act, and he'd have to call in the state police. "Damn it all."

One hand rests on the butt of the automatic holstered on his belt as he looks up from the dead trout to the adjacent hillside. With his other hand, he rubs his neck.

James Keefe steers his pickup truck along the gravel drive into the hatchery grounds. From this distance, through the truck's windshield, Callander looks to Keefe like a gunman about to draw down on a foe, not his former student who became the regional game warden and never fired, even drew, his weapon once in the line of duty.

Most of Keefe's former students have disappeared from his life. Or rather, he has disappeared from theirs. Always a bit aloof, he spent little time chatting with students after class or during the office hours he was known throughout Sherwood Community College for frequently missing. He walked his students through the basics of English composition or introductory literature classes. He became nearly a recluse when his wife died in a car accident just a few months after he had cajoled her into abandoning her house in Sherwood for a little streamside bungalow on the other side of the hillside at which J.D. Callander now stares. Since his retirement ten years ago, hardly anyone saw him, except on occasional trips into town for supplies. He lived a private, modest life on a modest pension in his modest bungalow on the Ripshin River, upstream from the reservoir, on the edge of the national forest.

He had, however, maintained a continuing, if casual, relationship with J.D. Callander. From time to time, they'd run into each other, mostly along the stream around Keefe's bungalow in the course of the game warden's official rounds. What amused Keefe most about his former student, perhaps endeared J.D. to him, was the game and fish warden's insistence on formality. He still referred to Keefe as *Professor* or *Dr. Keefe*, titles Keefe had not expected or felt comfortable with even when they applied.

As Keefe slows for a rut in the gravel drive, he watches Callander and a grin that might indicate fondness or sympathy spreads across his face. He recalls how grateful J.D. had been for the orderly formula of the five-paragraph essay. Topic paragraph, thesis statement, three body paragraphs—three main points—and a conclusion. J.D. could speak within this form. He produced controlled, flawless, and utterly unimaginative statements as long as he could fit what he said into those comforting, predictable five paragraphs. Keefe remembers how disconcerted J.D. had become when Keefe once suggested he try something a bit less formulaic, perhaps start at the end and work his way back. In the cab of his truck, approaching the pens where Callander stands with his hand on his gun, Keefe chuckles, remembering the terror in J.D.'s eyes when he made the suggestion.

"Looks like you're getting ready to gun someone down," Keefe says, stepping from his truck.

"Think I would, professor, if I knew who to shoot."

"Saw you from the road and thought I'd swing by and say hello. What's got you so ready for gunplay?"

"See for yourself." J.D. nods to the pen full of floating bodies.

Keefe walks to the troubled warden's side and looks down into the pen.

"Oh, for heaven's sake. They're all dead," he says.

"Real dead," J.D. says, "and a lot more of them this time."

Keefe cocks his head sharply and looks at J.D.

"This time?"

"Yeah, happened once before. Two months ago. We thought it was a problem batch of fish or some impurity in the pen. But this. Every single trout in this pen is dead. This is no accident."

"What do you do now?" Keefe asks.

"State police. Destruction of state property."

Keefe nods and lightly pats Callander on the shoulder.

"Why, Dr. Keefe? Why in the world would anyone do this?"

"Beats me. I'm just an old school teacher, fishing, tying flies, and living out my days alone in the woods. Can't seem to understand most people anymore these days. Best to leave that to you crime and science boys down here."

"What would Walt Whitman say about this, professor?"

"I don't think Whitman had much experience with hatchery trout, J.D. More of a saltwater fisherman, if memory serves."

A large pickup truck with a tank in its bed emerges from the garage of the hatchery office and rumbles up the drive to the trout pens. A man in a camouflage ball cap and a white t-shirt hops from the driver's side of the truck. He is the hatchery manager and lives with his wife and son in the double-wide beside the garage. His teenage son steps down from the passenger side. He wears a black t-shirt, frayed baggy pants, and no hat. His hair is dark and spiky with blond tips.

"Well, sorry about your mess here," Keefe says. "I better be heading on home now."

J.D. Callander removes his hand from his gun and walks toward the gravel drive and the hatchery truck with Keefe.

"How are you feeling these days?" he says.

"As well as can be expected, I suppose," Keefe says, "for a man who spends too much time standing in cold water and crawling over rocks."

The hatchery manager is removing two large nets from the bed of the truck as Keefe and Callander approach. The teenager grunts "hey" as he walks past them toward the pen with the dead fish.

"Still gonna have to get these others on out today," the manager says to Callander. "Got plenty for the reservoir and the downstream spots. Guess we'll have to forget upstream again."

"Guess so. I'm going to put in a call to the state police now."

"Good," says the manager. "Getting goddamned aggravating working up these rainbows just so some son of a bitch can kill 'em."

"We were going to drop a load of these upstream, professor," J.D. says to Keefe. "Doesn't look like we'll be able to now. Have to stock the main spots first. Not that many people fish up your way, and you know how people can get."

"Don't fret yourself, J.D. I'll get along."

J.D. moves toward his SUV and Keefe begins to walk to his truck as the hatchery manager's son returns from the lethal pen and takes one of the nets from his father.

"Like you said, they're all dead."

"That's what we said," the manager says as he hands his son one of the big nets. "Dead or not, we still got work to do."

The son shrugs as he accepts the net from his father. He takes a step toward the other hatchery pens, pauses, looks briefly over his shoulder toward the pen full of dead trout, and speaks in a near whisper.

"Awesome."

* * *

One week after she said goodbye to Margie and moved to the little vinyl-sided house on Willard Road outside Damascus, on her first day off from her new job at the Damascus Nursing and Rehabilitation Center, Sandy stands in the only place she could want to be on her first free day in a week: knee-deep in an Appalachian trout stream. The bow in her rod relaxes as she draws to hand and releases a modest brook trout. From the knees down she feels the chill of the mountain water wick through her waders. Above the knees, the late spring sun weaving through hemlocks and sycamores warms her as she reels in her line and slips from the water onto a streamside rock.

Before moving here, Sandy had fished most often in the tailwater of the Ripshin River, below the dam, where the trout were larger, trickier, and the product of successful fisheries management. Today she decided she should begin to learn the waters of the upper Ripshin, above the reservoir, within the national forest—begin to learn the cascading, gradient stream flowing within natural banks and the wild, native brook trout that had finned these waters for centuries. Her buttocks settle upon the rock, and its heat softens the flesh within the waders. Her booted feet remain to the ankles in the cold stream, and she relishes the split sensations in her body, sensing no contradiction or conflict. Her eyes follow the twisting band of water up the hillside until it disappears behind the next tier of boulders. She imagines the Ripshin at its source, an underground spring issuing from the ground near the spine of Rogers Ridge, winding down its slopes, picking up strength and volume from a dozen feeder streams along the way, until it merges with Hogback Branch and drops into a gorge of its own making to flow several miles down to where Sandy sits on a warm rock in a spot of sun. Never before has she fished this far upstream, but as the small river rushes down to where Sandy's boots slice the current, she feels as if she has, in some way, always been in this one spot at this one time. New, but old—ancient. An émigré in a strange landscape, yet utterly at home—indigenous. She imagines in an instant a million variations on this moment, this place, yet she cannot imagine her life before she picked up a fly rod and stepped into another trout stream, in this same watershed. She feels like a shining new and wild child, pushed raw from a rock, elegantly born into a venerable place. This place, for which she was intended all along.

Sandy rises from the rock and glides back into the stream. She thumbs her earring, peels line from her reel, and stalks up on the next pool. A good brook trout cruises the edges of a patch of sunlight, slipping from the shadows and slicing the gleaming surface to suck in passing insects. She spots it, squats, and remains still, watching, getting its rhythm. When she is in sync with the trout, she moves in a crouch to a gnarled tree overhanging the tail of the pool and, still crouching, lodges her boots into the tree's exposed roots, presses her back to the trunk and pushes herself up. The fish is no more than fifteen feet away and has not seen her.

When the trout curves into the glassy patch of sunlit water, Sandy sees the gleaming ivory-trimmed orange of the pectoral fins. She remembers how stunned she was by the brilliance of these fins when she caught her first brook trout in Dismal Creek. How many years ago now since her life began? She thinks how much brighter the orange will be in the fall when the fish are spawning. She watches the brook trout slip into the shadow, nose a fleck of floating leaf, then dip back into the light. The breath flows deep and regular into her lungs. Silent, without numbers, she counts out the fish's rhythm. Breath in. Count. Breath out. Count. Repeat. Repeat. Her breath, the rhythm of the trout, the light through the water, her arm and the rod—Sandy holds pressed to the tree until there is no separation, no gap, between any of it before she makes her cast. A barely perceptible roll of her wrist, the rod feints forward, and the line flips out and drops the fly in the center of the light. Unstartled, with ease and predatory confidence, the trout turns to Sandy's fly and sips it in, impaling its bony upper lip on the fraudulent bug when Sandy sets the hook.

Her breath is still in rhythm with the trout's movements as she takes the fish gently in hand, unhooks the fly, and releases the fish back into its pool. She watches the trout hold for a moment at her feet, regaining its equilibrium before shooting off deep into the shadow under the rim of a rock.

She recalls the facts of her life, but feels none of them. She looks upon the events of her past as if she is leafing through a stranger's photograph album left on her kitchen table. She can feel her own presence in none of her memories prior to first stepping into Dismal Creek with a fly rod clutched in her fist. She can't recall ever believing in anything until she escaped from that clearing along Dismal Creek just as Vernon burst from the rhododendrons and stumbled into the creek.

Sandy moves further upstream along a deer path. She notes the plum-sized cloven tracks of deer, steps over droppings when she notices, and ducks under thin branches that would lightly graze the backs of deer but catch a human in the chest, neck, face. The wind is gentle today but strong enough to be noticed. She feels it lift the wisps of hair that have escaped her cap and dance against her cheeks. She hears it rustle the branches overhead. A large dead sycamore, washed out and felled by the early spring run-off, lies across the path, and Sandy straddles the trunk, slides over it, and begins walking again when she hears a crackling of brush and something breaks from the deadfall behind her. A mink shoots from the tangle of sycamore branches along the stream, hops onto a moss-covered rock, pauses just long enough for a brief, fearful glance at her, and scurries off downstream along the deer path.

A half-mile further upstream, Sandy limps along the deer path. She'd twisted her ankle because of Margie.

After taking two good fish she'd drawn out from under a deadfall branch that cut at an angle from the bank into the center of a nearly perfectly round pool, Sandy had moved on up the path. Margie had slipped into her thoughts. She should get her phone connected so she could call her, she thought. Though she could barely admit it to herself, she missed Margie. Missed her unabashed sincerity and the rough and rowdy way she handled her sons. Sandy had chuckled to herself, wondering how long it took those two boys to devour the leftover sheet cake. Distracted, she had taken her eyes from the path and caught her boot in the curve of an exposed tree root, twisting her ankle. She stumbled, caught herself, and emitted her standard self-reprimand for these rare occasions of carelessness.

"Pay attention, stupid."

* * *

James Keefe's feet are sore, as they often are. He stands on the porch of his bungalow, barefoot, rocking on his feet, stretching them, flexing his toes. The big toe on his right foot seeks out the knothole in the worn planking of the porch and inserts itself, anchoring Keefe. He stands, one hand stuffed in the pocket of his baggy pants, the other holding a coffee cup, rocking, stretching, flexing, and watching the upper Ripshin River spill down the mountainside in front of his isolated little house.

He sips his third cup of coffee of the day and is thinking that at his age he should probably switch to decaffeinated when the loop of a fly line shoots from behind the streamside stand of hemlocks. An angler is approaching from downstream. Keefe brings the coffee cup to his creased lips again as Sandy wades into view from behind the trees.

Her long hair is pulled back under her cap, and, even from this distance, Keefe can easily recognize her unusual jewelry. The pattern and color are unmistakable—the red and white swirl of a Dardevle spoon, dangling from her ear. Nothing else looks like that.

Keefe considers Sandy's odd earring and watches. Her casts are elegant, precise, and efficient. No wasted motion, no needless flurry of false casts. Her work is tight and on target. On her third cast after emerging from the hemlocks, her rod arches to a strike. In the nonchalant way she holds her rod up and strips in her line, it is clear the fish is a small one. Only a few moments and she has the fish in hand and removes the fly from its lip. Even from Keefe's distance on his porch he can tell. Eight inches long, its sides an amorphous, dull silver. One of J.D. Callander's stocked rainbows has made it this far upstream into the pools of native fish. Keefe's toe probes deeper into the knothole.

The young woman glares briefly at the fish in her hand. Keefe recognizes a look of contempt on her face. He watches her shake her head slowly from side to side and flinches in mild surprise as she inserts her thumb in the little trout's mouth and jerks her wrist upward, snapping its spine. She pitches the dead fish high into the brush on the opposite bank and wipes her hands on her waders. She sees Keefe observing from his porch and nods to him as she begins to reel in her loose line. Keefe returns her nod and flexes his toe in the knothole.

A young man wearing jeans, a gray hooded sweatshirt, and an Atlanta Braves ball cap appears on the path upstream from Keefe's bungalow and wobbles down the bank to the head of the pool. He carries a spinning rod in one hand and tilts slightly to his side from the weight of the yellow plastic bucket he carries in the other hand. A bit of water sloshes from his bucket when he sets it down. From the pouch of his sweatshirt he removes a light blue plastic container, opens it, and removes a worm, which he quickly impales and loops around the hook on the end of his line. He has not seen Keefe, standing behind him on his porch, and the young man has cast his worm into the pool before he notices Sandy, partially obscured from his angle behind a rhododendron.

"How do, bud. . ." He pauses. "How do, ma'am. Doing any good?"

Sandy sets her line and rod for another cast, tilts her head just barely forward, and says, "little bit."

"Get any natives?" the young man asks. "I caught me a bucket full of 'em."

He tilts his head and the bill of his cap points to the yellow bucket on the ground beside him.

After removing his toe from the knothole and setting his coffee cup on the porch rail, Keefe grasps a smooth, wooden walking staff that leans by his door. As he steps down from his porch, he hunches his shoulders and head forward and down, seeming to decrease his height and increase his age significantly in a single motion. He limps and shuffles in his bare feet across the rough grass and stones before his bungalow, leaning heavily on his staff, and arrives at the edge of the bank behind the young man just as Sandy begins to speak.

"You know, this is special regulation water," she says.

"Say what?" says the young man.

"Not supposed to use bait up here."

The young man scoffs and shrugs.

"So? Don't make much sense to me. Catch a bunch more fish with worms than with that fancy business you're using."

"You will that, young fella," Keefe says as he plants his staff and slowly inches himself down the bank to the pool.

Startled by Keefe's presence, the young man jerks his head to see the old man complete his stumbling approach. He nods to Keefe and says "How do" again as Keefe limps to the young man's bucket, locks both hands on his staff, and peers inside.

"Well, now," Keefe says, "looks as though you truly have caught a bunch of fish."

"I have that," says the young man.

"Must be, say, nineteen or twenty brook trout in here."

"Yup, nineteen."

As he speaks, the young man's line jerks and he sets his wormed hook into another fish.

"Looks like twenty is on the way," he says.

He makes a few quick turns on his reel, then lifts his rod and yanks a small, writhing fish several feet free of the water and flings it flopping onto the bank. He tears a small chunk from the trout's tongue as he tugs the barbed hook free and pitches the fish into his bucket. Keefe continues staring into the choked, churning mass of the green-blue backs and orange fins of twenty brook trout barely able to move in the yellow bucket.

"Yes sir, quite a catch," Keefe says. "What you going to do with all those fish?"

"Pickle some, fry up the rest," he says.

The young man flicks the remaining shreds of worm from his hook and again removes the blue plastic container from his sweatshirt pouch.

Squatting, he sets the container on the ground and begins poking around for a fresh worm.

"Ought to be a few more in here," he says.

"Damn it, you're not supposed to use bait here." Sandy has moved out from behind the rhododendron into the main current of the pool.

"Look, lady," the young man says, his fingers still in the bait container, "I ain't bothering you. So why don't you go back to your fancy-pants, girlie fishing and mind your own business."

"This water is my business. And there are rules for this water," she says.

"Humph, women fishing," the young man says, turning a knowing glance up at Keefe. Keefe does not acknowledge the young man's glance. He continues staring into the trout-clogged bucket.

Sandy's cast shoots out tight and quick, and the young man falters and slips onto his rear as her fly zips before his face and lands on the blue bait container. His fingers remain pinched together and motionless when Sandy pulls on her line, hooks the fly to the edge of the container and flips the remaining worms into the pool, where they sink in a murky cloud of mud.

"What in the . . ."

Recovering from the shock of Sandy's action, the young man leaps up, his pinched fingers transforming into a clenched fist. His sudden motion apparently throws Keefe off balance. One hand breaks free of the staff, his footing slips, a knee gives way, and he stumbles against the bucket, knocking it on its side and dumping its contents back into the pool. Twenty brook trout shudder in a moment of confusion, then scatter in a starburst for the cover of the deeper water.

"Damn it. Damn it," shouts the young man. His fist is still balled up, and he turns his growl from Sandy to Keefe.

"There're rules, buddy," Sandy says, reeling in her line and sliding to the far side of the deeper water of the pool.

"You bitch," says the young man, grabbing his bucket and righting it. "And you, you clumsy old goat. Damn it."

Keefe has regained his footing and his hold on his staff. His shoulders appear to have hunched even lower.

"My, but I'm so sorry, young fella," he says. "So sorry. Getting to be even more of a clumsy old man than I thought I was."

"Damn it. That's a whole morning of fishing, shot all to hell, thanks to a crazy bitch woman and a stupid old man."

"Now, I'm very sorry, young man. But accidents do happen. Let's not get carried away. I'm sure the lady is sorry as well."

"Not a bit sorry," Sandy says from the far side of the stream.

The young man clutches his spinning rod and snatches up his empty bucket.

"Lucky you're an old man and you're a woman. Otherwise, I'd flatten the both of you."

He stomps up the bank and turns back to Keefe and Sandy.

"No need to be mean, young fella," Keefe says.

"Shut up, old man. Get on back to the nursing home, where you belong. As for you," he says to Sandy, "you'd best keep clear of me if I ever run into you again."

The young man smacks his bucket against a tree and curses to himself as he storms off downstream. Keefe and Sandy watch him in silence until he disappears around the bend in the trail.

Sandy wades slowly around the deep channel of the pool and comes out on the bank by Keefe. She winces and pulls up on her twisted ankle as she steps on shore.

"Are you hurt?" Keefe asks.

"It's nothing," Sandy says. "Twisted my ankle a little."

"Let me help."

Keefe straightens his shoulders, places one hand gently at Sandy's elbow, digs his staff securely into the earth, and leads them both easily up the embankment. He releases her elbow when she lifts it free of his hand and moves off toward his bungalow, walking briskly with his staff casually over his shoulder. Sandy glances at him with curiosity as she begins to hobble up the trail. Halfway to his house Keefe stops, and his shoulders rise as he inhales. He turns his eyes on Sandy limping away. He hesitates before he exhales and speaks.

"Why don't you come on up to the cabin and rest that ankle? Would you like some coffee?

"Thanks anyway, but there's no need to bother. I'm alright."

"No bother at all. Besides, you'd best let that fellow put some distance between you and him before you head downstream—if you're heading downstream."

"Yeah, I suppose I'd better call it a day after that."

"I'm afraid you may have made yourself an enemy of that fellow today."

"Won't be the first time I've pissed off some man on a trout stream."

Sandy lowers herself onto the top step of Keefe's porch, leans her rod against the railing, and reaches to rub her injured ankle. Keefe hops up the steps, picks up his coffee cup, returns his staff to its place, and slips into his house.

"Here we go," Keefe says, emerging from his house, handing Sandy a steaming cup, and sitting down on the step beside her.

"Thank you," Sandy says. She hesitates for a moment over the coffee, not particularly fond of it. But the cup Keefe has handed her is warm and smells rich and savory. She sips at it tentatively.

For a moment they watch the river in silence, sipping their coffee. Keefe lifts his cup up toward Sandy in a feigned toast and speaks.

"That was some pretty snazzy casting back there."

"Not so snazzy. I was aiming for his nose."

"Pretty snazzy nonetheless."

Sandy takes another sip from her cup and turns slightly toward Keefe.

"And judging by the way you're moving now, I'd say that was a pretty snazzy impersonation of an old codger, too."

Keefe smiles over the lip of his coffee cup.

"Recognize your limitations, and they can become your strengths. And it's not entirely an impersonation."

Sandy nods, sets her cup down and rubs her ankle with both hands.

"Suppose I'd best give you a ride down to the gate," Keefe says. "Are you parked there?"

"Yes," Sandy says, eyeing Keefe's old truck. "But I think I'll be okay."

"Recognize your limitations," he says.

"Thanks."

"Keefe."

"Excuse me?" Sandy says.

"My name. Keefe. James Keefe," he says, extending his hand.

"Sandy Holston," she says, meeting his hand with her own.

"Pleasure to meet a woman who can take out a bait can with a single cast."

"Pleasure to meet a man who can knock a bucket of illegal fish back into the water and make it look like an accident."

"Making use of my limitations."

"I'll get his nose next time."

2

Where a Woman Just Goddamned
Wasn't Supposed to Be

A half moon and two mercury vapor lights illuminate the grounds around the black water in the hatchery pens, and he watches through binoculars, hidden in the trees up the hillside. Gentle wind shushes through overhead branches, tree trunks creak and bend, dead leaves and twigs fall to the forest floor, water runs through underground springs, insects hum in flight, deer tear leaves from bushes and low branches, nocturnal rodents comb the hillside for food, an owl swoops down upon a foraging field mouse. He marvels at how much sound fills a sleeping forest in the middle of the night.

This time the county newspaper, always eager for anything to report, had run a single-column story about his latest killing. The what, when, *and* where *of the killing were adequately covered, but the* how *had remained a bit uncertain, pending results forthcoming from the state fish and game laboratories. Nothing of the* who *or* why. *He knows that* who *is the only concern of law enforcement officials and J.D. Callander, the local fish and game warden. He doubts they give much thought to or could even understand* why.

He'll have to be careful. For the last two weeks he has kept his vigil through the night on the hillside above the hatchery, watching. With only four deputies on staff, the county sheriff has only one cruiser and one officer to patrol through the night. He's seen a deputy swing his brown and white car through the hatchery only twice in the last two weeks. A state police cruiser drove through, flashing its spotlight over the pens, twice a night for three consecutive nights immediately following his last killing and hasn't returned since. The game warden has apparently been unable to convince traditional law enforcement authorities that the slaughter at the hatchery merits priority attention.

He has plenty of time. The fingerlings now in the troughs won't be ready to stock for another few weeks. Letting the binoculars rest against his chest, he lies back on the hillside and listens to the noisy life of the forest around him until the gap between the sound and his ears collapses, dissolving the night air into a single solution.

* * *

Some time ago, Inmate #52674 at the Bland County Correctional Facility wrote and mailed the following letter:

Dear Sandy,

So we're divorced now? They brought the papers and made me sign them today. Traitor. After all I've been through, after all the wrong you've already done to me, you just throw me away like trash. I never did anything but love you, want to be with you forever, take care of you, and now you betray me again, like this.

I signed your papers. They made me. But they don't mean a damn thing to me. You're my wife. Mine, do you understand? And no damned legal piece of paper will ever change that. Do you think you're going to get some other man? Or have you already, you slut? Well, forget it. As long as I say you're my wife, you are. Mine. Always mine. Right up until the moment I kill you.

   Your loving husband,
   Vernon

The letter was duly delivered but received no response.

* * *

Late spring is melting into early summer around the little house in the pine trees on Willard Road, and Sandy sits on the small front deck, sipping a cup of herbal tea and listening to Stink growling under her porch. Over the last couple weeks, she has arranged her few possessions and pieces of furniture in the little house and has settled into the pace of her new life and job rather quickly. Nothing unexpected about that to Sandy. But, as she drinks her tea and watches the rising sun behind the ridge begin to turn the undersides of clouds pink and orange, she thinks about the few things in her new life she did not expect. Stink growls again, more of a grumble really, and cautiously pokes his face out from under the porch, inching toward the bowl of dog food Sandy has set out for him.

   The woman who rented her the house neglected to tell her that Stink came with the property. Sandy first noticed him the day she moved in, sitting just at the edge of the trees around her house, watching her. He looked to her like a hodgepodge of spare dog parts melded forcefully into a single body. His fur, a splattering of so many shades of brown and yellow and orange that no one hue predominated enough to say he was a particular color. His body, thick in the chest and narrow in the hind quarters. One ear stood straight up, jagged on its edges, the other ear, slightly larger and flopping down. One eye dark brown, the other half blue and half black. Around his face and the ruff of his neck, small gray spots. His tail had likely been broken at some time in the past; the last few inches of it were crooked, the tip bent down at an odd angle. The left rear leg seemed slightly longer than the right, giving Stink an awkward, hobbled gait when he walked. And when he panted or growled, he revealed his most striking feature—perfectly-formed, blazing white teeth, not a single tooth snaggled, missing, or out of place.

"You may be too ugly and strange looking to be so mean," Sandy had said to him that first day as she carried two boxes of clothes into her house and Stink growled from the trees. "Nice teeth, though."

On her third day in the house, Sandy had asked her landlady about the dog when she stopped by to drop off an extra set of keys and see how her new tenant had settled in.

"Who? Stink?" she had said.

"That's his name? Stink?"

"Yeah. Rotten old mutt. Smells like every skunk he ever killed, all of 'em at once. He was my daddy's dog. Old Stink loved my daddy and daddy loved him, but that darned mutt pretty much hated every other living soul around here. Wouldn't let no one but daddy anywhere near him. I suppose some dogs could be partial to just one person, but Stink, he took things to extremes."

Sandy nodded and listened, saying nothing as the woman continued.

"When daddy died last fall, well, Stink sat out yonder there on that damned pile of old tires and moped for days. Couldn't no one get near him, much less get him away from the place."

"This was your father's house?" Sandy asked.

"Yeah. Mine too, I suppose. Did some of my growing up out here. Daddy had a heart attack and died on the spot. They figure he was unloading some old tractor tires, and the weight was too much for him and his heart just quit on him. We didn't find him for a whole day. Laying out there, under this big tractor tire, and there was Stink, sitting on his chest, inside that tire with his head poking up, just howling away. Was a sight to see, and I still don't know which smelled worse, them old tires, daddy, or Stink."

"I'm sorry for your loss." As a nurse, Sandy had spoken this phrase or heard it spoken so many times.

"Say what?" the woman said. "Oh yeah, thanks. Anyway, I wouldn't worry about Stink. He ain't going to come near you. Since Daddy died, he just lurks around out here, living off skunks and squirrels and whatever he can find in other folks' garbage or mashed on the road. If he ain't bothering you, I'd just ignore him. Or shoot him if you want. You want I should have my husband come out and shoot him?"

"Uh, no, that won't be necessary. He's no bother. I was just curious."

Sandy decided the dog had as much right to be there as she did, probably more. She bought a large bag of dog food, kept one bowl of food and another of water on the ground by the porch, and by the end of the first week, Stink had begun to creep in under Sandy's little deck to eat and lie in the shade for brief periods of time. He still wouldn't let Sandy get closer to him than to sit above him on her porch, and she didn't try. If she began to step down from the deck, he grunted and hobbled off to the trees. In his own good time, Sandy thought, though she realized that at some point she would have to get her hands on him once she realized that the gray spots around his face and neck were not spots at all, but rather a mass of blood-swollen ticks.

* * *

She leans forward in her chair and watches Stink begin to eat, hearing his perfect teeth crunch the nuggets of dog food. His neck is now particularly thick with bloated ticks, and from her perch above, Sandy can actually see tiny legs wriggling out from the sides of some of the more engorged parasites. She leans back, blows steam from her tea cup, and fans the air around her with her hand, a futile attempt to disperse the rank odor rising up through the deck planking from Stink's fur.

"If you're going to keep hanging out down there, at some point, I *will* be giving you a bath," she says to the dog.

The bottom-lit, sparse morning clouds blaze at their peak of orange and pink. Sandy knows the display will last only another five minutes or so and watches intently. And she watches her driveway. A simple gravel track runs thirty yards across the clearing from Sandy's house to a sparse band of trees and weaves another twenty yards through the trees to Willard Road. The remainder of Sandy's "driveway," as she considers it, continues directly on the other side of Willard Road—a narrow footpath leading through thickening brush another thirty or forty yards down to the banks of the lower Ripshin River. She sips her tea and knows that the surging water should have reached her path by now. Ten minutes ago she heard the siren at the Ripshin Dam a half-mile upstream from her house announce the increase in water levels as they began to generate power, pushing water through the enormous turbines in the dam, more than five hundred cubic feet of it every second. On a warm morning like this, there would have been a mist hovering over the glassy surface of the river from warm air meeting the cold water. Sandy pictures how the mist would have been dispersed and the glassy surface shattered once the water was released, in a matter of moments transforming the placid river into a rushing torrent. The torrent would arrive downstream at Sandy's path about ten minutes later. The water level in the reservoir is still high from spring run-off, and they'd be generating power for the next twelve hours. There'd be no fishing in these treacherous waters today.

The Ripshin churns within its banks, and Sandy watches her driveway. Without recognizing it, she is practicing, rehearsing, asking questions. Will it be like this when Vernon comes for her? Will she be sitting on her porch, watching the inflamed clouds, sipping tea, and smelling Stink when Vernon turns his white van up her driveway into the clearing? Will she hear his approach before he appears? Will the morning air be warm, indicating a warmer day to come, or will the early fall have begun to assert itself, cooling the temperatures and turning the leaves? Will the water in the Ripshin be running fast and high, producing electricity, or slow and smooth, inviting the trout fisher? Will it be morning? Afternoon? Night? Will Stink still be around? Will he stand forth, her rank protector, or wobble off into the trees to grunt and growl at the arrival of yet another stranger?

She finishes her tea and steps down from her porch. Stink slinks back deeper under the porch, grunts once, and waddles to the surrounding trees as she retrieves his empty food bowl.

"Ungrateful little bastard, aren't you?" she says, and walks back up the steps and into her house.

* * *

Sandy's skin glows under the stream of hot water in the shower, as she works the shampoo in her wet hair into a thick froth and thinks about the men she's encountered along the banks of the Ripshin River. Already, after only a few weeks, she has two enemies, one suitor, has been shot at by a neighbor, and is intrigued by one barefoot older man living alone on the upper Ripshin above the dam.

Another person might have been surprised to make enemies so quickly in a new place, but not Sandy Holston. Since she first picked up a fly rod and stepped into a trout stream, she noticed how most men viewed her, at best, as a curiosity, and at worst, as a dangerous anomaly, at times provoking their shock and anger. She still recalls the look of horrified confusion on Vernon's face, glimpsed only for a moment as she fled Dismal Creek. His horror sprang as much from the sight of his fleeing wife clad in waders and fishing vest, a fly rod in her hand, as it did from her betrayal.

The man in camouflage, whose spinner she had mutilated a few weeks back, and the young guy with the bucket of brook trout a couple weeks after that—one of them was definitely local, and the other likely was as well. She hadn't seen the younger one whose bait she had trashed. He seemed the more threatening of the two, but nothing she would lose sleep over. The camouflage man she had encountered already, and he would clearly be no more than a nuisance at most. Last week she had come upon him while putting gas in her truck at the Citgo. Sandy pulled to the middle pump behind another small pickup. Just as she began pumping her gas, a minivan drove up to the pump behind her, pulling to within a foot of her rear bumper, and the small pickup in front of her drove off. She had finished filling her tank and was returning the nozzle to the pump when he slipped by her in an orange Camaro with one gray fender. He had looked right at her and any doubts she had as to whether or not he recognized her evaporated as she walked in to the cashier and watched through the window while he backed his Camaro up to the first pump and stopped only an inch or two from her front bumper. He had her blocked in. After paying for her gas, Sandy slipped between the rear of her truck and the mini-van, stepped into the cab, and waited. Rather than engaging the catch and letting the pump do the work, the camouflage man pumped his gas by hand, slowly, sporadically, squeezing the handle and letting it go, over and over again, whistling and staring directly into the cab of Sandy's truck. She returned his stare without flinching. After about a minute of the game, the minivan behind Sandy backed out of its spot and Sandy did the same, as the camouflage man clicked the catch on the pump, flipped her the finger, and mouthed *bitch* as she pulled away from the Citgo. A fool and a nuisance, nothing more.

If she'd been a man, she wonders, would those two have responded differently to her vigilante discipline? Would they have come directly to blows, resolving the confrontation through force, or tucked their tails and retreated before a dominant peer? Did their shock and anger twist and fester because they could identify no acceptable response when their opponent was a woman in a place where a woman just goddamn wasn't supposed to be?

* * *

Sandy tilts her head forward into the shower stream and feels the lather slide from her hair, over her shoulders, back and breasts, down her stomach, and along her legs, swirling down the drain in the tub. Her hands squeak over her hair as she pushes it back from her forehead, wipes water from her eyes, and reaches for the soap.

J.D. Callander could prove to be a nuisance of a different kind. At first, Sandy saw no problem with him. She was a passing curiosity in the simplest way—a woman fly fisher. She'd seen the mild surprise, the brief flurry of gender confusion, on enough male faces to pay scant attention. However, once her contact with Callander moved beyond the river, the situation presented other complications.

She'd seen the state stocking truck drive up the road the evening before, so the next morning as she fished upstream from the foot path across from her house she wasn't surprised to see a game warden appear from the brush on the bank and ask to see her fishing license. They came out in droves on stocking days. With the denser population of anglers, a diligent game warden could write far more citations than usual in far less time. Sandy was downstream from the main stocking spots, but if Callander was anything, he was diligent.

"Could I see your license . . . ma'am?" he called from the bank.

Sandy nodded, reeled in her line, and began wading from the far side of the river toward the bank as she probed an inside vest pocket for the waterproof envelope containing her license.

"Won't be necessary, ma'am," Callander said. "If you just hold it up, I can read it from here." Callander lifted a pair of binoculars he had slung over his neck.

"That makes it easier," Sandy said, and held up the little square of official paper for inspection. The game warden seemed to keep his binoculars trained on her license longer than might be necessary to check its authenticity.

"Seeing what you need to see?" Sandy said.

Callander brought his binoculars down quickly and nodded awkwardly.

"Yes. Thank you. Sorry to have troubled you, ma'am."

"No trouble at all," Sandy said, stuffing her documentation back in her vest pocket. "Glad to see you out here checking. Anyone out here not fishing according to the regulations, well, I want them out of the water just as much as you do."

"Appreciate it."

Sandy began stripping line from her rod, preparing for her next cast.

"If you don't mind me saying, I've come across more than one person fishing with bait and spinners in the special regulation water, downstream from here and above the dam. You ought to be checking those spots as well as the stocked stretches. If you don't mind me saying."

"I try, but it takes a lot longer to cover those spots, and, thanks to state budget cuts and everything else that's going on, I'm spread pretty thin. Do my best."

Sandy nodded and began to move upstream.

"Have a nice day, Miss Holston," Callander said, and Sandy, halted by the unexpected familiarity, looked back to Callander on the bank.

"From your license. Your name on your license," he said.

Sandy nodded in acknowledgment and began to move again, but Callander stayed put on the bank.

"Doing any good?" he asked, and Sandy kept moving, beginning to be annoyed by his refusal to leave and continue his rounds.

"Little bit," she said, and continued wading, having spotted a rise about twenty yards ahead.

"You ought to head further upstream, closer to the dam where we stocked yesterday. Catch a lot more fish up there right now."

"I usually like my fish a bit wilder than that," Sandy said, still moving upstream.

"Suit yourself, I suppose," he said, and Sandy thought from the tone of his voice that she might have offended him. "But the way things are going lately, I don't know from month to month if we'll be able to keep stocking at the usual rate."

He seemed sincerely concerned, and Sandy paused in her wading, her rod held stationary, parallel to the river's surface. This had to be the damned chattiest game warden she'd ever encountered, but he'd gotten her interest now.

"What's the problem? Those budget cuts?" she asked.

J.D. Callander pulled himself up straighter, seemingly happy to talk of things that mattered deeply to him.

"Not that so much. We've had a couple incidents at the hatchery recently. Someone's killing trout."

"Really?" she said, and stood straight and looked squarely at Callander, genuinely interested. "How?"

"Not sure, but according to the state lab, we think somebody shocked them. Electrocution. It's happened twice now."

"Electrocuted? Interesting."

"I can't understand it. Just can't understand it."

Sandy could hear a definite pain in the warden's voice now.

"Why in the world would anyone do such a thing?" he said and looked down at the ground, shaking his head slowly.

"Couldn't say," Sandy said, returning to her fishing as Callander finally wished her a "nice day" again and disappeared back into the brush.

* * *

Sandy runs the towel one last time over her wet hair, drapes the towel around her neck, and walks naked from the bathroom to her kitchen to heat water for a second cup of tea. That first meeting with J.D. Callander admittedly had its moments. The killing of hatchery fish had gotten her attention. But it remained primarily an official encounter, offering no problems as far as she could see and easily forgotten. Complications began to crop up when she met Callander again about a week later.

According to her file, Ada Callander had been a resident of the Damascus Nursing and Rehabilitation Center for almost a year. Alzheimer's. According to other members of the nursing staff, her son J.D. came to visit her there maybe once or twice a month, usually on a Sunday. Not an overly-dutiful son, but more attentive than many children who parked their decrepit parents there and were hardly seen or heard from again, except for obligatory cards on birthdays and holidays or the occasional signature on a check or Medicare form. The old dump-and-run, the nursing staff called it.

Sandy had just finished checking Ada's blood pressure and was still leaning over her, removing the velcroed strap from her arm, when J.D. entered. His mother did not acknowledge his appearance. She was engaged in a quiet, unintelligible conversation with something invisible. He had seated himself in the chair by his mother's bed and greeted her before he recognized Sandy.

"Hello," Sandy had said, as she turned to leave the room.

"Hello . . . oh, hello, Miss Holston," J.D. said, clearly surprised.

Sandy recognized him, not so much by his face or voice as by the fact that he still wore, even on a Sunday visit to his mother, his game warden's uniform, including his gun.

"Sandy," she said, extending her hand.

"J.D. J.D. Callander," he said, rising too quickly, yanking his cap from his head, and reaching his hand to hers. "Nice to see you again. This is my mother."

"I gathered," Sandy said. "Unless you're here to check my nursing license, too."

Callander looked confused for a moment, then got the joke, smiled and turned his eyes to the floor.

"So you work here? I haven't seen you before," he said.

"Just started a couple weeks ago," she said.

Sandy found it only mildly curious that the game warden came to visit his mother armed and in uniform. Of more interest was that following that first encounter by his mother's bed, J.D. Callander became the most dutiful of sons. Every couple of days he stopped by to check on his ailing mother, spending a few minutes at her bedside, listening to her private conversations, and spending several more minutes than that, hanging around the nurses' station if Sandy was on duty. Since both of their lives were closely attached to rivers and fish, J.D. saw an opening for conversation.

"So you fish," he said.

"Yes."

"And fly fishing, no less."

"Uh-hunh."

"Been doing that long?"

"A while."

"You know, I don't see many women fishing," he said. "Certainly not fly fishing."

"I get that a lot," she said.

Sandy saw no reason to be any more forthcoming here than she was on stream. J.D. was, as far as she could see, a decent enough fellow, and if she had been interested in another man in her life at the time, she thought he might have done as well as the next one. But for the moment, as far as she was concerned, he was a relative of one of her patients, nothing more. If he had any special importance to her, it was only as the official representative of the angling rules and regulations she valued. By the end of last week, he had asked her if she'd like to join him for a movie that weekend at the cineplex over in Sherwood. Sandy had to work that weekend. She always worked weekends, and gladly so. Too many other fishers on the streams and rivers for her taste on weekends, so she took her days off during the week. All she required was the truth to keep him at bay this time, but she knew this wouldn't be the only time he'd ask, and she tried to turn the conversation back to rivers and rules.

"So, did you bust any of those bait fishermen in the special regulation waters?" she said.

* * *

Her hair hangs wet and loose, leaving small damp spots on the shoulders of her t-shirt. Through her kitchen window she sees Stink trot off into the trees. The remains of her second cup of tea have grown lukewarm, and she smears another dollop of blueberry preserves on her English muffin. She had the same breakfast a few days ago, the day she crossed paths with her neighbor, Tommy Akers. He lived about a half-mile upstream from Sandy on the remains of a farm that had been in his family for five generations, ran a fence-building business, raised a few black Angus cattle on the side, and was, as far as Sandy could recall, the only person who ever shot at her.

The air that day had been warm and still, the river's surface smooth, glassy, and the fishing slow. She'd taken only one fish all morning, but Sandy had long since ceased to gauge her fishing in numerical terms. Moving effortlessly through the water, she laid her line gently on the still surface, bisecting and rippling the mirrored reflection of the streamside trees, and settled into the peace of watching her fly drift slowly on the current. The roof of an old barn had been visible above the trees and brush on her right for several minutes, and her eyes played back and forth between the actual barn and its reflection in the river. Just as she dropped another cast onto the surface, a sharp blast resounded behind the tree line, leaves tore and exploded, and a spray of buckshot peppered the water only a few yards in front of Sandy, like a hundred tiny trout rising in unison.

Instinctively, she pulled her rod back, dragging her fly over the shattered surface, and retreated downstream from the shot, not frantically, simply a reverse of her graceful upstream wading.

"Hey," she shouted. "Hey. Someone's over here."

No second shot followed, and a moment later the brush parted again, less explosively. A man carrying a pump-action shotgun, the barrel pointed at the ground, appeared above the slope of the river bank, as Sandy continued her retreat. He wore a ball cap and a t-shirt with no sleeves, sported an enormous pot-belly that flopped far over his belt, and chewed ferociously on a wad of tobacco in his cheek. A pair of binoculars hung from a strap around his neck, resting on the hump of his pot-belly. His eyes were wide, his face flushed red, and even from her distance Sandy could recognize the concern and fear on his wide face. He spat a large brown gob before he spoke.

"Y'alright, ma'am? Y'alright? Didn't hit you, did I?"

Strictly as a reflex, Sandy looked down at her body to check and stopped her retreat.

"I seem to be in one piece," she said, "but watch out. Be careful with that damn thing."

Maintaining a certain caution, Sandy began to wade back upstream closer to the man. After a few steps she could read "Akers Fencing Service" stenciled on his cap.

"I'm real sorry, ma'am. Didn't know no one was back here. Real sorry. Sure you're okay?"

"I'm alright."

"I was shooting at a groundhog in my garden."

Sandy remembered the level at which the shot burst through the trees and thought it must have been a remarkably tall groundhog, or else this pot-bellied man was a remarkably lousy shot.

"I sure didn't mean to shoot at you. Thank the Lord you ain't hurt," he said.

"I'm okay," she said. "Just be careful. You ought to know people could be fishing through here."

"Well, I wouldn't shoot 'em just for that. Especially a woman."

The fear on his face evaporated, leaving a stern blankness. He jammed his finger inside his cheek, repositioned his chaw, and spat again. The shotgun remained pointed at the ground, loosely cradled in the crook of his arm.

"Though Lord knows, they's times when I feel like shooting someone."

Sandy kept moving upstream. She wanted to be away from this man and back to her fishing, but she thought, given the circumstances, she'd do best to keep up a little casual talk with this chatty, tobacco-chewing armed man who spoke wistfully of shooting people and had, accident or not, just taken a shot at her.

"That doesn't make me feel too secure," Sandy said. "Maybe you'd let me get out of range before you start firing again?"

"I'm sorry ma'am. I'm just jawing," he said. "I wouldn't ever shoot no one. Just that sometimes I can't think of much else to do, what with what all they done to the river."

"What did they do?"

"What they do? Look at it. This ain't the way this river supposed to be."

The man's eyes lifted from Sandy and gazed upstream. Sandy kept moving, but her pace slowed. She was listening.

"I'm old enough to remember before they put the dam in."

Sandy only now noticed the crows' feet around the eyes and a couple days' growth of white stubble on the round, red face.

"Used to be chock full of catfish. Best place around here for catfish. Now, ain't seen a catfish in here since I was a little one."

Sandy froze when he moved the shotgun but relaxed when he set the stock on the ground, leaned on the tip of the barrel, and continued.

"Built the dam, the water got cold, they filled the river with them trout and poisoned and shocked out all the catfish. I do love eatin' catfish, and there ain't nothing compares to one you fresh caught."

"Trout are pretty good, too." Sandy thought she should say something, and that was the best she could muster at the moment.

"I fish for 'em sometimes, but never could get partial to trout. Too fussy. Except maybe for the natives up in the headwaters, and they's too small and too far away for the bother. Used to come right down here when I was a boy, with my daddy and granddaddy, and we'd catch enough catfish for a big old catfish dinner in no time at all. Anytime we wanted."

He leaned forward and shot another fat, brown gob of juice from his mouth. From the middle of the river, Sandy could hear it splat on a leaf.

"If that ain't bad enough, the fish and game people expect me to buy a fishing license to fish in my own river. Last year that Callander fellow wrote me up a ticket for just that. Imagine, making me pay to fish in my own river. Akers been on this farm since my great-great-granddaddy. Five generations. That'll be the day when I buy a fishing license. Let 'em try to make me to pay that fine."

"I met him a couple weeks ago. Just doing his job."

"Humph," he said, and spit. A dark strand caught on his lip and dripped onto his chin. He spit again before wiping his arm across his face.

"Hell with his job, excuse my language, ma'am," he said. "Couple years ago them fish and game people was out here. Drove their trucks right across my pasture. Said they had to repair, what was it, ree-parian habitat, cause run-off from the cattle pasture was bad for the fish. Imagine that. My land, my cattle, my river, and they just come right on in here and do what you will. And I'm supposed to pay for it."

He paused and looked back over his shoulder in the direction of what Sandy assumed was his pasture. Sandy thought this might be a good time to say nothing and tried to inch her way further upstream, but he hadn't spent himself yet.

"Nowadays, seems it's mostly outsiders like you, no offense, with fancy fishing tackle and expensive cars. Not so many local folks fish the river anymore."

"I live just up the road," Sandy said. "And I drive an old pickup truck."

"Oh, you the woman moved into Calvin Linkous' place, God rest his soul?"

Sandy nodded and reeled in the line that had drifted down behind her.

"Tommy Akers," he said, touching his hat.

"Sandy Holston," she said.

"What brings you to these parts, if you don't mind me asking?"

"Fishing, mostly. When I'm not being shot at."

He grinned sheepishly, looked down, and spat.

"Sorry about that again. Not a real neighborly way to welcome you, I suppose."

"All's forgiven. I work at the nursing home in Damascus."

"That daughter of Calvin's get rid of that old dog Stink?"

"He's still hanging around. Still stinks."

"Pitiful animal. How about that pile of tires out back?"

"Still there, for the time being."

"Well, no offense again, ma'am, but from where I'm standing, you still a bit of an outsider. Moving to a place don't necessarily make you part of a place. But welcome anyway."

Sandy breathed a bit easier and resumed her upstream course as Tommy Akers turned to walk away, but before she could proceed very far, he spoke again while he walked off into the brush and trees behind his barn.

"And keep that smelly old dog away from my cattle. Shot him once and I'll shoot him again if he comes down here running meat off my herd."

* * *

Sandy puts her breakfast dishes in the sink for later and wonders if Tommy Akers's buckshot had anything to do with Stink's hobbled walk. She walks out to her truck and takes a pair of work gloves from the bed. The gloves are noticeably new, yet the palms are dirty, soiled a dingy black. She throws them into the cab, climbs in, and starts the ignition.

"You going to sit there all day and growl again, or are you going to help me, you old mutt?" Through the open truck window she calls to

Stink, sitting at the edge of the trees, as she backs up the drive behind her house to the huge pile of old tires.

According to her landlady's version of the story, Calvin Linkous' plan had been fairly simple. Let anyone who wanted to dump old tires behind his place. Start a tire retread business. The pile of old tires grew surprisingly quickly over the last few years, but the retread business somehow never got up and running. As it turned out, Calvin Linkous was quite adept at collecting and piling old tires but didn't know the first thing about the retread business.

"Of all the fool things he ever did," his daughter had said, "them tires was one of the most foolish."

With her landlady's blessing, Sandy took it on herself to get rid of the tires. They were a fire hazard, mosquitoes bred in the stagnant water collected in some of them, and they smelled. Since it appeared that here in her new home she would have to live alongside an odd-looking dog that reeked of every skunk he'd ever killed, she saw no need to cohabit with a mound of smelly old tires as well. The Goodyear store over in Sherwood said they'd recycle them if she brought them in, and she'd already dropped off two pickup truck loads. Sandy estimated it would take her another ten or twelve loads to move her pile to Goodyear's pile. She could only take them at their word that the tires wouldn't end up behind some other Calvin Linkous's house.

Car and pickup tires presented little problem. She could lift them easily, sometimes two at a time. Sandy had always been a fairly strong woman, and after eight years or so of lifting patients from beds into wheel chairs, bloodied accident victims from ambulance gurneys to emergency room tables, some old tires were no sweat. Except, maybe, for the tractor tires, piled in two stacks separate from the mound of other tires. Enormous and heavier than she had thought, she'd have to lever, roll, drag, and shove them. The tractor tires could wait. There weren't that many of them, but they were so large her truck wouldn't be able to carry more than three at a time. She'd work on the car tires for now. Besides, Stink seemed emotionally attached to the tractor tires. A single tractor tire lay loose on the ground by the stacks of the others, and each time she had started lifting and loading tires into her truck, Stink had come from the trees and sat inside the tire, growling low, his eyes fixed on Sandy, occasionally sinking his perfect teeth into the worn black rubber. She wondered if that were the fatal tire.

Sandy wipes her face on the sleeve of her t-shirt and lifts the last two tires of this load into the truck bed. Stink grumbles from within the ring of the tractor tire. Sandy closes the tailgate, removes her gloves, and leans against the side of her truck, tilting her face down toward Stink. He gnaws tentatively on the tire.

"I can't decide if you're sadly tragic or just pathetic," she says. "Either way, you're one disturbed dog. And stay away from the cattle today."

After moving the truck back down the drive to the front of her house, Sandy puts fresh water in Stink's bowl and dumps her fishing gear in the truck's cab, wedging it against the passenger door to allow room for herself behind the wheel. With the day off from work and the water running high and turbulent in the tailwater all day, she decides to drop this load of tires in Sherwood, then drive back up above the reservoir to the headwaters of the Ripshin. She should be able to make it in plenty of time for the afternoon stonefly hatch. The clouds have dissipated and the late morning sun has risen high above the ridge. Stink barks once as Sandy pulls out of her driveway onto Willard Road. She wonders if she'll see the barefoot man, Keefe, up there again today.

* * *

In just a month's time, in an out of the way place where she thought she would be left alone, where she went to avoid a vengeful husband, she has been forced to contend with more problem men than any woman should have to face in a lifetime. Then again, they were all men, weren't they? But Keefe had aroused her interest. Compared to other men with whom her life had intersected, there was something different about him, something present or lacking in him she couldn't identify and hadn't encountered before.

He seemed to grow like moss on the river rocks of the upper Ripshin, to be shaped by the terrain he inhabited. Though they only spoke briefly over their coffee the day they met and double-teamed the young man in the Braves cap, something in his voice lingered in her ears. Not what he said. Not the pitch or tone of the voice. No, it was the rhythm of his voice. It rose and fell in time with the waters pouring down the mountainside in front of his cabin. But within the voice she sensed something, some one thing, broken. Like a single piece of flood-trash—a crumpled plastic soda bottle or a rusted bicycle, in a pristine gradient stream—something out of place, out of balance, cut the current of Keefe's voice.

If a bit distant, which Sandy could certainly appreciate, he'd been amiable enough when they met. He'd helped her walk to the steps of his cabin, given her coffee—good strong coffee—and driven her back down the fire road to her truck. More than most strangers would do for another. More than Sandy might have done if their positions had been reversed. But the broken thing hidden in his voice could be heard when she asked to use his bathroom. His face went stony and his voice caught in his throat, stammering out the reluctant *yes* that he couldn't decently withhold, given the circumstances. Though it took her only a minute to step through his small home and use the tiny bathroom, Keefe stood by the door and watched intently the entire time, except when she disappeared behind his bathroom door. Keefe was clearly on edge, feeling invaded, and Sandy thanked him and apologized for the intrusion as she exited. The river-rhythm in his voice returned as she stepped back out onto his porch.

"No intrusion at all," he lied.

But during her brief passage through Keefe's bungalow, Sandy, too, had been alert. Perhaps more than the cadence of his voice, the interior of Keefe's modest home provoked Sandy's fascination.

Whereas Sandy's new home was sparsely furnished, pared down as a result of her recent move, the cluttered interior of Keefe's cabin indicated a resident with no intention, or hope, of any manner of relocation. Walls of pine paneling surrounded what was little more than a single room, a room that by conventional standards might have qualified as a fairly large room, but had been shrunken substantially by the density of its contents. From floor to ceiling, along each wall, stacked in corners, the room was clogged with books and fishing gear. Bookcases packed with volumes shelved at all angles, wedged into any available space, with more books piled on top of the cases and across the mantle of a river-stone fireplace through which Sandy could see into what appeared to be a bedroom on the other side of the wall. Fly rods leaned in corners and rested on hooks on the walls. A fishing vest hung from a nail near the door, and waders and boots sat in a pile nearby. An old wicker creel dangled from a pair of discarded antlers on the wall above a woven basket filled with what appeared to be river rocks. At the center of the room, a small oasis was formed by a single lamp, a small sofa of cracked brown leather and a matching armchair sitting at a right angle to it around a heavy but simple pine coffee table. Like the rest of the room, the table was cluttered, covered with books, fly boxes, a reel, river rocks, a squirrel tail, a pack of non-filter cigarettes, and a glass ashtray with one cigarette butt stubbed out in it. The sofa faced away from the front door toward the back wall, against which sat a fly-tying bench. At the center of the bench, a magnifying loop and vise, and around that center, scattered on the bench surface and spilling from drawers and shelves, a motley, multi-colored mass of feathers, fur, string, thread, scissors, pliers, bottles of glue and paint, trays of hooks, several more squirrel tails, one rabbit hide, and other indecipherable materials. The room had the look of an arena in which an ongoing battle had been waged for some time now.

As overwhelmed as Sandy was by the chaotic jumble of the main portion of Keefe's home, she was equally engaged by its islands of order. At one end of the bungalow, a small kitchen area, simple and clean, divided from the rest of the room by a counter. A few canisters lined the countertop along with a toaster oven and an unusually elaborate coffee maker. Three polished copper pans of varying sizes hung from the wall. A tea kettle and a cast iron skillet sat on the stove

At the opposite end of the room were the only other separate rooms in the cabin. A small bedroom, containing a bed, neatly made, and a simple night stand holding a brass lamp. Opposite the bedroom, the bathroom, narrow, clean, with matching towels neatly hung on a rack, a toothbrush in a glass, and no noticeable film or grunge on the sink, toilet, or tub.

Leaving the bathroom and carefully picking her way through the rubble of Keefe's main living area, Sandy noted one other enclave of orderliness. On the top shelf of Keefe's fly-tying bench, hovering over the whirl of feathers and fur, a crystal lamp and a polished silver canister, wider at the top, narrowing to its base. Even with only the momentary glance she gave it as she stepped past it, Sandy could see the shelf, the lamp, and the canister were meticulously free of dust.

* * *

Scattered clumps of clouds have moved into the afternoon sky. It took Sandy a little longer to dispense with her load of tires than she predicted, but she should still be in time for the afternoon hatch. She casually rubs at a black smudge on her t-shirt as she turns onto the fire road leading into the headwaters of the Ripshin. She parks her truck at the gate, removes her gear, and begins to step into her waders, wondering if she'll see the barefoot man again today by his cluttered cabin that both intrigues and confuses her. Keefe's bungalow is not a home, really, but rather a repository of sorts, a place for storing the material supplies of a life that occurs elsewhere. And yet the cabin seems to mark him as a creature who could exist nowhere else but right there.

"I think I feel like the inside of his house looks," Sandy says.

The springs far up along Rogers Ridge pump waters into the upper Ripshin like blood into robust arteries, and Sandy feels the stream gush into her like a transfusion. As she drops down the bank and steps into the current, she looks behind her, as if to locate visually the weight of men lurking at her back. She targets a back eddy beside a chute of water plunging into the pool, strips line from her reel, and reminds herself to call Margie when she gets home tonight.

* * *

Not that long ago, Inmate #52674 at the Bland County Correctional Facility wrote and mailed the following letter:

Dear Sandy,

Maybe I should have told you this right off the bat. Maybe if I had told you then, things would be different now, and I wouldn't have to do what I have to do. Or maybe I'm only just now realizing what it really was that made me crack, made me have to make a run for it.

I shouldn't have been sent here in the first place. I never belonged here. I wasn't a criminal. I was an honest man, a working man, a free man. I was protecting my wife, protecting what was mine. What still is mine. Remember that. But not anymore. Now, thanks to you and that kid, I'm just what they say I am, a convict, a criminal. Guess I better tell you about the kid.

It happened years ago. It was July. I'd been in for 3½ months. I remember. Everyone here remembers time real clearly. I was getting along as well as can be expected, I guess. A few fights, but nothing I couldn't handle. I've always been able to hold my own. And I always will be able to.

We were sent out on road detail. About 15 of us and 3 guards, packed into one of them blue buses with bars across the windows. Back then I never looked out the windows. I couldn't stand looking through the bars. I just looked down at the floor. It didn't matter where we were going. The whole world looks just the same through those bars.

They took us over to a long stretch of route 100, about ten miles away, to pick up trash. Trash people, picking up people's trash. They gave us each an orange trash bag and one of those orange plastic vests to wear, like they'd give a shit if someone didn't see one of us and ran us down. All those vests were good for was making us hotter than we already were, and after we'd been out there a couple hours, we were sweating like pigs. Like pigs, we're digging around in the dirt for garbage while the guards just stand there, their shotguns jacked on their hips, talking and laughing, telling us what to do, what not to do, and not one of them any better, any different really, than us, just luckier.

I was near the end of the line. A guard was standing maybe 20 feet away, watching off down the line. As we spread out working, the guards spread out too. Like I said, it was hot, and I stood up straight, just for a second, to wipe the sweat off my face, and a car went by. Cars had been going by us all morning, but I had to look up just then, at that car, one of those minivans.

There was a kid in the back seat. I don't know how old. Just a kid, like a million kids. Just as I was wiping my face the van drove by and the kid was looking right at me and I looked right at him and I saw in his face exactly what he was seeing. The guards with the shotguns, the blue bus with bars across the windows, all of us strung out along the road in orange vests and prison blues, and me. He saw me. Looked right at me and saw me, all of it that was me now. Not me as a kid like him, not me as a hard-working, free man who could build a house from the ground up if he only had the chance, not me married to what I thought was a good woman. No, he only saw a convict. A criminal. That's all he saw. All anyone saw. And just then I knew. Maybe I couldn't say it like I am now, but I knew. It didn't matter a damn anything else I was. To that kid, to all those kids in all those minivans, kids that could have been my kids in a van I was driving past a road gang, to anyone on the outside—I was a con. Nothing else. Never would be anything else. And just then I knew I had to get out. Get out while there was still some me other than a convict left.

And you know the rest. Maybe if I'd told you this, you'd have felt different, done what you were supposed to do, what you promised to do. If you had known, really known what this place was like, what this life did to a man, you wouldn't have, couldn't have left me there. And now there's nothing else left for me do. I may be a convict, but I keep my promises. And you can count on me. See you soon, traitor.

Your loving husband,

Vernon

The letter was duly delivered but received no response.

* * *

"What? Did you just tell me you got shot at?" Through the phone, the rise in Margie's voice sounds like a knife slicing into stiff styrene.

Sandy leaves the remains of the salad she's been eating sitting on the kitchen table and takes the phone and her tea cup outside, pushing the screen door open with her rear end and settling down onto the concrete stoop behind her house. The sun has been down for more than an hour, but a band of light remains above the trees behind her house, enough light to see the pile of tires up the hillside to her left, where Stink has resumed his place inside the old tractor tire. Sandy can see that Stink is watching her, and through the metallic hum of cicadas in the surrounding trees, she can just hear his low, sporadic grumbling.

"It wasn't that big a deal, Margie," Sandy says. "An accident. He was shooting at a groundhog."

"I don't care if he was shooting at a groundhog or whatever other furry creatures you have crawling around there. He almost shot *you*."

"But he didn't. He missed me by at least ten yards. Besides, after that buckshot went through all those trees, it was pretty spent. Even if it had hit me, it wouldn't have done much damage."

"Oh, well, no problem then. You'd have only been shot a little bit. Anything like being a little pregnant? Jesus, girl, what kind of wilderness are you living in?"

Sandy smiles and laughs silently, sipping at her tea.

"It's hardly a wilderness," she says. "Nothing to worry about."

"Nothing to worry about? Uh, let's review. You . . ."

Margie's voice drifts into the distance as she pulls the receiver away from her mouth.

"Luke, stop poking your brother. Stop it. Matthew, stop whining. If your brother pokes you, well, poke him back."

Sandy hears Margie's breath in the receiver as the phone comes back to her mouth.

"Where was I?"

"You were about to conduct a review."

"Oh yeah, let's review. You've lived in this god forsaken wilderness for, what, a month or so now? And, I'd like to point out, I'm about the only friend you have, and about the closest thing you have to any sort of family, as far as I know, and I still don't know where the hell that god forsaken wilderness is."

"Not yet."

"Uh-hunh."

"At least I finally called."

"And for that I am truly blessed."

"Don't be snotty," Sandy says, smiling, as she watches Stink in his tire, scratching at a tick in his ear.

"Sorry. I get a little testy when I'm abandoned," Margie says. "Okay, you've lived in who-knows-where for a month or so, and in that short time, in this mysterious place where you went to get away from it all, you can't seem to turn around without bumping into some fool man, who you then proceed to royally piss off. Am I getting it right so far?"

"Only pissed off a couple, really."

Margie's voice drifts away again. "Luke, what did I just tell you?"

Sandy stretches her legs out from the stoop and massages one thigh as Margie's voice comes back into the receiver.

"Maybe you could teach me to use that fly rod of yours on these boys before they drive me completely nuts."

"Maybe."

"Where was I this time? Yeah, you've got a couple fishermen pissed enough to spit nails. And if that isn't enough, before you can blink an eye, your neighbor, if you can call him that, comes out of the trees, blasting away at you with a shotgun. Accident or no accident."

"His name's Tommy Akers."

"Well, do send Tommy my regards the next time he shoots at you."

"His family's lived on that farm for five generations."

"Oh, that changes everything. By all means, let him fire at will. He's got the right to, eh?

Sandy is draining the last of her tea when Margie says this and breaks into a laugh, choking on the liquid in her throat.

"You okay?"

"Fine, fine."

"Now, review almost complete. On top of all this, there is the real fish police. What's his name again?"

"J.D. J.D. Callander. He's the local fish and game warden."

"J.D. What's the J.D. stand for?"

"Don't know. Didn't ask."

"Figures. Okay, J.D., it turns out, doesn't shoot at you and isn't pissed off at you. In fact, quite the opposite. J.D., who is apparently the only man in who-knows-where who doesn't want to kill you, good old J.D., it seems, appears to have a thing for you."

"I don't know."

"You don't know? Uh, he shows up where you work, hangs out at the nurses' station, sweet-talking you, and, in fact, asks you out on a date. A date, girl. Remember those? When's the last time you went out on a date?"

"Been a while."

"A while? More like ancient history."

"Been a while for you, too," Sandy says.

"That's different. I'm a single mother, with two sons. Nothing will turn a man off faster than a woman who comes with children. That, and the fact that my ass is the size of Kansas."

"It's not that big, Margie."

"Don't avoid the issue, girl. We're not talking about my sex life or my ass. We're talking about you. You're alone, and a perfectly decent guy—he is decent, right?"

"He's fine."

"No warts on his face? Doesn't get his jollies pulling the wings off flies or kicking puppies?"

"Not that I can tell."

"So, this perfectly decent guy, J.D., is always hanging around. Face it, he doesn't come see his mother every other day, his mother who,

85

according to you, doesn't even know he's there . . . he doesn't come to see his mother that often all of a sudden because he's such the good son. He's got a case for you, girl, he asks you out, and you just brush him off. Why?"

"Just not interested."

"Not interested? Aren't you at least horny? God knows I am."

"Not that often. Besides, there's other ways to take care of that."

"Please. I'm an expert on sexual self-maintenance. But it gets old. Wouldn't you like a little of the real thing?"

"Sometimes. Maybe. But that tends to come with extra baggage."

"True. Can't argue with you there. But it's just not healthy for you to be alone so much. I worry about you, girl."

The evening has gone dark. Sandy can no longer see Stink, but she can hear him, curled up in his tire, his growls mingling with snores.

"I'm not alone."

"Right. There's Stink. You're all alone, just you, your fish, and your watershed. You're a good-looking thirty-two-year-old woman, free and available, and your most enduring relationship with a male is with an old dog who smells like skunk and hates you."

"He doesn't hate me. We're just working out our differences. Margie, I appreciate your concern. Really I do. But you're forgetting something."

"What?"

"I didn't come here looking for a man. I'm trying to avoid one."

"Maybe so, but for a woman who's doing all she can to avoid men, you sure have a talent for attracting a flock of them around you."

"I don't mind being alone, Margie. Prefer it most times."

"So you say, but if that's the case, how come most of what we've been talking about is the men, good and bad, you've come across since you disappeared?"

"I could tell you about the fishing. It's been great here."

"No, thanks, honey. I love you to death, but if you start that fish-talk of yours, lord, I'll be asleep before either of us know it. Like listening to a foreign language to me."

"Okay. And I didn't disappear. I just moved," Sandy says and stares off into the dark trees, wondering for just a moment if Margie could be right. If she might be just a little lonely.

"No forwarding address, girl. Unlisted phone number. To me, that's disappeared."

"Sorry. I'll let you know sometime soon."

"But I miss you, god knows why."

"Miss you, too."

"So, review complete. Have we covered everything? There aren't any other men angry with you or lurking around after you there?"

"Not really."

"Excuse me? *Not really*? Give it up, girl. You're holding out on me. Who else is there?"

"Well, there's this one other person who's kind of interesting. That older man I mentioned."

"Whoa. The old coot and the bucket of fish? Now you've really got my attention."

Sandy hears one of Margie's sons begin to wail in the background.

"Matthew, stop crying, honey. Luke, behave," Margie says, not moving the phone from her mouth. "I'll be right there. Look, Sandy, if I don't get these boys to bed now, they may kill each other."

"That's okay. It's getting late," Sandy says.

"Not on your life, girl. You don't drop something new into the story and just leave it lying there, expecting me to ignore it. No way you get off that easy. It will take me exactly thirty minutes to get these monsters to bed, wash up, and pour myself a big old glass of wine. Call me back then."

"Alright."

"Promise?"

"I promise," Sandy says, rising from her stoop.

"Good," Margie says, "because if you don't, I'll star-69 your ass all night long until you do pick up."

Sandy's ear is sweaty and sore from holding the phone against it for so long. She rubs her ear and is reminded why she's never been very fond of talking on the telephone.

"Good night, Stink, my darling," she calls as she steps inside her kitchen.

Sandy washes her few dishes, hangs her work clothes for the next day on the hook on her closet door, and takes a quick shower. There are still a couple of black smudges that she missed on one arm from the morning's load of tires, and she scrubs them until her skin is almost red. She pulls a t-shirt from her dresser. The shirt has a picture of a Royal Wulff on the front, and the lettering reads "Check Your Fly." She slips into the t-shirt as she walks back into the bathroom. She squeezes a pool of moisturizer into the palm of one hand and rubs it into the skin of her hands and forearms. Still rubbing her arms, she walks into the living room, scoops the latest issue of *Fly Fisherman* from where it lies beside the mahogany fly box—Margie's gift—on the coffee table, and walks back to her sparsely-furnished bedroom. The evening remains warm, and through the open windows she can hear the cicadas, the crickets, and the occasional grunt from Stink. She pulls the covers back but lies uncovered on top of the sheets, feeling the cool cotton on the back of her legs and buttocks, as she flips through her magazine until it's time to call Margie again.

Sandy has had a long, good day. The air in the hills around the headwaters had been cooler than at her house on the tailwaters, and the native brook trout in the upper Ripshin had been responsive and feisty. But a day full of hefting heavy old tires and hiking up trails and over streamside boulders has left her tired and drained. Tomorrow she has a full shift at the nursing home, and she wants to sleep. Margie's enthusiasm and curiosity are beginning to wear her down, but Sandy can't bring herself to cut off the conversation. After repeating the story of the young man in the Atlanta Braves' cap at the pool in front of Keefe's cabin, emphasizing Keefe's role in the episode, Sandy feels the muscles in her legs and arms melt into the sheets.

"So, is he old or not?" Margie asks. Sandy can hear the snap of Margie's cigarette lighter and her long exhale through the receiver.

"Well, yes and no," Sandy says.

"Come on, you're a geriatric nurse now. You ought to be able to figure this out."

"That's just it. He changed. When we were rousting the guy from the pool, he looked ancient. I'd have sworn mid-eighties at least. But when we went back to his cabin, he got younger. Stopped using his staff and stood up straight. I wouldn't have said he was more than sixty or so then."

"You went to his house? Hah. I've had a sneaking suspicion all along that you were into this fishing stuff for the sex. But geezer sex?"

"You have a hopelessly dirty mind, Margie."

"I'm a single mother with a big ass. The dirt in my mind is my only pleasure. It keeps me entertained."

"I'd twisted my ankle a little. He let me rest on his porch and use his bathroom, then gave me a ride back to my truck. That's all."

"Sounds nice enough, but not that interesting, except for the old coot act."

"I don't know. There was something about him. Can't put my finger on it. He just sort of interested me. That, and his cabin."

Sandy drops her head back on her pillow and listens to Margie slurping wine.

"The inside of his cabin was, well, I don't know, interesting."

"Details, girl."

"Well, the place was packed. Full of stuff. I could hardly walk through the room."

"Packed with what?"

"Books. Books everywhere. And fly fishing gear. Fly rods and gear all over the place. And a fly-tying bench, piles of feathers and squirrel tails and the like."

"Squirrel tails? Ugh. Okay, he's a lousy housekeeper."

"Just the main part of the cabin. The kitchen and the bedroom and the bathroom were neat as a pin."

"Ah-ha. You were in his bedroom. I knew it."

"Oh, stop it. I could see it when I went into the bathroom. It's just a little cabin."

"Well, why not," says Margie. "All the men you know either want to kill you or you don't want anything to do with them. At least this guy interests you."

"Stop it. It's nothing to do with that. Besides, he's probably twice my age."

"Well, maybe that's the way to go. Seems to take men about twice as long to grow up as women. Maybe he's Mr. Right. God knows, he needs a housekeeper."

"I'm no housekeeper," Sandy says.

"No shit."

"There was just something about his cabin. About all that stuff piled all over the place."

"What?"

"Don't know. It didn't feel like a mess. Felt like everything was exactly where it was supposed to be. Felt like there was a whole life right there in the room. I don't know. It was like . . . forget it."

"Like what?"

"I know it's silly, but . . . well, it felt like a room in the ICU."

"Uh, the last time I worked in ICU, I didn't see any rooms equipped with squirrel tails."

"I said it seemed silly. But all that stuff, it felt like IV drips and monitors and respirators keeping a critical patient alive."

"Whatever works for you, honey."

"I told you it sounded silly."

"So, have you seen the coot since then?"

"His name's James Keefe."

"Okay, have you seen old James Keefe since then?"

"Once. Today."

"And? At this mysterious cabin again?"

"No. Came across him lying in the tail of a pool upstream from there."

"Uh, *lying in a pool*? Of water? Dare I ask, was he alive?"

"Yes, alive. In a wet suit, with a swim mask and snorkel. Just lying there in the tail of the pool, not more than a foot of water."

"What? What was he doing? Scuba diving in a foot of water?"

Sandy chuckles and props herself up on her elbow.

"No. Just lying there. Looked like a huge beaver."

"Just lying there. What'd you do?"

"Nothing. Watched him for a minute. I was curious."

"I'd say."

"Then he saw me and got up. Think I startled him a little."

"The mighty huntress stalking the wild, codger-beaver in its natural habitat. You should have your own show on the Discovery Channel. So, did you ask him why he was scuba-diving in a foot of water?"

"Not in those words, but, yes."

"What'd he say?"

"That's what was interesting. He said *keeping an eye on things.*"

"*Keeping an eye on things.* Weird. Then what?"

"That's it. Then he left. I told you, I think I startled him. And, in a way, he seemed maybe a little embarrassed. I don't know."

"Weird. An old coot with a messy house who scuba-dives in puddles of water. Weird."

"Yes, but interesting, you have to admit."

"Yes, interesting. And weird."

Margie emits a long yawn, and through the phone it infects Sandy, who yawns in response.

"Guess we better call it a night," Margie says.

"Yeah, it's late and I have to work in the morning," Sandy says.

"Did we cover everything of interest in your mysterious little wilderness?" Margie says. "Leave anything out?"

"Don't think so," Sandy says. "Someone's been killing fish over at the hatchery."

"Oh, christ, Sandy. What in the hell kind of place are you living in?"

3

Penance

Stepping through thick, prickling summer brush onto the bank of the lower Ripshin, Sandy freezes, her weight shifting forward onto her right leg, and feels her scalp tighten under her cap. Only a few feet in front of her, a water moccasin lies loosely curved in the shallows at the river's edge. The black and brown snake draws its head back and up at Sandy's emergence, coils itself slightly, locates the source of the disturbance, and opens its wide, white mouth. The moccasin is a big one, maybe five feet long, and Sandy attempts to calculate the distance between herself and the viper as her scalp grows tighter and a chill runs down the outside flanks of her legs. If it strikes, is the snake long enough and strong enough to reach her? If it does, can its fangs pierce her waders? If they can, will she be able to make it the mile and a half back up the trail to her truck before the venom in her blood makes her too weak to walk? The water moccasin closes its mouth, uncoils, slithers backwards into the deeper water, and is quickly gone in the downstream current.

Sandy releases the weight from her right leg, relaxes her stance, and discharges the air locked in her lungs. Only snakes could elicit such a response from her. In all her years stalking trout in the waters of the Rogers Ridge watershed, no other wildlife but snakes ever froze Sandy in her tracks. From angry men with mangled fishing tackle to deer, skunks and raccoons, herons and kingfishers, tail-whacking beavers, mink and muskrat, even a black bear a couple of times—none of these were ever more than a minor caution to her, at worst, and at best, and most often, they crossed her path as confirmation that the watershed remained alive and in good health and that she inhabited the right place. Whether an innocuous water snake swimming in midstream, a small ring-necked snake asleep on streamside stones or the admittedly more dangerous copperhead or water moccasin, her response was the same. Every cell in her body ground to a halt. Once, a startled black snake coiled itself up into a corkscrew at the side of the path she walked, and she actually let out a tiny shriek and dropped her fly rod. Sandy chastised herself the rest of the day for being frightened by such a harmless creature as a black snake, but the fear remained. She heard anglers' yarns of the *biggest goddamn timber rattler ever*, sunning itself on a riverside rock. Like everyone else who heard such tales, she scoffed at the dubious narratives, but she checked those rocks carefully just the same.

For the last month little rain has fallen in the Rogers Ridge watershed. The brush along stream banks has grown stiff and dry, stalks and leaves brown and crinkled. Water levels are low in other streams and maintained at a minimum here in the lower Ripshin. The hydroelectric dam has virtually shut down, only rarely releasing any water for power generation, keeping the lake level up for the water-skiers and pleasure boaters. For the last couple of weeks, Sandy has fished below the dam more often than in the headwaters, taking advantage of the consistently smooth and gentle current to learn better the tailwaters of the lower Ripshin. After the water moccasin's retreat, she takes a few deeper breaths to relax her lungs into a calmer condition. She rubs her earring and waits a moment longer, giving the snake ample time to slink downstream, then glides into the river, her balance restored, and begins to wade upstream.

She had tied on a hopper pattern before she began the hike down the path to where she entered the river, and the hike confirmed her choice. Grasshoppers popped and exploded from the brown grass and brush. The crackling buzz of their black wings filled the air with a din that accompanied Sandy's footfalls on the dusty path. She smiled at the dull click of frantic grasshoppers bouncing off her waders, knowing that this same leaping frenzy would send many of the insects flying into the seam of water along the riverbank. The proliferation of such large, volatile insects on the surface of the water would stir up the trout in the lower Ripshin. In particular, as Sandy knows, large numbers of these frenetic grasshoppers, flapping desperately on the river's fringes, would catch the attention of even the huge, hook-jawed hogs that inhabit the deeper holes. Older, savvy, and normally cautious trout could be enticed by such big bugs to abandon their usual wary ways, to venture out from their guarded cover to feed recklessly on this seasonal fare. Today she has come for big fish.

The carefully controlled waters in this stretch of the lower Ripshin could be tricky. Occasional riffles, sections of modest rapids churning around boulders, and chutes of rushing water plunging into pools punctuate the more prevalent and dominant feature of the river—long, tranquil, mirror-like expanses of seemingly still water, flowing at such an even, steady pace, through a riverbed so free of obstacles, that the water often appears not to flow at all. When the water is like this, and it almost always is, a vigilant trout can see a careless angler's approach from a hundred yards. Sandy was not a careless angler, and still, after two hours, in the midst of fish feeding ecstatically on grasshoppers, she has landed only two brown trout. Good fish, respectable fish, but not the lunkers she stalks today.

With the sun pasted high into the morning sky, Sandy's body is split. From her thighs to her feet, even through her waders, she feels the deep chill of the water she stands in, water released from the dark, frigid bottom of the reservoir. The three miles it has flowed from the dam, past Tommy Akers's family farm, past Sandy's little vinyl-sided house, to where she now stands mid-stream has not been enough to much alter the cold temperatures at the bottom of Willard Lake. Above the water, from her thighs to the crown of her head, Sandy bakes, as the day's heat rises rapidly toward its peak. She tilts the bill of her cap back, drops her sunglasses, and drags her shirt-sleeve across her face, wiping beaded sweat from her forehead and eyes. As her sunglasses settle back onto the bridge of her nose, she sees a massive boil in the pool behind a large snag by the opposite bank. A big fish is scarfing up careless grasshoppers under the protection of a fallen, blight-dead elm. Sandy rubs her earring, locks onto her target, and moves up and across the stream, sweat drying around the wisps of prickled hair under her ponytail. The fish she has come for today is in her sights.

A deep hole lies between her and her prey, and Sandy's feet inch deftly along the ledge around the hole, her body stooped to nearly half its height, until she reaches the far side and slides into casting position. The fallen elm has broken the previous glassy flow along the bank, sending a bubbling tongue of water around it toward the middle of the river for a brief stretch until the force of the river pulls the errant current back in line with the main flow. But behind and beneath the triangulated arch of the fallen trunk, the water retains its original stillness, and the enormous trout has grown delirious in the glut of grasshoppers and his presumed safety under the snag. And, for the most part, the old boy is safe. The opening under the elm trunk is only about six feet around and the water under it is deathly still. With such a large, cagey fish in such a small and delicate spot, Sandy knows that, despite his feeding frenzy, she will have one, two casts at best before he shoots back to the security of deeper waters. And if she does seduce him to her fly, she will have only a couple of seconds to steer him out from under the snag. If she doesn't move him quickly into the open water downstream to run himself out, if she tries to bring him to hand by mere force, he'll tear the hair-fine leader to shreds and escape.

Her feet set firmly on the ledge above the deep hole, Sandy sees only her target, feels only the flex of her rod, the rhythm of the trout rising. Now she is the predator, the one to be feared, and she turns her rod upstream toward her precarious target and fires a low, tight loop at the big trout's pool. Sandy locks her legs in a crouch, reaches straight out with her rod, and the hopper fly strikes the fallen elm. It pops back and hovers in the air for a split second like a befuddled, tumbling insect, then drops gently to the still surface of the pool. The first ripple of the fly's falling has barely formed before the big trout strikes, and Sandy leans her rod and hips back and away from the snag.

She knows immediately that he's bigger than she thought and that if he'd chosen to dive under the snag or flee upstream, she would have lost him. But his instincts have sent him running downstream, exploiting the power of the current in his flight. Curving downstream and across, the fish comes back on Sandy, dropping into the hole under the ledge and stopping, lying still, as brown trout will do, in the hopes that the danger will disappear. For the moment, Sandy has the privilege of a clear view of the fish's bright golden flank, a sight to match the shuddering tension running up her line and rod and into her arm. She takes advantage of the moment to inch her way back around the hole to the shallower side of the river, but as she moves, the big trout takes an additional, momentary dive. The shift in weight and force draws

Sandy off balance and her foot slips from the ledge. Her arms shoot out and she wobbles on one foot, rod held high, over the deeper hole. The flurry of her movement to regain her balance spooks the trout from his sanctuary, and just as Sandy's drifting foot regains the ledge, the fish takes off downstream. She lifts her finger from her line and gives the trout free rein into the open water. Her reel hums as he runs away with her line, and Sandy moves quickly now around the hole and into the shallower water.

Coursing out in a long, downstream arc, the trout runs and Sandy pursues. For at least ten minutes their play continues, the trout seeking escape from the hook firmly lodged in his lower jaw, Sandy hoping her leader will survive the contest and hold until she is able to draw him to her net. When the fish pauses, Sandy draws in line until her fish flees again. He is beginning to tire, she can tell, and she might draw him in further, but still she plays him, luxuriating in the electric quiver of the trout's fearful force in her arm. She knows this is unwise if she hopes to release him with as little damage done as possible, but after so much time spent with the little brook trout of the headwaters, she is losing herself in the thrill and titillation of this much fish weight and fish fight on her line. A wise old fish, well-caught on a single cast, and Sandy regrets the sensation must be momentary, that she cannot slip beneath the surface of the Ripshin and follow this massive trout forever.

Once in her net, pulled from his subsurface world into Sandy's world of air and men, the trout's weight and size increase and deaden. His tail spills over the handle of her net. Some of the red and blue spots on his gold sides are nearly as big as Sandy's fingernails. She frees the hook of the mangled hopper fly from the long, hooked jaw, nicking one fingertip on a razor-sharp tooth. With one hand she cups the trout's dense belly, with the other clutches his tail, and gently cradles him in the flow of the shallow water, allowing him to reclaim some of the oxygen lost in the fight. When the huge and heavy trout begins to resist her grip, she releases him. He fins the gentle current for a second, senses the returned control of his own body, and rockets across the river, gone in an instant.

Sandy rises from the water feeling satisfied, complete, her big fish caught and caught well. Yet, as she gathers in her net and loose line, a creeping sense of shame slithers into her satisfaction. She had played the fish too long, more than necessary, simply for her own pleasure. She had unduly endangered the well-being of a creature already threatened by her capture of it, a creature whose presence was a matter of life and death to Sandy. The contest, the subterfuge, these she accepted, but within limits. There were rules, her rules, and she had broken them for a moment of indulgence.

She hooks the tattered fly to the fly catch on her rod and resumes her course upstream. She would fish no more today. She didn't deserve to. Rounding a bend in the Ripshin, she moves slowly through a gentle riffle, the rippling water splashing against her ankles and shins. Her gaze wanders upstream, away from the rises of other trout sucking in grasshoppers. Her guilt sends her gaze further upstream, past her house, past Tommy Akers' family farm, beyond the controlled flow of the tailwater that swallowed Tommy Akers' catfish river, over the dam, across Willard Lake and the jet-skiers and pleasure boaters, to the wild headwaters of the upper Ripshin, up the gradient, over boulders and pools of native brook trout to James Keefe's bungalow. She feels the press of something at her back, of something following her.

From the opposite bank and behind her, the deafening smack of something large hitting the water rings out across the stream. Sandy twitches and turns suddenly toward the noise just in time to see a beaver slip beneath the surface and disappear into its lodge at the river's edge.

She scolds herself for her foolish fears and continues upstream, her rod idle in her hand.

* * *

Not long ago, Inmate #52674 at the Bland County Correctional Facility wrote and mailed the following letter:

Dear Sandy,

It's been a while, I know. And I know you won't write back. You never did, not once in all these years. Then again, there hasn't been much new to say to you for some time. Just more of my anger and hate. Funny, isn't it, loving someone so much and hating someone so much at the same time. Loving you and hating you felt pretty much the same to me most times. Well, I still love you. That will never change, I promise. But all that hate is gone, washed out of me by the Blood of Lamb who reached into my heart here in this place and cut the hate from my body like a tumor. Hate and anger are behind me now. I am saved in Jesus Christ and live now to glorify Him. Only to glorify Him.

I have much to atone for. So do you. But Jesus has forgiven me, opened my eyes to His loving light, and offered me the opportunity to make amends for my sins. I have nearly paid my debt to the government of men. My debt to God will require the rest of my life to repay. Praise Him for finding me just in time, before my hate could be let loose in the world again. All my days will now be blessed with love and devotion.

His plan for me is clear, and I will follow it to the end of my days. To atone for all I've done wrong in my life. When I'm released in October, I'll go to my parents, kneel before them, beg their forgiveness, and promise to be the devoted son they so deserve. This has all been such a burden to them. My mother especially, such a good Christian woman, has suffered so. Then I'll be coming to you to do the same. And happily I'll grant the forgiveness that I know you'll ask of me, too, when you see how I am redeemed. My faith is so strong. When

Jesus is truly present in our lives, he cannot be resisted. You will see the strength of my salvation and I know, I have faith, that you will be moved by it. You will know that God has ordained that we be together, and you will join me in the blood of his salvation, and we will begin our lives anew, cleansed and reborn. I have such faith in it.

What God has joined together, let no man pull asunder. Till death do us part. I'll be coming for you soon, my one true wife, as intended. Be ready.

Your loving husband, in Christ

Vernon

The letter was mailed but returned unopened two weeks later, marked *Addressee Moved, No Forwarding Address.*

* * *

Sandy sits on a low, streamside rock beneath a hemlock with her feet in the water, tying on a stonefly pattern. It's cooler here along the headwaters, just downstream from Keefe's cabin, and she is glad to be free of sweat in her eyes for the first time in days. When the door of Keefe's bungalow creaks open and he steps onto his little porch, she creeps up the bank and settles behind the trunk of the hemlock. This is the first time she's seen him since the day she stumbled across him, lying belly-down in a pool in a wet suit, swim mask and snorkel. She had fished past his little house several times during the last couple of months, but Keefe had been nowhere to be seen. She had noticed a light through his kitchen window once, and his battered truck had always been parked in the graveled space just off the fire road snaking up behind his cabin. On a couple of occasions, a fly rod leaned against the wall by the front door and waders hung over the porch rail. But never Keefe in the flesh. At the moment, it appears to Sandy that he has not seen her. She lays her rod softly on a bed of moss, rubs her earring, and leans into the tree trunk, studying Keefe through the brush and branches.

He stands on his porch as he did the first time she saw him, rocking gently on bare feet, his hands thrust into the pockets of baggy pants. His khaki shirt is noticeably wrinkled, the shirt-tail hanging loose, and his gray hair is disheveled. He still has not noticed Sandy. She hunkers deeper into her hiding place. His gaze is fixed, unmoving, riveted on the rush of the upper Ripshin flowing before his cabin. Without altering his gaze, the toes on his right foot begin to bunch up and flex, pulling his foot a few inches to the right until his big toe sinks itself in the knothole Sandy recalls stepping over when she entered his house that day. Keefe continues to flex his toes, to sway softly forward and back, to watch the river's descending course, anchored by his rooted toe.

From her hideout behind the hemlock, Sandy scrutinizes him—a man on the back slope of his life but peaceful, relaxed, at home in both his body and bungalow. One hand comes free of its pocket and rises to the back of Keefe's neck, rubbing it as he tilts his head from side to side, and Sandy sees a different man, resting for a moment from whatever contest he wages in the arena of the cluttered interior of his cabin. The other hand comes out of the other pocket, both arms cross loosely over his chest, and Sandy sees a gatekeeper, guarding the entrance to a chamber she longs to enter.

Keefe relaxes his arms, pulls his toe from the knothole and slips back into his cabin, leaving Sandy behind the hemlock, sunk into the assortment of Keefes she's just witnessed and wondering why in the hell this man is so appealing to her. She is about to rise and continue her fishing when Keefe's door creaks open again and he reappears. He remains barefoot, but his pant legs are rolled to the knees, his shirt-tail is now tucked into the waist of his pants, and a weathered brown fedora covers the matted gray hair. He carries a fly rod, which he leans against the outside wall by the door, then steps back inside, leaving the door ajar. After only a few seconds, Keefe reemerges, carrying now a thick book with a black cover in one hand. Cradled in the other arm is the silver canister Sandy remembers sitting atop his fly-tying bench.

Sandy is again surprised by the smooth, easy progress of Keefe's barefoot gait over the stony ground between his bungalow and the river. He stops on the bank and opens his book to a marked passage, carefully retaining his hold on the canister in his other arm, and begins to read aloud. Her distance and the sound of the river's rushing water keep Keefe's words from reaching Sandy's ears. She can only watch the movement of his lips.

Keefe closes the book, lays it carefully on a dry rock, and steps into the water. His bearing slows and becomes more cautious, negotiating the more slippery stones of the riverbed until he comes to a stop, calf-deep in the stream, just to the side of where the pool's main current fans out over the deeper water.

He lifts the lid from the silver canister, dips his right hand into it, and brings the hand back out. As far as Sandy can see, the hand remains empty, but the thumb and forefinger are pinched together. Keefe extends his arm over the main current and opens his hand, then appears to brush the tips of the thumb and forefinger together. To Sandy, he looks for all the world like a chef, dropping a pinch of spice into a vast cauldron of soup.

Keefe puts the lid back on the canister, wraps both arms around it in a tight embrace, and bows his head. Fascinated as she is with this strange man, Sandy has now grown uncomfortable and ashamed of her voyeurism. She begins to fidget behind the tree, wishing for a line of escape that would not reveal her presence, when Keefe lifts his head and walks out of the river.

Sandy remains in hiding after Keefe disappears back into his cabin. She is oddly immobilized, both by her sense of shame for spying on his curious ceremony and by her fear of exposure and embarrassment. She had, after all, been watching him, an uninvited and deliberate intruder. Should she simply slink back downstream, avoiding the old man's stretch of the river entirely? There would be several hours of good fishing upstream yet today. Or should she just wait where she was? Wait long enough before continuing upstream to preclude any suspicion, in case Keefe might see her passing, that she could have been present for his ritual?

Berating herself for the absurdity of her situation, the foolishness of her feelings, Sandy reaches for her rod and is about to rise from her hiding place when Keefe steps back outside his bungalow and she drops sharply back down behind the hemlock. As before, the old fedora is on his head. But the hat is all that remains from his previous appearance. James Keefe stands on the porch of his little house, utterly naked, hat on head, toes flexing. Sandy attempts by sheer force of will to make her body smaller, to shrink further behind her tree, as Keefe takes the fly rod leaning by the door in his free hand and returns to the riverbank.

Deep in her shame and embarrassment, Sandy tries at first to avert her eyes, even pinches them closed for a moment, but no use. Her curiosity overwhelms her sense of impropriety, and she peeks out from behind the hemlock, through the gap in the rhododendrons, at the naked man on the bank of the Ripshin. She feels nothing that would qualify as lurid or perverse, certainly not enticing, only the crassness of her intrusion into something clearly private.

After fourteen years of nursing, the mere sight of a human body, in and of itself, male or female, old or young, beautiful or ugly, healthy or diseased, could no longer elicit much in the way of an emotional response from her. She had cleaned clogged stents implanted in the chests of cancer-ridden infants, swabbed fungus from under the hanging breasts of paralyzed old women, wiped black feces from the sphincters and thighs of feeble, incontinent old men, helped push the jagged edges of broken bones back into place beneath the skin and tissue they had pierced, held partially dismembered limbs while emergency room surgeons attempted to keep them from detaching entirely, and watched the face of a red-haired man explode into pulp on a bar top. To Sandy, the human body alone was no more than a fragile amalgam of bone, blood, and skin in constant need of repair. That the mere sight of it could engender an emotional reaction of any kind was, at best, pathetic. The graphic photographs in her textbooks in nursing school never disturbed her the way they had many of her classmates. Pornography mystified her.

Yet here she hunches behind her hemlock tree, peering at a naked man, and she cannot deny the increase in her rate of respiration. Fear of exposure, she tells herself, nothing more.

Keefe lodges his fly rod under one bare arm and retrieves his book from the rock he had placed it on a moment ago. Again he reads aloud for a moment, and again Sandy cannot hear the words, can only hear the moving water and see the moving lips. After reading for only a moment, Keefe closes his book, returns it to the rock, shifts his rod to his right hand, and steps into the cold current.

The body of James Keefe is the body of a man his age, ordinary in every way. The face is cragged, not extensively wrinkled, and tanned from the hat brim to just below the base of the neck. The torso remains fairly slender, lightly muscled, pale and unsunned, a few tufts of gray hair over a breast of softened, dimpled flesh, a small spare tire of fatty tissue barely plumping at the waist. His arms are thin, but the sinewy muscles retain definition beneath a layer of loose skin. From the elbows down, the thin arms are deeply tanned. The buttocks are small, sloping inward rather than protruding. Unlike the chest hair, the pubic hair is dark and sparse. The scrotum droops but begins to tighten a bit from the cold temperature of the water, and the penis hangs taut but limp to the side. The legs, like the arms, are thin but the delineation of the muscles shows through skin that is tight and smooth. The ordinary body of a man Keefe's age.

However, when Keefe strips out his line and lifts his rod into play, Sandy recognizes immediately that all that is typical about him has vanished. His movements are precise but relaxed, minimized to only what is necessary to place his fly on the water in this particular pool. No false casts, no long, flamboyant rocketing of line in tight loops. A mere flick of the wrist, a quick whip of line, leader and fly above his head, then lightly down to the surface, the fly dropping onto the current in exactly the same spot over which Keefe had opened his hand a few minutes before. No motion Keefe executes is beyond Sandy's own abilities, yet she feels a faint quiver of what she can only think of as reverence, not for the ordinary man, not even for the extraordinary fisherman. Her reverence is for the integrity and humility of the cast. In this man's hand, the fly rod is neither weapon nor tool. It is an extension of the entire man, an integrated limb. He casts a second time, and Sandy sees that the first cast was no fluke. She emits a long, soft exhale as Keefe casts a third time, and a fish strikes.

His rod arcs and he draws the brook trout gently to hand. Squatting to scoop the fish from the water, Keefe's testicles nearly skim the surface of the chill stream. He slips the hook easily from the trout's mouth and cradles the small fish in his hand for a moment. Keefe's back is to her now, and Sandy leans out from her hiding place to get a better look at the fish, her guilty caution momentarily succumbing to the lure of the fish. She can just make out the orange glow of the ivory-trimmed fins, already taking on brighter color for the fall spawning, when Keefe releases his fish and her foot slips on a patch of loose stone, sending Sandy skidding down the bank to the river's edge.

Keefe turns quickly, but does not appear particularly startled. Sandy has tumbled to a spot just outside the rhododendrons through which she has been peering, and Keefe shows no discernible reaction on his face when he locates the intruder. Sandy is paralyzed, embarrassed and ashamed, unable to speak. Keefe calmly turns back to the pool and retrieves his line. When he turns back toward her, Sandy tries to speak, to say something, anything, to offer up even the most feeble apology for her transgression, but the air is frozen in her throat.

The hint of a sympathetic smile twitches at the corners of Keefe's mouth as he touches the brim of his fedora and nods to her.

"Hello again, Ms. Holston," he says and walks out of the river, collects his book from the bank, and disappears into his house. Sandy remains immobile, an exposed interloper, splayed out on her ass in the shallows. Her head droops and she groans, hiding her face beneath the bill of her cap, feeling as if she just farted in church.

* * *

He stands alone at the edge of the trees, the straps of the heavy pack frame scoring his shoulders. Through the night and his binoculars, he looks out at the hatchery pens in the clearing and sees that tonight's killing will have to be delayed, perhaps postponed.

"What in the world is that fool kid doing?" he whispers to himself.

Through his binoculars the answer to his question comes quickly into focus. The hatchery manager's son sits cross-legged on the ground beside the trough of trout furthest from the house and hatchery buildings, outside the light from the nearest mercury light. He intermittently rocks slowly, smoking what appears to be a joint and drinking from a large brown glass bottle. With each rocking motion forward, the boy's face dips over the black surface and pauses briefly as he gazes into the trout-packed trough and drops a large gob of spit into the water. Each time the boy spits he speaks to the water below him. Through his binoculars from the edge of the trees, he sees the boy's lips move, but the sound of the voice falls far short of his hearing.

He retreats a few feet back into the trees, quietly removes the heavy pack frame, and leans it against the trunk of a poplar. Bracing himself with his hand on the tree trunk, he sinks slowly to the ground, crosses one leg over the other, lifts the binoculars from his belly, and watches the boy and waits.

The boy continues rocking, smoking, drinking, spitting, and speaking. He is just visible outside the ring of light. A lurking half-moon has slipped behind the ridge above the hatchery. He drops the binoculars back to his belly for a moment, kneads the sore strands of muscle on his shoulders, then slides his hands into his boots and rubs at his aching ankles. Glimpsing some shimmer of motion in the distance, he jerks the binoculars back to his eyes.

The boy has risen from his sitting position. He sways as he walks but does not stumble. Stepping to the end of the trough, the boy takes a last drag on the joint, inhales deeply, and flicks the nub into the air. A miniscule red ember arcs out into the night before the boy and vanishes in the black water. He leans back, downing the final dregs of his bottle, turns and flings it against the wall of a small, cinder-block shed near the pens. A second later, the sound of shattering glass arrives at the edge of the trees.

Now visibly wobbling, the boy turns his face back to the trough, unzips his jeans, fumbles for his penis, and urinates into the trout pen. His face is not visible through the binoculars, but the shaking of his head and shoulders indicates he is laughing. After an excessive amount of bouncing and shaking, he zips up and turns in an awkward circle, seeming to search for something out in the night around him. He locks onto the nearby shed, totters to it, enters, and reappears a moment later, his hands gripping the long handle of a large net.

He makes an awkward stab at the surface of the water, comes up empty, and slaps at the water with the net, nearly losing his footing. The boy recovers his balance, pauses as if thinking. He readjusts his grip, extends the net down into the water, and begins to walk decisively toward the far end of the trough. Through the binoculars, he knows what is happening in the pen—he has seen it before. The terrified trout are rushing away from the looming shadow above them in the only line of escape available to them. When the fleeing fish reach the end of the pen, they turn frantically in the only remaining direction and swim directly into the boy's lowered net. His knees buckle, he widens his stance, and hefts the sagging net of captive trout out of the water and dumps them on the ground. The boy's chest heaves and he is clearly laughing again. He reverses his direction, drops the net in the water again, and comes up with another load of trout, quickly netted on their return flight. The boy dumps his second load of fish onto the pile of the first, shifts the net handle to his right hand, and fires the net like a javelin into the darkness.

The boy bends forward, places his hands on his knees, and shouts at the heap of trout in a voice loud enough to be just audible when it reaches the edge of the trees a second later.

"Fuck you fish. I hate you goddamn fish. I hate you."

The shreds of light that persist in the night are scattered, fragmented and twitching, shimmering in erratic flecks on the writhing bodies of hundreds of gasping trout.

The distant reflections dance on the lenses of the binoculars as the boy gets to work. He jumps at the pile of fish and, continuing his loud curses, begins to kick the slick, shivering bodies. Like a maniacal soccer player, he attacks the pile with feverish sideways kicks, spraying trout bodies up into the night air. A few land back in the water of the pen. He shifts from kicking to stomping, pouncing on the mound of fish in a cruel caricature of a war dance. Most fish are mashed beneath his heavy boots; some squirt out from under a poorly aimed stomp.

"I hate you goddamn fish," the boy shouts.

He slips on one body and falls backward, his feet flying out from under him, but leaps immediately back to his feet and continues his assault.

Tim Poland

Hidden in the distance at the edge of the trees, he brings the binoculars down and drops his head to his chest, sickened by the sight of slaughter for the sake of hate.

Lost in the thrill of his massacre, the boy does not notice the porch light of his house switch on at the far side of the hatchery, nor does he see his father emerge from the house, brandishing a flashlight. The boy's curses mix again with laughter as he continues to stomp and kick the dead and dying trout. He remains oblivious to his father's shadowy form, bolting across the hatchery grounds toward him behind a bouncing beam of light. The boy has cocked his leg for another kick as his breathless father arrives behind him and delivers an open-handed blow to the back of the boy's head, sending him face-forward down into the massive smear of mangled trout carcasses and fish goo illuminated by the beam of the father's flashlight.

He watches the father's administration of consequences for a moment longer, then lets the binoculars hang from the strap. The boy's father strikes him only once more as he lifts him by his collar and begins to lead him back to their house. As father and son retreat into the darkness, he rises and straps on the heavy pack frame. He knows that once inside the house, both hatchery manager and son will be well distracted by the tumult of discipline and contention. He will have to work fast, but what was before a delay is now an effective diversion.

At the moment the father drags the boy into their house, he steps from the cover of the trees and advances on the trout pens. It should go fairly quickly, he tells himself. Fewer fish to kill now. As he nears the first trough, he firms his grip on the long handle of the cathode wand and reaches back to the pack frame and switches on the motor. Through his strained back he feels the low vibration of the motor and the throbbing weight of slaughter for the sake of love.

* * *

The smaller the pile of tires behind her house became, the less widely Stink ventured from his tractor tire. Eventually, he left his tire only to relieve himself, leaping back inside it the moment he finished. A few days ago, Sandy moved his bowls next to his tire, and Stink now ate by draping his front legs over the tire and extending his head and neck to reach his food and water. His growling was no more frequent, but Sandy thought she detected a deeper tone to it.

"Keep it up," she says to the dog, "and you're going to end up with a nasty case of laryngitis."

The late summer sun has long since cleared the ridge in front of Sandy's little house, and nothing remains of the pile now but a few tractor tires. She has already dispatched one three-tire load today. Only four tractor tires now remain, including Stink's. Her truck's suspension is still settling under the weight of the second tire she has hefted into the bed as she wipes the sweat from her face with the front of her t-shirt and turns up the slope for the third tire. Squatting, sliding her hands under the tire and lifting, straining, Sandy raises it up onto its worn tread, as she had the previous two, and rolls it slowly down the short patch of slope toward the pickup bed, standing in front of it, inching cautiously backward, easing the huge tire closer to the truck. A drop of sweat falls into her eye. She dips her face to her shoulder to rub out the sweat, her foot slips on a loose rock, her grip on the tire loosens, and she stumbles backward against the tailgate of the truck as the tire leaps away from her and bounds toward her house. She has collapsed to one knee and can already feel a bruise taking shape where the small of her back collided with the tailgate as she turns her torso just in time to see the tractor tire crash into the screen door and topple back on its side. The screen door is left buckled, hanging from a single hinge, the screen mesh torn, the latch ripped apart. Her knee still on the rocky ground, one arm draped over the tailgate, Sandy tilts her head back and sighs loudly.

"Shit," she says, and pushes herself up from the ground.

Stink lets out a sharp bark and Sandy looks to where he is ensconced in the last tractor tire. He barks once more, and she is certain he is smiling at her.

"I'm sure this is all very amusing to you, you rotten old mutt." Stink growls low and rests his jaw on the side of his tire, his eyes locked on Sandy.

The screen door creaks and rattles on its remaining hinge when Sandy tests it. It will hang in place for the time being, but it is beyond repair. She'll have to replace it. Stink continues to watch her closely as she squats to lift the tire again. His ears twitch briefly when she emits a groan and hefts the tire upright. Her arms spread wide, the tractor tire tilted slightly toward her body, Sandy sets her stance and begins rolling the tire back up the slope to the truck. Sweat falls into her eyes again, but she ignores it. Only halfway up the slope to the truck, her hands sweat profusely inside the work gloves, her shoulder muscles twitch, and she wonders how much longer her penance should last.

She had, at least in part, been lurking along the headwaters of the upper Ripshin near Keefe's cabin in search of an ambiguous absolution for her guilt in overplaying the big brown trout. All she had managed to find was an additional guilt for intruding upon and desecrating Keefe's naked ceremonial. Since that day she had locked her life into a self-imposed course of contrition and atonement that seemed to broaden and proliferate her sense of her own responsibility in the infractions of her life rather than to relieve her of any of that guilt. A husband abandoned in dire straits. A friend ignored. A string of men confronted, then angered, rejected, or insulted. At last count, she estimated that she owed everyone she had encountered an apology of some sort, but for exactly what she wasn't yet sure. Now the screen door on the back of her house was mangled beyond repair, she had a large bruise forming on the small of her back, Stink still viewed her with suspicion from within the stronghold of his tractor tire, and she hadn't been fishing in two weeks.

* * *

She began her penance by throwing herself into her job because that was one of the things people often did in times of distress and uncertainty, and it seemed to her as good a place to start as any. In the months she had been working as an LPN at the nursing home in Damascus, Sandy had not acquired a reputation as a compassionate caregiver or a congenial colleague. "A cold fish, that one," Sandy overheard one nurses' aide say to another one morning. She was in the restroom, about to come out, and the two nurses' aides stood outside the door. Sandy paused for a moment before exiting, allowing them to move on, to avoid embarrassment for all three of them. Leaning against the wall, looking at her reflection in the mirror, she wondered if the aide's assessment of her was correct and knew almost immediately that it was.

As she heard the two nurses' aides pass on down the hall, she placed her hand gently on the doorknob and considered her reflection, imagining herself as a wily and elusive solitary trout, holding in slow current under an overhanging tree branch. In nursing school, she had been instructed in the hard-and-fast rule to remain emotionally detached from her patients. Sandy turned the doorknob and slowly stepped into the hallway, wondering if she had taken that particular rule too far, wondering if she had, in fact, learned that rule in nursing school at all.

Over the past weeks of her penance, Sandy had nearly exhausted herself in providing care to the residents of the Damascus Nursing and Rehabilitation Center. She had worked double shifts to allow one of the other LPNs to take some extra time off for a long weekend away with her husband, with whom she had recently been reunited after a long estrangement. Sandy had bandaged cuts, salved rashes, replenished

IVs, and kept all records exact and up to date. She had tended to Mr. Portman, kept him stationary and soothed, and helped lift him onto the ambulance gurney when he fell and broke his hip. She had been one of the two LPNs to officially confirm and pronounce the death of old Mrs. Quesenberry, offer her own condolences to the family members in attendance, and sign the official sympathy card sent by the nursing home administration and staff. She had performed all her assigned functions with expertise and skill, dispensing all the necessary care required by the home's residents without, she realized, actually caring much about them at all. Did her self-imposed penance demand that she change in this regard? After all these years of cool, detached care-giving, could she learn to care, even if she wanted to?

Walking back to her station, she glanced into Mrs. Moser's room and saw the old woman doubled over in her wheelchair, half-dressed, straining to pull up the pink flannel slacks crumpled around her ankles. On any other day, according to standard procedure, Sandy would have called a nurses' aide in to help the old woman get dressed. Watching Mrs. Moser battle her petulant pants, she could hear the echo of the aide's comment. "A cold fish, that one."

"Let me help you with that," Sandy said, walking into the room.

Mrs. Moser stopped her struggle, raised halfway up in her chair, and looked quizzically at Sandy.

"Here, let's sit you up straight and take care of these," Sandy said.

"Who are you?" Mrs. Moser said.

Her eyes pinched tightly together and she stared at Sandy's face. Sandy pulled back, surprised by the question.

"I'm Sandy. Sandy Holston, the LPN for this wing."

"I don't know you," Mrs. Moser said, and Sandy realized that in the two months since the woman had been moved into the nursing home, she very well may not have been in her room a single time.

"You must know me," Sandy said. "I'm here almost every day lately."

"Now you listen to me, young lady. I may be old and weak, and I may not be able to pull my own damn pants up, but I'm not senile. And I'm not stupid. And if I say I don't know you, then I don't know you."

Sandy took a deep breath, knelt before the old woman's wheelchair, and reached for one of Mrs. Moser's thin, purple-veined hands. Taking the old hand into her own, she squeezed it gently and introduced herself.

"I'm Sandy Holston, one of the LPNs here."

"Edith Moser. Very nice to meet you, Sandy. Now, could you help me get these damn pants on?"

Sandy slid the pink flannel up the legs and over the sunken haunches. Mrs. Moser's blouse was buttoned askew. Sandy redid it, smoothed the rumpled fabric, and without thinking, reached to the woman's nightstand, picked up a hair brush, and brushed the woman's mussed hair into place.

"Thank you, dear," Mrs. Moser said. "Damn nuisance being so useless. Could you push me over to the window and open the blinds? It helps to have something to look out at."

Sandy rolled the woman into place and opened the blinds, letting in the incipient light of the early morning.

"Another morning, and I'm still here," Mrs. Moser said softly. "It's a surprise every day."

Leaving the room and returning to her station, Sandy felt curiously unaltered. She pulled a clipboard from the rack and began to examine a resident's chart, feeling she had behaved much the same as when she overplayed the big brown trout. Apparently, changing from a cold fish to a caring human being would involve more than helping one old woman get dressed. As a nurse in a hospital, her charges came and went, and Sandy's clinical attitude posed no problems for her or her patients. Here in the nursing home, her charges were permanent residents. They stayed put, at least for a little while, and like it or not, Sandy had entered into an ongoing relationship with them. On a trout stream she was a flawless reader of the water and other conditions. But here, where she was supposedly a professional, a professional with official responsibility and authority, she had badly misread the situation. Some adjustments might have to be made, if she could only determine how.

She had come no closer to a knowledge of how to be caring, but she tried. If deeper understanding was not forthcoming, then superficial action would do as a substitute for the time being. When she had a free moment from her usual duties, she began making casual rounds of the rooms, looking in on residents. Whereas before she would have looked into the room, made assessments and assigned tasks to nurses' aides, now she knocked on doors, walked into rooms, introduced herself, asked how an old man or old woman was doing that day, asked if there was anything she could do. But her actions remained on the surface. She was a robot of mercy, and she knew it. Why could she not muster for these old, sometimes abandoned, people a fraction of the compassion she felt when she looked into the waters of a trout stream, when she thought of the Rogers Ridge watershed? Since she had taken up a fly rod and stepped into the fishy waters of Dismal Creek, she couldn't recall any recognizable feeling of compassion for much of anything else, and she wondered if things had gotten out of hand now. If she was beyond rehabilitation. If she, in fact, wanted to be rehabilitated.

On one of these robotic rounds of counterfeit mercy Sandy had run into J.D. Callander again. She hadn't seen him for several weeks, hadn't noticed that she hadn't seen him for several weeks. He had long since given up asking Sandy out and had either decreased the frequency of his visits to his mother or had been coming, by accident or design, when Sandy was off duty. Or both.

Sandy overheard one of her nurses' aides tell another that she'd better go down the hall and check Mrs. Callander's diaper.

"God, I hope the old girl has already emptied herself out," the aide said.

"The last time I changed her she shit right in my hand, bless her heart."

Sandy stepped out from behind her station as the two aides pinched their faces into a combination of disgust, pity, and laughter.

"I'll take care of it," Sandy said. "I'm heading that way anyway."

The aides watched Sandy walk off, each looking as if she had just awoken to find a complete stranger lying in bed beside her.

Neither gentle nor rough, Sandy's motions were methodical and precise, exactly what was required—no more, no less—to tend to Mrs. Callander's immediate needs. She rolled the flannel nightgown above the waist, slid the padded panties from the shrunken loins, disposed of them, and cleaned the soiled flesh. As she unfolded a fresh diaper and slid it under Mrs. Callander's backside, the old woman spoke in a cracked, gurgling voice.

"No, not that one. I want the blue one today."

Sandy looked to the old woman's face, the eyes watery and locked onto a spot on the wall behind Sandy. Sandy was not Mrs. Callander's audience. Blue incontinence pants were not the blue thing she desired. J.D. Callander knocked once on the partially closed door of his mother's room and stepped inside as Sandy was snapping on the clean diaper.

"Oh, excuse me," J.D. said, and stumbled awkwardly back out into the hall, mortified by the sight of anything beneath his mother's waist.

Sandy smoothed the nightgown over the legs and pulled the blanket up over the shrinking body.

"It's okay now. Come on in, J.D.," she said.

J.D. Callander poked his head sheepishly through the cracked doorway and shuffled into the room, removing his cap as Sandy wiped a trail of encrusted drool from his mother's chin. In one hand he clutched a small, cheap vase containing three pink carnations.

"How is she today?" he asked.

"Pretty much the same," Sandy said.

She stepped aside as J.D. moved to his mother's bedside, set the flowers on her nightstand, and tentatively, clumsily brushed a strand of hair from his mother's forehead.

"Mama? It's me. J.D. How are you feeling today?"

Sandy paused on her way out of the room, studying the fragile mixture of genuine love and simple obligation in J.D.'s actions, searching for clues to the core of his caring. In a moment she realized her mistake, but too late. Before she could escape, J.D. turned his eyes from his unresponsive mother to Sandy.

"Not ever going to get better, is she?" he said.

"No," Sandy said, retreating toward the door.

J.D. leaned over his mother and looked down into her vacant eyes like a man staring helplessly under the hood of his stalled car on the side of the road.

"Bye, mama. See you soon," he said. He kissed her lightly on the forehead and left the room, pulling his cap back down on his head and following a few steps behind Sandy on her way back to the nurses' station.

After reviewing basic aspects of his mother's ongoing care with Sandy, J.D. pushed the bill of his cap up from his forehead and glanced back down the hallway toward his mother's room.

"Ought to be something more that could be done," he said.

"Sometimes there's nothing else we can do."

"But there should be more. Some drug or something."

"Well, for now all we can do is keep her comfortable," Sandy said, and returned Mrs. Callander's chart to the rack and pulled out another clipboard.

Aware that J.D. lingered at her station though he apparently had nothing else to add about his mother's care, Sandy tried to keep herself occupied with the chart she held. He pulled the brim of his cap down onto his forehead again and dipped his hand into his pants pocket and fumbled with his keys.

"Haven't seen you around much," he said. "How's fishing been?"

"Okay, I guess. I haven't had much time to get out lately."

"I'm surprised to hear that. I got the impression that fishing was pretty much your main occupation. Too bad. Water levels have been down, but the fishing has still been good."

"I've been kind of busy," Sandy said, cautiously turning her eyes up to meet J.D.'s. "Putting in a lot of hours here, doing some work around the house."

"That pile of old tires getting any smaller?"

"It's getting there."

She tried to turn back to her work, to cut the conversation off, but couldn't. The tall, awkward man in his dark green warden's uniform, nervously jingling the keys in his pocket, was part of her penance. She would have to see this through. She let the words from her mouth as if she were releasing a wild animal that she longed to keep for a pet but knew, for the animal's sake, she couldn't.

"Haven't seen you around here much either."

J.D. continued to fidget with his keys and looked down at his boots, shuffling across the linoleum.

"I've been pretty busy, too, I suppose. Haven't been able to get by so often. But I've been here a few times. Maybe I just came when you were off or something."

"Maybe."

J.D. looked up, lifted his keys from his pocket, and checked his wristwatch.

"But, I'm off now and it's getting to be time to eat. Suppose I'll head on over to the diner and get some dinner."

As he spoke, Sandy's stomach turned and emitted an audible growl. She hadn't had but a cup of tea and an English muffin that morning. She was famished. Penance and contrition made one hungry, she was discovering.

"Sounds like you could use some dinner, too," J.D. said.

"Sounds like it," Sandy said, gently laying her hand on her stomach.

J.D.'s eyes darted over the walls around the nurses' station and came back to rest on Sandy. Then, before speaking, his eyes dropped casually to the desk top of the station.

"Well, you could, uh, join me if you like, if you're getting off work and got nothing else to do. Might have a good special today."

In spite of her best efforts, Sandy found J.D.'s efforts to appear casual and indifferent sweet. And she was hungry. And her shift would be over soon. And, by her tally, she owed this clumsy man something. Of all the men who had dogged her, at least this one didn't hate her or want to kill her. What could it hurt to have one little meal with him? Yet, she cringed as the words slipped between her teeth.

"Might not be a bad idea. I get off in about fifteen minutes. Meet you there?"

She turned her eyes quickly back to the clipboard, so she would not have to see J.D. trying to hide his surprise and delight that she had actually accepted one of his invitations.

"Sure," he said. "Okay. See you there in fifteen minutes or so."

"Okay."

Sandy had eaten at the Damascus Diner a few times since she moved. A good place for the kind of large, greasy breakfast Sandy ate only occasionally and only at the beginning of what would be a long day of fishing. The wooden booths were thick and shiny from many coats of paint applied over the years, and the tables were covered with tattered calico-print vinyl tablecloths. Slender tree branches bent into wreaths and paint-by-number watercolors decorated the walls. Punctuating the wreaths and watercolors were framed Bible verses, the same sort of pithy, inspirational, and informational verses that were printed intermittently on the laminated menus. The glass display case on which the cash register sat contained an assortment of candy bars, mints, chewing gum, and small, heavily-varnished wooden plaques sporting more Bible verses. On the wall behind the cash register hung a small painting—a blue-tinted portrait of a thickly-bearded, husky Jesus sporting his crown of thorns. Sandy had always thought the portrait bore a suspicious resemblance to Jerry Garcia. She glanced at the portrait as she entered the diner, noted that the similarity remained between this particular Jesus and the dead guitarist, and walked toward the booth near the back of the diner where J.D. sat bolt upright behind his plastic menu. Though she had clearly spotted him already, he raised his hand to wave her on back to the booth, then removed his cap and laid it on the bench beside him. As Sandy slid into the booth, he raked his fingers over his thinning hair, trying to push it into some kind of shape that didn't indicate it had been under a cap all day. Sandy noticed that he pawed at his own hair in much the same way he had fumbled with his mother's earlier.

"What's good?" Sandy asked.

"Most everything," he said. "Haven't you eaten here before?"

"Only breakfast."

"Well, most everything's usually good. Got a meat loaf special tonight."

Sandy scanned the menu, her eyes pausing on a verse from the Book of John:

I am the way, and the truth, and the life; no one comes to the Father, but through me. Her stomach tightened and gurgled slightly. Beneath this particular verse she located what she searched for, a vegetable plate of mashed potatoes, broccoli, and brown beans with cornbread. J.D. ordered the meat loaf special.

"Saw you unloading over at Goodyear the other day," J.D. said. "How's work on that pile of tires coming along?"

"Getting there."

"I already asked you about that, didn't I?"

"Yeah, but that's okay. I've got a few more loads to go, I think. That is, if Stink let's me finish."

"Who's Stink?"

"My dog. The dog I inherited when I moved in."

"That's right. Calvin's old dog. I forgot about him."

"He's got an unnatural attachment to those tires. Growls at me every time I touch one of them. Sleeps in one now. Won't hardly ever get out of it. I may have to leave him that one tire. Sort of a peace offering."

Sandy sipped from her water glass and J.D. took a gulp of his Diet Pepsi. They each leaned back in the booth, symbolically making more room, when the waitress brought their dinners. J.D. laid the side of his fork into the meat loaf and levered off a large bite. Sandy dipped her fork into her mashed potatoes and released a runnel of gravy that flowed down the mound of potatoes and curled around her broccoli.

"How are things at the hatchery?" Sandy said after she swallowed her first bite of potatoes and speared a piece of broccoli. "Any more mysteriously dead trout?"

Sandy wondered if there weren't a slightly amused tone in her voice when J.D. stopped chewing for a moment. A look of uncertainty fluttered over his face before he continued chewing and answered.

"Nothing since last month. But I'm still trying to figure it out."

"Any leads?" Sandy said, keeping her tone of voice deliberately flat.

"No. Hard to come up with much of a lead or an idea about who might have done it when I can't for the life of me figure out why someone would want to do something like that in the first place."

Sandy broke off a piece of cornbread, laid it into her mouth, and thought of her occasional practice of killing stocked fish she caught in wild waters.

"I'm none too fond of stocked fish," she said. "I'd rather go for wild fish, native trout."

J.D.'s fork paused before his face, a chunk of meat loaf skewered on the tines. A drop of gravy fell to his plate.

"Do you think killing those trout was okay to do?" he said. His voice was soft, fearful.

"No. That's pretty extreme. I was just trying to give you a reason why someone might want to do that. Am I a suspect now?"

J.D. smiled sheepishly, popped the meat loaf into his mouth, and shook his head.

"No," he said. "Sorry."

"Have the police come up with anything?" Sandy said.

J.D. snorted and dropped his fork onto his plate.

"Cops couldn't give a damn. Think it's just a prank. Seems they've got more important things to do."

"Maybe they do."

"I suppose so, but it's still damage to state property. Hundreds of dollars worth of state property. They ought to do something. I'm pretty much on my own with this one."

Sandy wondered if the sympathetic look she tried to paste onto her face was convincing as she chewed her last piece of broccoli.

"There's this one good old boy I was suspicious of at first," J.D. said. "Every time I see him he complains about the tailwater below the dam, about there being no catfish in the Ripshin anymore."

"Sounds like Tommy Akers."

"You know Tommy?"

"He lives up the road from my house."

"Oh, that's right," J.D. said and pushed his empty plate to the side. "Anyway, he's always griping about trout and crying about catfish. Geez, there haven't been any catfish in that part of the river for years. Tommy couldn't have been but a little kid when they finished the dam and shocked out all the catfish and replaced them with trout. Back in the early fifties. But he ain't about to let it go."

Sandy dipped the corner of her last bite of cornbread into a dollop of gravy and slid her plate a couple inches toward the middle of the table.

"Couple years back," J.D. continued, "we were building up a bank that had washed out along his property. We were out there for two days, and he never let up once. Trout this, catfish that. Griping about our trucks driving out to the riverbank across his pasture. Stood out in his yard watching us through those binoculars he's always got with him."

The waitress came by, tore the green ticket from her pad, and slid it onto the table by J.D.

"How's your mother doing these days, J.D.?" the waitress asked as she lifted their plates from the table.

J.D. leaned backed in the booth and pursed his lips.

"About the same," he said.

"Well, we're all praying for her here," she said.

"Thank you," J.D. said. The waitress carried their plates into the kitchen and J.D. turned back to Sandy. "Where was I?"

"Tommy Akers and his binoculars," she said.

"Anyway, thought at first it might be him, but Tommy Akers couldn't ever pull a thing like this off. Probably never think to, for that matter. He's mostly too busy complaining."

"He does like to go on," Sandy said.

"Yes, and seems like I do, too. I must be boring you with all this."

"No. I asked about it, didn't I? Anything about the fishing around here interests me."

J.D. smiled with relief and poked at his hair.

"I guess I just don't really understand why anyone would get that angry about hatchery trout. What's wrong with it? Folks like it. Expect us to keep fish in the rivers around here."

"Well," Sandy said, "I suppose some people are looking for something else in the rivers, something, I don't know, something closer to what was there before we started growing trout in hatcheries."

"That's sounds like something the Professor would say."

"The Professor?"

"Professor Keefe. He was one of my teachers when I was at the community college. Lives up the fire road by the headwaters on the edge of the national forest line. You know him?"

"I met him once when I was fishing up that way. He was your teacher?"

"English teacher. Always a little weird, but I liked him, I guess."

"What was weird about him?" Sandy asked, now sitting up and leaning slightly toward J.D., physically showing more interest than she had throughout the meal.

"Nothing really. Seemed to be somewhere else sometimes. I guess he was just sad mostly."

"Why do you think that?"

"Probably his wife. The way I heard it, a few months after they moved out to that cabin, his wife was killed in a car accident. Guess he never got over it."

Sandy nodded along with J.D.'s words while she recalled in detail the clutter inside Keefe's cabin.

"He was a good man. Still is. Kind of particular about his fishing, though. Got a real thing for the little natives up in those headwaters."

The brilliant orange of a brook trout's flanks flamed across Sandy's imagination.

"Funny. It didn't matter what he was talking about in class, how to write a sentence or Walt Whitman—had a real thing for Walt Whitman, but I sure never could see what all the fuss was about. No matter what he was talking about, he usually found some way to work fishing into it."

Sandy reached for the ticket to see what her share of the meal was.

"Oh, no," J.D. said. "It's my treat."

"That's not necessary," Sandy said, feeling like she would like to crawl into that old tractor tire beside Stink.

"I insist," J.D. said. He snatched the ticket from Sandy's fingertips and lifted his hat from the bench and set it on the table. "I was wondering, maybe you'd like to do this again sometime, if you like?"

She felt her back press into the back of the booth as she inched her way out of it. She'd tried to be nice, to care, and all she was going to do was disappoint this man again.

"Maybe get some dinner and go to a movie over at the mall in Sherwood? If you like."

Dinner and a movie. Would he bring her flowers, too? She wondered if she would have reacted differently had he asked her to go fishing with him. They had just had an extended conversation about fishing.

He knew very well she was an avid fisher, possibly a fanatic. It would have been so easy. And yet, when it came to courting, J.D., like all the others, resorted to the conventional. So many possible choices, and all he could envision was dinner and a movie. Like Vernon, thoughtless in his thoughtfulness.

"I'm pretty busy these days. Working a lot. Don't really have much free time."

J.D. slid out of the booth, yanked his cap on, and looked down at his feet.

"That's okay," he said. "Just thought I'd ask. Guess I should have known better, hunh?"

Sandy thanked J.D. for dinner, said she needed to get home to feed Stink, and drove off in her truck, leaving J.D. tugging at the bill of his cap and fumbling with the keys in his pocket in the parking lot of the Damascus Diner. The entire ride out to her house, winding along the two-lane, through the trees, along the river, she felt as if she'd wasted the time and money of one man when she should have been talking to another.

* * *

After rolling the runaway tire up the slope and working it into the bed of her truck, Sandy sits on the tailgate and wipes the sweat from her face. Her penance has been a bust, a distraction, an indulgence even. All her efforts at apology and caring have, at best, gone unnoticed, at worst, backfired. She owes two apologies only, and she has made neither. One, she can likely never make to an abandoned ex-husband who might want to kill her when he sees her for the first time in seven years. The other, she can make simply and easily, with no need for any foolish penitential scheme that was beyond her scope anyway. And she needs to call Margie. She closes the tailgate and throws her gloves into the bed of the truck. Stink growls at the sharp catch of metal against metal.

"Get over it, you mutt," she says, and walks to the cab of the truck.

Later today she will walk to the end of her path and fish the tailwaters of the lower Ripshin until dusk. Early tomorrow she will walk up the fire road along the upper Ripshin, knock on the door of James Keefe's cabin, and tell him she is sorry. Just that she's sorry. Nothing else would be necessary. Maybe she will fish the headwaters for a few brook trout while she's up that way. No reason not to.

Sweat still beads on her forehead as she steps into the truck cab, and Sandy decides to clean up before taking the load of tractor tires into town. She leaves the truck door hanging open while she goes into her house to wash.

The damp t-shirt and bra lie in a lump on the floor at her feet as she stands before the sink and mirror, scrubbing. Under the pressure and movement of the washcloth soaked in cold, soapy water, the grit and film fall away, and Sandy's skin flushes taut, pink, and cool. She waits a moment before drying herself, relishing the chill of the water on her flesh. She slides the folded towel neatly back onto the rack after drying and walks bare-chested into her bedroom. Her shoulders hunch slightly forward as she slips on a clean bra and adjusts the underwires of the cups under her breasts. She slips a black tank top over her head and brushes her hair back. Walking through the kitchen toward the back door, pulling her slick hair back, she hears a truck rattle up the gravel of her driveway and jolt to a stop behind her house. She shakes out her ponytail, gives the mangled screen door a pathetic wiggle, and steps from her back door, raising her arm in greeting to Tommy Akers as he drops from his truck, his binoculars bouncing on his belly. His shotgun rests in a rack across the truck's rear window.

"Screen door's a mess. What happened?" he says.

"One of those tires got away from me while I was loading them," Sandy says.

"Well, isn't that a damned shame," he says, and steps around his truck, squinting at the wrecked door.

"Stupid, mostly," she says. "Nothing that can't be fixed."

"Oh, sure. But I might've saved you the trouble if I'd come down a little earlier, seeing as how it's tires I was coming to see you about. Now it looks as if I'm kind of late."

"How so?"

"I wanted to get a few tires from your pile. The wife likes to paint 'em up and use 'em for planters out in the yard, but damned if they ain't all gone, pretty much."

Tommy Akers looks from Sandy, past Stink, to the raw spot on the hillside where the tires had sat piled for years until Sandy moved in.

"I've been getting rid of them all summer," Sandy says. "Taking a load or two into Goodyear in Damascus when I have the chance. This is the last of them. If I'd known. You're welcome to these last few, if that'll help."

"That'd do just fine," Tommy Akers says. "Don't need but a few anyway. Sure appreciate it."

"My pleasure. Saves me a trip into town. I can get to fishing sooner."

Tommy Akers walks around the front of his truck and lifts one heavy foot to the running board.

"I'll pull around and back up to your truck, so we can just roll the tires over into mine."

"Don't bother," Sandy says, walking to the cab of her truck. "They're already loaded. I'll just bring them down in my truck."

"Oh, now, I wasn't aiming to put you out none."

"You're not. You're just down the road. No need to do the work twice."

"That's true, but I sure do appreciate it though. Thank you."

Sandy nods, smiles, and lays her hand on the door of her truck.

"I'll just toss this last one into my truck," Tommy Akers says, "seeing how you're pretty full loaded."

Sandy turns her gaze to Stink, hunched down inside his tire, growling, his rear end down, his hackles up, his teeth bared ferociously.

"Get on out of there, you smelly old mutt," Tommy Akers says, stomping up the hillside toward Stink's tire.

"Tommy," Sandy calls. "I think we'll leave that one. Stink's gotten attached to it. Probably be better for all of us if we let him have it."

"Suit yourself," Akers says, turning back down the slope. "Crazy old dog."

"Yes, he is that," Sandy says. "But I suppose he's got it coming to him."

Tommy Akers is halfway down the slope to his truck when a powerful shriek pierces the air above the pine trees and he stops short and snatches his binoculars from his belly and whips them up to his eyes. Sandy's eyes follow in the direction Akers has aimed his binoculars in time to see a large pair of wings disappear over the pines.

"What is it?" Sandy asks.

"Red-tailed hawk," Tommy Akers says, dropping the binoculars back onto the hump of his belly. "Hope he's heading up to my place for a little groundhog snack. Them damn rodents is playing hell with the wife's garden."

"Think he'll have better luck than you and your shotgun?" Sandy says.

Tommy Akers blushes full red across his round face at Sandy's good-natured reference to their first meeting. He glances briefly at the shotgun in his truck window, then drops his chin to his chest.

"I still feel just awful about that," he says.

"Sorry," she says, smiling. "Just kidding, but I guess that was kind of mean of me. Come on, let's get these tires down to your place."

Sandy follows Tommy Akers down the gravel driveway. As she turns onto Willard Road, she can see in her rearview mirror that Stink has risen inside his tire and stands with his front paws on the side of it, his tongue lolling out of his mouth. Sandy turns in her seat and looks directly out the rear window, not trusting the reflection of the mirror to tell her she is actually seeing Stink's tail wagging.

* * *

A dim line of light remains over the ridge behind Sandy's house. She drops her damp waders over the porch rail and enters her front door, hanging her cap on the hook by the door as she enters. The cool water from the bathroom sink refreshes her as she washes her hands and face and brushes back her matted hair. Walking into the kitchen, she takes a scrunchie from one of her vest pockets and pulls her hair back, feeling cleaner than she's felt in weeks. She had fished the tailwater of the Ripshin at the end of her path for two hours this evening, thinking of nothing but the fishing, focused only on the late glint of light on the water and the trout holding beneath the shimmering surface. Four good fish had come to her Caddis fly, and she had played them well, gracefully and efficiently, releasing each easily and quickly back into the darkening flow.

She turns the flame on under the kettle to heat water for tea, but as she takes the green mug from the cupboard, she thinks differently. Cutting off the flame under the kettle, she reaches to a bottle on the back of the counter and pours the green mug half full of red wine. Sandy drinks little, and hopes the bottle hasn't gone too sour since she opened it a month ago. Her palate registers the slight tang as she takes a sip—on the edge but still drinkable. She runs her tongue over her teeth and carries the mug out to her back stoop to watch the stripe of last light dissolve into the trees on the ridge.

The green ceramic mug makes a grating clunk when Sandy sets it on the stoop. The concrete still retains enough heat from the afternoon sun to warm her rear through the worn denim of her jeans. Forceps and scissors dangling from her vest clink together, emitting a flat jangling sound as she removes a fly box from one pocket, pinches the dried Caddis fly from her drying patch, and returns it to the box. She sips from the green mug and feels the wine bite into and warm her stomach as the last strand of light vanishes, leaving the ridge behind her house a dim outline in gray and black, a vague seam between earth and the field of a few large stars in the hazy night sky of late summer. Stink, too, sitting upright within the circle of his tire, has faded into shadow. Behind her, down her driveway, down her path to the riverbank, Sandy imagines she hears the hushed, persistent current of the Ripshin at night, imagines the familiar sound she knows she is not hearing through the click, buzz, and hum of nocturnal insects in the air and trees around her house. She cocks her ear when the sound of agitated water actually does mix with the insect hum. From the shift in the shape of the shadow, Sandy sees that Stink has leaned out of his tractor tire to lap at his water bowl. She runs her thumb over the form of the trout etched into her mug, takes another slurp of wine, and wonders how Keefe will respond when she comes to apologize tomorrow afternoon. Wonders if he will accept her apology. Wonders if he will care that she has hiked to his hideaway to lay her private guilt at his bare, knobby feet.

She pushes herself up from the stoop and slips into the house, returning in a moment with her telephone and a citronella candle. She lights the candle with a kitchen match she takes from a small plastic bag in one of her vest pockets. As the candle flickers and flares up, she runs her thumb over the smooth red and white surface of her earring, drinks again from the green mug, and punches Margie's number into the telephone.

The click and hum of whirring insects fades into the background as Sandy presses the receiver to her ear and listens to Margie's phone ring on the other end. One ring. Two rings. No answer, and Sandy's grip on the mug tightens, though she is unaware of her hand's reflex. Three rings. Four rings, and the answering machine clicks on. She sets the mug down on the stoop and looks up at the invisible ridge behind her house as the message plays. At the beep, Sandy pauses, speechless for a moment, before mumbling into the receiver.

"Hey, uh, it's me. Just calling to say . . ."

"Hey, girl," Margie says, breaking into Sandy's faltering message. Her voice is high-pitched and rushed, her breath coming in quick bursts.

"Hi," Sandy says. "You okay?"

"Just got out of the shower. Got the boys to bed early, for once. First minute all day I've had to myself."

"Sounds like I caught you at a bad time. I should let you go. I could . . ."

"Don't be an asshole. Don't you even think of hanging up on me. I haven't heard from you in weeks. Been worried about you. What's going on, girl?"

Sandy suspects that Margie could offer her exactly the right perspective on her recent period of imposed penance, but she can't imagine how to tell her about feelings she barely understands herself. And she'd be embarrassed to do so if she could.

"Nothing special," Sandy says.

"Oh, come on, Sandy. Forget that tight-lipped routine and talk to me."

Sandy softens under the persistent voice from the phone and lets Margie slip through into the still night air buzzing around the back stoop. Like a loop of coarse but strong rope, her voice encircles Sandy, tethers her, and draws her in. Tempered by Margie's voice, the red wine loses its sour tang, settling smoothly into Sandy's stomach as Margie leads her through the reconnection of the mundane details of two separated lives.

"Jesus," Margie says. "I'm telling you, Dr. Barton was all over her ass, which, of course, means she embarrassed him. What a little prick he is."

"I can imagine," Sandy says.

"I mean, he prescribed heparin to be taken orally."

"Orally? Since when?"

"Since never. It's always given subcutaneously. Who doesn't know that? The son of a bitch is, like, incompetent, but as usual, it's the nurse who catches grief when the doctor fucks up."

"How are things now?"

"Okay, I guess. He was wrong and he knew it, so he had to let it drop. But damn, girl, when he's on the floor, whew, you want to talk about tense?"

"Doctors," Sandy says.

"I bet that's one thing you don't miss, being in a nursing home."

"Yes, I suppose so. Doctors aren't around that often. Not so frantic. You know, once they get to a nursing home, well, there's not a whole lot of doubt about what's next."

"Ah, good old Sandy Holston. Warm and fuzzy as always."

Sandy grins and drains her mug of wine.

"Really, honey," Margie says. "You know, a lot of us would consider going from a hospital to a nursing home as kind of a step down. Are you okay there?"

"Yeah. Yeah, I think I am. It's different. The pace is more even. Less pressure, I guess. More of an ongoing thing. Your patients are around longer, for the most part. You have to get to know them more as people, not just another patient."

"Oh, there's a selling point for the warm-and-fuzzy Sandy Holston."

"Give me a break. I'm getting better."

"Really now?"

"A little bit."

Sandy hears Stink stir in his tire and knows that he has leaned out again for a drink as the sound of his slurping drifts down the slope.

"So, how's the old geezer with the snorkel?" Margie asks. "Spotted him in his natural habitat lately?"

"You're mean, Margie."

"No, I'm not mean. I'm vibrant. There's a difference. So, how is the old coot?"

Sandy squirms on the stoop from a slight flutter of guilt and a left buttock growing numb.

"Well?" Margie asks.

"Haven't seen him for a while. Haven't been fishing up that way for a while."

Sandy's open ear turns to a new sound in the night, and her body locks rigid on the edge of the stoop.

"Hold on a second," she says to Margie as she slowly pulls the phone away from her other ear.

The scuff of footsteps on gravel, the crunch of feet on dry grass. It happens before she can see it happening, before she can understand what's happening. Before she can understand who's coming. He steps slowly, with a hobbled gait, out of the dark and into the faint ring of light around the stoop. Sandy leans back involuntarily as his rank scent hits her nose and Stink waddles to the stoop and lies down with a huff at her feet.

Margie's voice is a distant screech as Sandy lifts the receiver back to her ear.

"Sandy? Sandy? Are you there? Sandy?"

"I'm here."

"You okay? What is it?"

"Nothing. Just thought I heard something. I'm okay."

"You sure?"

"Yeah. I'm sure."

Sandy reaches tentatively toward Stink and holds her hand above his head, which he tenses slightly, lifting his jaw just off the ground. She slips her fingers gently behind one ear and scratches lightly, feeling the taut body of one of the dog's more swollen ticks tap against one of her fingernails. Stink grunts softly and settles his jaw back to the ground.

"I saw Vernon's mother in the supermarket the other day," Margie says.

"What did she have to say?"

"Oh, like that old cow would talk to me. She knows we're friends. Far as she's concerned I'm the sidekick of the devil's spawn."

"Guilt by association, I guess. Sorry about that."

"Who gives a shit. Fuck her. But that ain't the half of it. You wouldn't believe what the old bitch did."

"What?"

Stink seems calmed under Sandy's scratching, perhaps drifting off to sleep, his breathing deep and steady.

"Well, there I am, going along, pushing my cart. Luke's in the kiddy seat and Matthew's toddling along, whining for me to get him every damn thing he sees that has too much sugar in it. I come around the corner, from one aisle to another, and nearly bump into her. Just standing there with her goddamn cart right in the middle of the aisle, looking at something, instant mashed potatoes or some such shit. Instant mashed potatoes. Jesus, who thinks of shit like that? How lazy can you get? Anyway, there she stands, like no one else might want to come down that aisle."

Sandy grins and shifts her fingers to Stink's other ear.

"So, what am I supposed to do? She's blocking the whole damn aisle, right? So, nice as can be, I just say 'hello' and 'excuse me' and try to push on around her. And do you know what that old bitch did?"

"I'm afraid to guess."

"She makes this little huffy sound, like how dare I fucking speak to her, and spits. And not some little spitting sound, just to let me know what she thinks of me, like there was any doubt or like I cared. No, she hawks up a big goddamn loogie and splats it right on the floor, not but a couple inches from my foot. Jesus."

"She always was a charming old girl," Sandy says.

"Damn, given the people he came from, it's a surprise Vernon isn't more of an asshole than he is," Margie says.

"He's not an asshole."

"Yeah, yeah. I've heard this before. So, when's he getting out exactly? I forgot."

"Middle of October. The fifteenth."

"Perfect. In time for Halloween. Trick or treat, girl."

"Something like that, I suppose."

Sandy unhooks her forceps from her vest and begins to stroke the fur around Stink's neck and face, searching out the biggest ticks.

"I still worry about you all alone, wherever you are," Margie says.

"I'm not all alone, Margie. There's people all over the place."

"Exactly my point. You work with however many people and there's your fish policeman and the neighbor with his shotgun, not to mention the geezer, and you're still alone. And don't try to bullshit me. I know you."

"I'm fine, Margie."

"Alone is one thing. Lonely is another. And I worry about you being lonely, sweetie. It's just not healthy."

"I'm not lonely."

Sandy slides her searching hand slowly down Stink's spine, feeling the warmth of his fetid body and the rhythm of his rasping breath.

"Well, maybe a little," Sandy says.

"You see, honey," Margie says. "I knew it. You don't raise two wild boys, pretty much on your own, and not get a sense of when there's something to worry about. And I worry about you, lonely in your goddamn wilderness. Your water bed."

"*Watershed*," Sandy says, chuckling softly.

"Whatever. That's not the point and you know it."

"So, I get a little lonely from time to time. It's not a big deal. Besides, I've got you. So you see, nothing to worry about."

"Yes, sweetie. You've got me, and *me* doesn't even know where the hell you are. Doesn't even have your phone number. Knew I should have sprung for caller ID. Do I have to hit you over the head with a goddamn hammer? I miss you, girl. Though for the life of me, sometimes, I wonder why. You don't give a person much to miss, if you get my point. "

"I guess you're right," Sandy says.

"I mean, you . . ." Margie begins to say, halting. "What did you say?"

"I said you're right. Maybe I took all this a little too far."

"Well, beat me, whip me, spank me with a spoon. We've had a breakthrough. Where are you, girl? Wait, wait. Let me go get something to write with. I'll be right back. Now, you promise me you won't change your mind about this in the next thirty seconds, okay?"

"I promise."

After she hangs up with Margie, two equal waves, one of fear, one of relief, sweep over Sandy. She is happy to have let Margie back in, the feeling undeniable. And just as much, she regrets succumbing to a moment of tenderness. With a disturbing certainty, she knows she's just done one of only two things—let her one faithful friend back into her life or guaranteed a world of trouble for both of them. For the moment, the sensations of relief and happiness are stronger. She'll go with that for now.

She spreads the fingers on her hand and rakes them through the fur on Stink's back, moving them over the coarse hair back up to his neck and pinching the first fat tick. With her forceps she tears the glutted tick from his neck, and Stink raises his head, mildly startled. But he remains relaxed, in fact, seems to relax further, lifting his snout calmly into the night air, as Sandy holds the first tick to the candle flame. She squeezes the forceps, and the blood-laden bag of the tick's body ruptures in the flame, a brief sizzling and spattering of burning dog blood and arachnid tissue. Sandy knows that, if Stink remains willing, she will have to search his body tomorrow in the daylight for the less gorged ticks that she can't possibly find in the thin glow of the porch light above her stoop. For the moment, she contents herself with killing the most bloated and obvious ones that she can see or feel with her fingertips. After twenty minutes, Stink is still calm under her touch, his eyes now closed, his nose still lifted peacefully into the night air. The tips of Sandy's forceps are black, charred by the flame and encrusted with bits of the scorched skins of the twenty-two dead ticks lying on the stoop around the base of the candle.

* * *

The weight of slaughter for the sake of love. It feels heavier tonight. The straps of the pack frame dig deeper into his shoulders and dew coats his boots as he is folded back into the trees and begins his ascent of the hillside. How much longer can he keep this up? The task itself is easy enough. A battery, an electrical generator, a voltage regulator, mounted on a backpack frame and all connected to a four-foot cathode wand. Dip the pole into a narrow trough of still water. He knows he can do that until the last gasp, if need be. The problem lies in the working conditions. Packing the heavy gear over the hill and down a slope that seems to grow steeper with each trek, the apparatus seeming to increase in weight and density with each deadly use. Then, after such work, the hike back up the hillside, which so drags at him now. And it can only be done at night. Deep night, with no help from the beams of a flashlight or a clearly-marked trail. But he has no other option. Only to stumble his way down the hillside in the dark, trudging under the weight of the heavy pack, sneaking cautiously through the trees along the gravel road by the tanks, then walking swiftly from the protection of the trees into the open, working quickly, escaping just as quickly. Heavy night work, incessant stealth, fear of exposure—to electrocute swarms of little trout trapped in concrete hatchery troughs. It takes its toll on a man, certainly on a man his age. Still, the job must be done. No choice in the matter. He wonders how he might go about taking on an apprentice for such specialized labor.

Tonight's killing was the easiest yet. The destructive dance of the hatchery manager's son had emptied one trough of at least half its population, making his task that much simpler. By the time he finished off the fish the kid had missed in that one and killed every trout in the next pen, the lights still burned bright in the hatchery manager's house. He gave little thought to the varieties of discipline being transacted in the manager's double-wide as he stepped to the third and final pen. Halfway down the length of the final trough, the house lights went out, and he completed his sweep beneath the distant glow of sheets of stars.

The choral hum of the forest night cloaks him, and the heft of the pack frame tears at his shoulders. The image of the kid's self-indulgent butchery is slow to fade. He is troubled by the messy brutality of the kid's actions, and he is troubled by what his actions hold in common with the kid's. Does his cool, precise technological slaughter for a larger purpose set him above the emotional fury of the kid's massacre? The result is the same. Do his methods and purpose somehow sanctify his hatred, make it honorable in comparison to the kid's simple rage? "Of the uncertainty after all, that we may be deluded . . . " Enough of this, he thinks. *The fish that needed to die had died, and the kid's mayhem, sloppy as it was, had helped in the process. That is all that matters at the moment. The job had gone more quickly than usual, for which he is grateful. He has a long hike up the hillside before him, and he is tired. His back aches and pinches under the strain of the pack frame. He needs to concentrate on the hike, on getting home while he still has some strength.*

Trudging up at an angle across the face of the hillside, he moves slowly along. The woods are dark under the canopy and the moonless sky. He can see and feel his way just enough to maintain his progress. Nocturnal forest sounds come to him as from a distance, filtered through the constant hum in his ears. The breath in his lungs begins to burn, and the straps of the pack frame feel as if they are scraping bare bone. His sore feet slip out from under him three times before he reaches the ridge, and he stops to rest his seared lungs for a moment, leaning his shoulder against what feels like the smooth, slender trunk of a young ash, before he begins his descent. The ache of his lungs and feet, the pain of his scored shoulders, are tempered by the sensation that he is here, at this place in this time, moving across the slopes of these glacier-pushed hills, down into the gorge cut by the rushing waters of the upper Ripshin, where the descendents of Ice Age brook trout fin safely. Safe, for the time being.

"They belong here," he whispers through his labored breath, as his sore feet set themselves onto the descending slope.

The effort of the downward trek always surprises him, reminds him. Rather than a relaxed surrender to the tease of gravity, he must push against the weight of the pack that dragged at his back on the upward climb if he is to keep from toppling face-forward. His exertion shifts trajectory but continues until he comes out on the streamside flats at the base of the hill.

In his back and feet the pain lingers, but once he comes off the slope into the sparsely-wooded flatter stretch of ground leading to the stream, once he can hear the gush and plummet of the Ripshin, his posture straightens slightly under the pack's more balanced weight and the burning air in his lungs cools. He can never be away from these waters for very long. Once a month he reluctantly drives his old truck into Damascus to deposit his pension check and purchase food and supplies. Even after such a brief absence, he feels a rush of relief once the old truck hits the gravel of the fire road to his bungalow and he can again hear the sound of the cascading current cutting through the whirring in his ears.

He sinks under the weight of the pack and shifts the straps, but the change only spreads the pain of the previous placement. Slipping down to the water's edge, he wavers under his burden. He is flagging and knows he needs to keep moving. He must yet cross the stream, walk up the short slope behind his bungalow, and store his cumbersome equipment in the little cave there before he is finished and can finally collapse onto his neatly-made bed. And he thinks it will be peaceful, restful before bed, after such a night, to linger on his porch, smoking a single cigarette, his sore feet freed from the heavy hip boots and bare, flexing and toeing the knothole. As he traversed the hillsides, clouds had rolled in and covered the field of stars. Rain is on the way, and he is glad for this. It is much needed after the long dry spell of late summer, but he would just as soon not get caught out in it right now. And yet, he pauses for a moment before crossing the river. From the darkness, the flowing stream seems to emanate its own light, the ghostly shimmer over deeper pools, the faint white bubbling of currents churning around rocks. The ringing in his ears disappears, perfectly masked by the hiss of rushing water. Looking over the quivering glow of the Ripshin in the night, he thinks of the native brook trout still safe and thriving beneath the surface. And he thinks that these waters remain safe and pure for her, to receive her. "Nothing collapses," he thinks. His gaze lifts from the water's surface to the other side of the stream, to the shadowy silhouette of his bungalow at the base of the next slope. He imagines the shining urn on the top shelf of his tying bench there and steps from the bank onto the network of exposed rocks that mark the course of his passage to the other side.

He tells himself he should have brought his staff along tonight after all, at the exact same moment he loses his footing. His right foot slips on a patch of slick moss he'd avoided on the night's previous crossing, twisting his body perpendicular to the bank and pitching him over beneath the bulk of his pack. His right foot slides into the water and wedges itself between the rock from which he slips and another submerged at its base. As he topples, he can feel the ankle wrench between the rocks, can feel the ligaments tearing. Still falling, he grows suddenly faint from the shocked rush of blood to the mangled ankle, but he is still conscious when the side of his head strikes an adjacent rock. Collapsed and still, he lies with his head and torso leaning against the rock, pulled slightly back at an awkward angle by the weight of the pack frame. The bottom half of his body is submerged in the cold, flowing water, and he remains conscious just long enough to feel the implacable, leaden weight of the water filling his boots, remains conscious long enough to see one last flash of the image of the kid dancing and stomping the pile of dead and dying trout into mush at the hatchery that night before all in his vision is sucked into a pinhole of fuzzy light. The first raindrop splats on his cheek as the pinhole closes and everything fades to black.

* * *

Sandy tosses her poncho in with the rest of her gear in the cab of her pickup. She slides into the seat, turns the ignition key, and switches on her windshield wipers. Runnels of gray water trickle along the edges of the windshield, and the wiper blades flick old dust mixed with new rain out to the side of the truck.

The rain had begun in the middle of the night, and Sandy had woken to the unfamiliar patter on the roof and the charged, invigorated air drifting through her open windows. For a moment she had thought to get up and close them, but she decided a little water pooled on the sills and floor was insignificant compared to the deliciousness of the ozone-rich air now filling her lungs. The weather forecast had predicted a much-needed, long, slow soaker that would last all day. Sandy had hoped the prediction would prove to be correct. Water levels were low in the streams, and the underground springs and aquifers that fed the rivers and streams of the

Rogers Ridge watershed needed the sort of lingering, steady rain that would soak down and begin the perennial process of replenishing the sources of those trout-thick waters that marked her heart's geography. She had begun to drift back to sleep with the smell of the rainy air in her nose, Margie's voice in her ears, and the feel of Stink's bristly fur in her fingertips. As her eyes fluttered shut, she hoped that Stink had left his tire and taken up his old position under the deck to get out of the rain.

Gazing through the clicking windshield wipers into the gray early light, she thinks the rain looks as though it will live up to the forecast. Stink sits under the deck, happily scratching at the itchy scars and scabs left on his face and neck by the ticks Sandy removed last night.

"Keep dry, you old thing," Sandy says to the dog as she closes the truck door. "God knows, but your skunk-stink is ten times worse when you're wet."

Stink ignores her, engrossed in his scratching, as she slips the truck into gear and rolls down her driveway. Bits of gravel shoot from under her rear tires as she accelerates and turns onto Willard Road, on her way into Damascus to gas up the truck before heading up to Keefe's cabin.

On the wet pavement around the pump islands at the Citgo, the workday life of Damascus is already out on the go, while the rest of the little town is barely up and moving. The gas station is crowded with heavy-duty pickup trucks, vans, and delivery vehicles. Every pump island is occupied, so Sandy pulls in behind a small flatbed with a roofing company logo painted on its doors to wait her turn. The canopies over the pumps provide some protection from the rain. Sandy switches off her wipers, rolls down her window, and inhales the rain-freshened air, now mingling with the scents of spilled gasoline and the fumes of internal combustion engines in varying states of repair.

Two men in caps, t-shirts, and well-worn jeans lean against the side of the roofing company flatbed. One drinks coffee from a plastic cup, the other handles the gas pump, clicking the nozzle grip spasmodically, topping off the tank. The pumper screws the cap back on the flatbed's tank opening and rams the nozzle back onto the pump as he speaks to the coffee drinker.

"Of all goddamn days to rain," he says.

"What do you mean? We're needin this rain bad," says the coffee drinker.

"You forgetting? We left that section uncovered yesterday. Never thought it'd actually rain."

"The weather forecast was calling for rain. Pretty definite about it as I recall."

"Well, still never thought it actually would. Damn. Best get on over there before their ceiling gets soaked. Be hell to pay. That woman's a goddamn bitch about every little thing."

"That much is for shit sure."

Sandy continues waiting while the roofers go inside the convenience store to pay for their gas. As they enter, a man with a red bandanna wrapped around his head, wearing heavy black coveralls over a smudged white t-shirt, comes out. He appears oblivious to the rain he walks through, intent on scratching with a coin at lottery cards in the palm of his hand. His eyes never rise from the cards as he walks in front of Sandy's truck to a white van on the other side of the gas pumps. Simple lettering on the side of the van indicates the name and phone number of a sheet metal company. The card-scratcher completes his scratching, sighs, crumples the cards, and drops them to the pavement as he climbs into the driver's seat of the van.

"Well, it's rainin like hell and it's another day I ain't gonna be rich," he says to another man in heavy coveralls in the passenger seat.

The white van squeals away across the wet pavement as the roofers return to their flatbed. Sandy pulls her truck beside the gas pumps when the roofers drive off. As she removes the gas cap and inserts the pump nozzle into the tank, she thinks that Vernon would have loved nothing more than to be among such working men at such a Citgo on such an early workday morning as this.

Unleaded regular pumps into Sandy's gas tank, and she watches a man in matching blue shirt and shorts pushing a hand truck loaded with cases of soda and bottled water across the lot from his truck to the doors of the convenience store. He moves quickly, his head and shoulders hunched against the rain. She notices J.D.'s dark green government SUV as the soda delivery man rushes past it and into the store through the door J.D. holds open for him. J.D. has already seen her as he and the delivery man exchange nods. Holding a hand over his plastic coffee cup, he walks carefully through the rain to Sandy and her truck under the canopy. He shakes sloshed hot coffee from his fingers as he steps around the truck while Sandy removes the nozzle from her full gas tank.

"Hello, J.D."

"Hi, Sandy."

"Finally getting some rain," she says, glad there is at least the common topic of weather to speak of.

"Yeah, suppose so," J.D. says, distracted, glancing through the rain at nothing in particular.

"Water levels as low as they are, we need this rain pretty bad."

"Yeah, guess so."

"J.D., I'll admit that talking about the weather doesn't make for the most dazzling conversation. But since you're the one who walked over to me, I thought maybe you might have something to say."

"Sorry," J.D. says, sipping from his coffee and turning his face from the rain to Sandy. "Didn't mean to be rude. Just that rain isn't my main concern right now. It happened again."

"What?" Sandy asks.

"The hatchery," J.D. says. "There was another kill last night."

"Oh. Same as the last time?"

"Don't know. Just got the call. I'm on my way out there right now."

Sandy leans into the cab of her truck and takes her wallet from the storage compartment on the door.

"Good luck. Hope you catch your killer this time," she says.

J.D. snorts and angrily throws his half-full coffee cup into the trash container beside the gas pump.

"Sooner or later, I'm going to get them. But I just don't get it. For the life of me, I can't understand why."

Sandy tries to shrug her shoulders sympathetically as she eases her way around her truck toward the entrance to the store. J.D. looks down, his eyes flitting sideways toward the trash container, embarrassed by his outburst.

"Sorry about that. Makes me mad I guess," J.D. says.

"Don't worry about it," Sandy says.

He looks back up at Sandy, trying to maintain a pleasant look on his face.

"Going to do a little fishing?"

"Yes. Thought I'd hit the headwaters. Haven't been in a while."

"Even in this rain?"

"Light rain like this, the fishing should be pretty good. Gets them all stirred up. Besides, this is why they make rain gear."

"Well, good luck."

"Same to you."

"Yeah. Thanks." J.D. trots off through the rain to his SUV.

As she enters the store, Sandy glances briefly at his retreating figure, surprised to see his fists clenched at his side as he runs.

* * *

By the time Sandy has hiked one of the two miles up the fire road leading to Keefe's cabin from the locked gate where she parked her truck, she is hot under the clinging plastic of her poncho. The rain continues to fall at a steady pace, but has decreased in intensity and is broken by the forest canopy overhead. She leans her rod against a tree at the roadside and removes the stifling poncho, stuffing it into the pouch on the back of her vest. Given the summer's long, dry wait for precipitation, she finds it incongruous, silly to keep the soft, enlivening rain off her thirsty skin with dead plastic.

The rain beads coolly on her bare arms as she walks, her rod riding parallel to the ground, the rod grip cradled loosely in her hand, its tip extended several feet before her, divining the way to Keefe's cabin. It had been a small crime, perhaps no crime at all. If she had simply apologized on the spot, said she was sorry for the intrusion and turned away, then that would have been that. Simple, direct, routine courtesy. Instead she sat on her ass like a lump, mute, staring at a naked man engaged in a private ritual. That the ritual seemed a bit odd did not change the fact that it was a personal, intimate moment, that it was his moment. Instead of apologizing and slinking away, she had nearly exhausted herself working extra shifts at the nursing home and feverishly clearing out the pile of tires behind her house, leaving her with a bruise the size of a fist on the small of her back and a broken screen door. Instead of doing the simple thing, the obvious thing, she had behaved like a fool, like someone other than the Sandy Holston she thought she was, and, in the process, had managed to spook her coworkers, hurt J.D. Callander yet one more time, and go for more than two weeks without fishing once. Enough of such nonsense, she thinks.

"Fool," she mutters to herself.

Now there remains only Keefe, waiting less than a mile ahead. Would he accept her tardy, pathetic apology? Be outraged or embarrassed by her intrusion? Would he even remember her? Would their combined assault on the young man in the Atlanta Braves cap outweigh her crude invasion of his ceremony? Would he brush it off as nothing and send her on her way, telling her not to worry about it? Tell her that she should be goddamn sorry and slam the cabin door in her face? Assure her that all was forgiven and invite her into the cabin for a cup of his strong coffee? Would she get to see once again the chaotic cabin interior that had so fascinated her the first time? Would Keefe even care, one way or the other?

Still, she is glad to be walking here in this rain on this road in these mountains along this river. The rush of the upper Ripshin's descending waters and the rain on her neck and arms conspire to cool her flesh and soothe the questioning prattle in her head. The hemlocks and pines glisten, droplets of rain coating their needles. The sound of Sandy's boots scuffing the damp cinder road is matched by the patter of those rain droplets falling from the needles to the turgid leaves of rhododendron, laurel, and the forest floor beneath the trees. A heron flies along the upper Ripshin, and Sandy follows the bird's course, marking its massive and graceful wing span until it disappears around the downstream bend. Chicory blooms along the fire road, the small purple blossoms wet and brilliant. Sandy looks at the moisture of the ground around the wild plants, squats and presses her palm to the damp earth, and imagines the water seeping steadily through the soil, down into the limestone, refreshing the springs feeding the current flowing beside her. She feels that the air would lock in her lungs and the blood would freeze in her veins, that she would cease to live if she could not walk here, breathe here, fish here, live here. The joy of being in this place and the terror of losing it mingle in her expanding lungs, her pumping heart. Perhaps her penance had at least given her that, allowed her the time and circumstance to realize this. To feel this. She recalls the voice of the nurses' aide through the bathroom door. "A cold fish, that one."

She tilts her head back as she walks and inhales the moist air deep into her lungs. The rain is gentle on her face, and her heart pulses from the uphill hike. Coming around a switchback on the road, she thinks of Stink and Margie and is surprised by how good it feels not to be alone anymore. She smiles, wondering how long it will be until Margie calls her, now that she has her phone number.

"Water bed," she says, chuckling softly at Margie's slip of the tongue the night before.

If Sandy remembers correctly, and she does, Keefe's cabin sits in a small clearing just around the next bend in the fire road, about a hundred yards ahead. She pauses at the edge of the road, looks into one of the Ripshin's larger, placid pools down the bank to her left, and again runs through the questions about what she'll encounter when she rounds that bend into Keefe's clearing. Ridiculous to be so anxious about this, she thinks. A simple thing to do. Apologize. Say it and be done with it. Besides, what does she really care about this old man's opinion of her, of her actions? Nothing at all, she tries to tell herself. She taps herself firmly on the side of her head, wipes rainwater from the back of her neck, and issues a final reprimand to herself to get it right the first time around in the future. Learn from your mistakes. A simple thing. She shakes herself and has taken only one step on up the road to Keefe's when she spots it.

In the tail of the pool, in water more shallow than she would have expected, holding in the slow current, a solitary brook trout. A big one. As big as the one at Dismal Creek, the one it took so many attempts to catch, so many years ago. She crouches, slinks back from the bank, and backtracks several yards downstream. Shielded behind a hemlock, she rigs her rod and ties on an ant pattern, her eyes periodically flitting up from her close work to mark that the big brook trout maintains its position. Carefully, very slowly, she lowers herself down the bank on her rear, gains her footing in the riffling water and, holding in her low crouch, stalks warily toward the big fish. It continues to hold in the same place. She marks a spot on the bank for her casting target. Her fly will have to hit the water at the target point, just a few inches in front of its nose, will have to hit the water lightly, will have to be delivered from close range, only the fly and a few inches of leader hitting the surface, no long loops of rocketing fly line, only rod and wrist, quick close work. A brook trout this big in water this shallow, she will get only one chance.

Rubbing her earring, marking the position of the fish and gauging the length of her line, her rod, her arm, Sandy takes one last squatting step and drops to her knees. The frigid water reaches to the middle of her thighs. The rocks in the streambed bite into her knees but she ignores the discomfort. There is only the fish. There is only the target, this one cast, this one chance. Her arm rises slowly, over her head and out to her side. Her wrist flicks the rod and line back, the rod tip moving only a foot or so. All that is necessary in this tight space. The rod tip and line twitch forward, and as the short line shoots out, she reaches after it, extending her arm and rod. The line unrolls to its full length, dead even with her target, catches the ant mid-flight, and drops it to the surface of the pool, just ahead of the brook trout's nose.

Barely a single ripple has risen from the impact of the fly on the water before the big brook trout strikes, and Sandy sets the hook, rises from her knees, and plays the fish out into the deeper water of the pool. Her rod bows nearly double as the brook trout dives and spins, desperate to rip free of the hook. Sandy holds her rod high, locks her elbow, and begins to retrieve line. Drawing the scrappy fish toward her, she is again awed by the ferocity of these small fish, as she was the first time she took a brook trout this size. The huge brown trout she caught a few weeks ago in the lower Ripshin, the brown trout she overplayed, the brown trout that started all this, that led her to this pool on this day, that brown trout, half again as long as this brook trout and three times as heavy, didn't put up half the fight this brook trout is now dishing out to her.

She does not overplay the fish this time. Each arch and tilt of the rod, each retrieve of the line, deployed to bring the fish to hand as quickly, as efficiently as possible. The tension in her arm is delicious, but she does not indulge it and brings the thrashing fish to hand in less than a minute. The blazing glow of its orange belly dazzles her as she hefts the lush body in her hand and removes her fly deftly from its upper lip. Cupped in her hand, she dips the brook trout into the rain-dappled water. It lingers in her hand for a moment, gasping oxygen into its depleted body through beating gills before it flashes away into the deeper recesses at the head of the pool.

Sandy shakes the water from her hand and reels in her line. Intent on playing the fish, she had been oblivious to the increased intensity of the rainfall. She squints into the downpour. Her shirt is soaked and clinging to her skin. The rain falls heavily through the open spaces and bounces in thick drops from the overhanging leaves. Climbing up the bank onto the fire road, she decides that at this point the poncho would be irrelevant. Perhaps Keefe will, after all is said and done, let her linger on his porch, even ask her in to dry off, have a cup of coffee. Perhaps. She wonders if he might have any tea in his bungalow as well.

There is no response to Sandy's first knock on Keefe's cabin door, no sound of movement within. She waits before the door on his little porch, rubbing her chilled wet arms, her rod leaning against the porch rail. Replaying all her anxious questions about Keefe's possible response to her arrival, to her apology, she lands on the one question she had omitted. Would he even be home when she came to ask forgiveness? Sandy toes at the knothole in one of the porch planks and sees the drops of water dripping to the planks from her hair. She removes her cap, sets it on the porch rail, and shakes out the excess water. Keefe's truck sits beside the cabin. Is he away fishing elsewhere along the upper Ripshin? Is he lying face down in a pool somewhere, in his wet suit, "keeping an eye on things"? Sandy knocks again. Still no response.

"Damn it," she says.

He must be somewhere within walking distance, she thinks. His truck is here, and he's not a young man, after all. She waits on Keefe's porch, hoping he will appear, afraid he will appear, glad to be out of the heavy rain for a little while longer. Her damp shirt wraps her chest like a wet second skin, but her arms and face are beginning to dry. Resisting a momentary temptation to test whether or not Keefe's door is locked, she leans against one of the posts supporting the porch roof and looks across the small clearing to the large pool where the upper Ripshin widens in front of Keefe's cabin.

At the tail of the pool something is wedged in the exposed rocks that break the still pool into a series of riffles. Straining her eyes to focus through the rain, she sees what appears to be some sort of machinery, a rectangular construction of metal and plastic. Must be flood trash, she thinks for a moment, before she remembers that since she's lived here there hasn't been enough water in the upper Ripshin to wash down such a large piece of refuse. She takes one step down from the porch and squints again through the sheet of rain. She spots something brown, not a part of any machine, just above the edge of what now looks like a metal frame, and steps off the porch and out into the rain. Three more steps and she can tell that the brown thing visible above the metal frame is a hat, a brown fedora. She walks briskly now, with long strides, and sees that the hat is askew under a head covered in tangles of wet, white hair. She is running when she reaches the bank and jumps down into the water. Her breath comes in short, hard bursts as she wades swiftly to Keefe's partially submerged, still body, lying twisted against the rock and the bulky pack frame. She squats at Keefe's side and lifts his face into her hands. His fedora falls away and rolls onto its crown, collecting rain on top of the rock.

"Mr. Keefe. Mr. Keefe," Sandy says, loudly, slapping his face lightly.

One hand slips from his face, and her fingers probe his neck for a pulse. His body is cold, clammy, but the pulse is there.

"Mr. Keefe. Can you hear me?"

She shakes him, and his eyes flutter half open, then roll back in their sockets. He mutters something unintelligible. The only word Sandy can understand is "luckier."

Keefe slips back into unconsciousness, and Sandy, almost instinctively, becomes the nurse, and Keefe another damaged body in need of care. She reaches into the water and carefully frees the trapped foot from between the rocks. The hip boots are full of water and heavy. She undoes the loops at his belt and tugs the leaden boots carefully from his legs. They sink immediately, the loops drifting in the current beneath the surface. Sandy runs her hand down the length of Keefe's leg, feeling for any swelling or fracture. Probably a severe sprain. Hard to tell just yet. She releases the shoulder straps and pulls them to their full length, so she can pull Keefe's arms loose without bending them excessively. The cathode wand trails from the pack, floating on the riffle behind them, and Sandy recognizes the apparatus as a shock pack, the perfect device to electrocute hatchery trout trapped in their pens. Tiny streams of rain course down her face, and she blinks her eyes against the water. A pair of binoculars still hangs from a strap around Keefe's neck, one of the lenses cracked. Sandy slips the strap over his head and flings the binoculars to the bank. She breathes the rainy air deep into her lungs, slides one arm under Keefe's twisted back, one under his knees, and braces herself to lift his body from the stream. Dipping her head down to collect her strength before lifting, her earring catches on a button on Keefe's shirt. Thrusting her strong body upward, hoisting the heavy mass of immobile flesh, the earring tears away from her ear lobe and falls into the current. A sharp pain inflames her ear and shoots down her neck. A trickle of blood begins to mingle with the rain on her ear and neck, but she continues to lift, stands upright, feeling a twinge at the bruise on her back. The shock pack slides from the rock and settles half submerged in the water. She secures Keefe in her arms and wades out of the current and up the bank before collapsing to her knees, laying Keefe heavily onto the sodden ground.

"Mr. Keefe?" she asks again, knowing she has, at once, carried both James Keefe and J.D. Callander's hatchery killer from the chill waters of the upper Ripshin.

Sandy pulls the wet socks from Keefe's feet, pushes up his pant legs, and examines the ankles and lower legs. She holds his frigid feet, one in each hand, trying to warm them against her own wet skin while she looks for damage. A massive purple bruise has formed on the right foot and ankle. The swelling would begin soon, now that the foot was out of the cold water. She touches her fingers lightly to a pink, raw bump on his right temple. A concussion, perhaps.

She knows she must get him out of the rain, out of the wet clothing, into the dry warmth of his cabin, but she knows as well that she will not be able to lift him again, will not be able to carry him all the way across the clearing and into his cabin. She puts the socks back on his feet, pulls the pant legs down, and runs her arms under his armpits, locking her hands over the center of his chest. Lifting only his torso from the ground, Sandy hauls him slowly across the clearing toward the cabin, watching carefully not to drag his injured ankle over any rocks or tree roots. Her chest pressed to his back as she pulls, she can feel his fever setting in through their soaked shirts.

Sandy feels a palpable relief when the unlocked cabin door gives way as she turns the knob, still holding Keefe's limp body with her other arm. Dragging Keefe through the clutter of the cabin interior toward his bedroom, she reprimands herself when she realizes she has divided her attention between Keefe and the alluring contents of his cabin.

Once she has his body on the bed, she acts with speed and precision. She removes the damp clothes and throws them to the floor. She brings two towels from the bathroom beside the bedroom and begins to dry him, vigorously rubbing the flow of blood back into the dimpled, pruned flesh. She misses no part. Face, neck, ears, chest and back, buttocks and groin, thighs and calves and injured feet. She dries and rubs every inch. A damaged body in need of care. Nothing more.

She finds a third towel in a cabinet in the bathroom and dries Keefe's hair, pushing the wispy white strands off his forehead with her fingertips. Searching the drawers in the solitary dresser in the room, she comes up with a sweatshirt and a pair of flannel pajama bottoms, both well worn. Slipping the sweatshirt over Keefe's head, she can feel that his flesh is now burning. The fever has set in fully. Anxious to get him under the covers of his bed, she slides the pajama bottoms up his legs too quickly, catching the waistband under his scrotum. With one hand she tugs the waistband back down a few inches, and with the other she tucks his genitals inside and pulls the waistband into place.

Once Keefe is safely under the covers, his head on one pillow, his injured ankle elevated on the other, Sandy feels again the acute chill of her own wet clothes on her skin and the sharp pang at her ear lobe. In the bathroom mirror, she confirms that the earring has torn fully through the lobe, but the bleeding seems to have stopped. She leaves it, allowing the clotted blood to do its work. She soaks a tattered washcloth in cold water and returns to Keefe's room. He is breathing easily, steadily, but his fever is raging. She lays the cool cloth across his forehead and turns to his dresser, removing an old woolen sweater, gray with holes worn in each elbow. She could apologize for this theft when she finally apologized for her first crime.

The sweater in one hand, another towel in the other, she walks into Keefe's living room. Amid the clutter of books, fishing gear, animal skins, and fly tying material, Sandy drops her vest to the floor and peels off her wet shirt and bra. A rush of cool air sweeps over her naked torso. Her skin tingles into a taut sheet of goose flesh, her nipples grow tight and hard. Running the towel over her skin, her neck, breasts, back, arms, her wet hair, she steps through the exquisite mess of Keefe's cabin to the open door and looks through the rain across the clearing to the river. She can just make out the top of the submerged shock pack lodged behind the rock.

Her hands drop to her sides, the towel draped on the floor. She knows she must retrieve it. It sits midstream, its presence and purpose glaring. Evidence. If J.D. should wander up this way today, angry as he is.

From the waist down, still in her waders and boots, she is warm and dry. From the waist up, she is cool, dry, and naked. She drops the wet towel over the back of the cracked leather sofa. The cool air continues to bathe her bare chest, and she looks at the woolen sweater, trailing her fingertips over the rough weave. Foolish to put it on now, she thinks. Just one more wet thing to dry. It would take only a moment to dry her naked skin again. She does not even consider the slick wet poncho stuffed in the back pouch of her vest.

The porch planks creak quietly under her boots as she takes two tentative steps out of the cabin door. The downpour remains heavy, constant. She glances briefly across the clearing and up the fire road, then steps bare-chested from the porch into the rain. She strides across the clearing, the rain pelting her hair, face and chest. Rainwater drenches her skin, dripping from the ends of her hair, flowing in tiny rivulets over her shoulders, down her back and between her breasts. She pauses when she reaches the bank, her eyes involuntarily scanning the rain-pocked pool for sight of the brook trout that she knows have taken refuge in the deeper holes, terrified by the force of the torrent on the surface. Her eyes rise from the surface of the pool, checking both upstream and down from the shock pack. It occurs to Sandy that she has never before stood bare and exposed in the open air. She breathes deep the rain-laced air and delays one more moment, relishing the sensation of the air and rain on her naked skin, the exhilaration of her exposed breasts floating above the waters of the upper Ripshin. For a moment, she thinks she understands some small particle of Keefe's naked, streamside ritual as she leaps down the bank and wades to the shock pack.

After hefting the dead weight of Keefe's fallen body from the river, the weight of the pack barely registers in her throbbing arms. She grips the metal frame and lifts the pack out of the water. She moves back toward the bank, picking up Keefe's fedora from the rock as she wades around it. The cathode wand drags behind at the end of its wire in the current. She puts the fedora on her head, draws the wand in with her free hand and carries the contraption to the bank. The boots. Wading back in, she hefts the submerged hips boots from the water, one at a time, empties them of water, and heaves each one to land and follows them out of the stream. She slips the strap of the binoculars over her head, hanging them from her neck. Gripping the shock pack with her right hand and the hips boots with her left, she heads back across the clearing. For one brief moment, she feels an odd sensation of being followed, pauses and looks back over her shoulder toward the river, then shakes off the feeling and continues to the cabin. The loosened shoulder straps of the pack and the cathode wand trail along the ground, and the tingle of her bare, dripping skin begins to subside as she steps back into the cabin and sets the shock pack and the boots on the floor behind the sofa. She will hide the pack, stash it more securely, later. She removes the fedora and binoculars and places them on the pine coffee table.

Taking the damp towel from the back of the sofa, she rubs herself dry again and lingers for another minute at the open cabin door before she slips the baggy old sweater over her head, gingerly pulling the neck opening away from her torn earlobe. The wool feels coarse but soothing. She should put a kettle of water on the stove, check on Keefe again and fashion a wrap for his ankle, she thinks, as she closes the door on the rain falling outside Keefe's cabin.

* * *

Not long ago, Inmate #52674 at the Bland County Correctional Facility wrote and mailed the following letter:

Dear Margie,

Has Sandy moved? My last letter came back to me, unopened. Funny, that unopened letter is the only letter I've ever gotten from her in all these years. The only one. When I got the letter back, I called my parents, and they told me they hadn't seen or heard from her since she brought my van back years ago.

Well, I figure if anyone knows where she is, it would be you. I don't suppose I could blame you if you think I'm still angry and a danger to her. But I promise you, I'm no longer a danger. To anyone. Sincerely, I am a changed man, redeemed in the blood of Christ. Please send these letters I've enclosed here on to her. If need be, I can find her. But tell her there is no reason to hide, from me of all people. I wish only to beg her forgiveness and to share with her the light of reborn Christian life and love.

Yours, in Christ

Vernon Adams

The letter, in a manila envelope containing two other letters, one previously postmarked, was duly delivered to the addressee, but received no response.

4

As Long as the River's Here

The alarm clock begins beeping into the dawn dark of her bedroom at the same moment the banging begins at the back door. As her eyes flutter open, still groggy from deep sleep, it seems to Sandy, for an instant, that her alarm clock has developed a new, louder, more demanding ring. In another instant her waking mind separates the beeping clock from the noise at her back door. She slaps down the alarm button and sits upright in bed, her eyes wide now, her senses alert. Another bang at the back door, as if it has been kicked. She hears the broken screen door rattle and slowly slides her bare legs out from under the sheets. Someone is there.

Sandy jams her legs into a pair of jeans that lay crumpled on the floor and emerges from her bedroom in a crouch. Inching silently through the kitchen toward the back door, she grasps the handle of the green mug in the dish rack and hoists it like a hammer, her arm cocked. She eases her body along the edge of the countertop, her shoulder pressed to it. At the end of the counter she rises from her crouch and peeks around the end of the kitchen cabinets to the window in the back door. Nothing. She can see nothing through the window but the scant hint of the slope behind her house in the budding dawn light.

Looking at the mug tensed in her hand, she smirks and sets it back on the counter, wondering just what in the hell she thought she was going to do with it anyway. She takes a step toward the back door, feeling the steady, firm beat of her heart in her chest and rubbing the red, scarring crease on her earlobe, when the broken screen door bangs and jumps again. The sudden rattle and clank slam into her chest, exploding her even pulse into a wild thumping.

"Shit. What the . . . ?" She resumes her crouch and creeps to the door.

Her hand reaching for the knob and resting on it, she gradually raises her forehead and eyes above the lower edge of the back-door window and flips on the porch light.

"Oh, you goddamn dog." She stands up, shaking her head, her heart rate calming, and opens the back door, quickly slamming it closed again.

"Oh, god," she says, holding one hand over her nose while the other swats at the air before her.

Stink sits happily, proudly outside the door, panting and looking from Sandy's face in the window to his prey lying on the back stoop. A skunk, a very dead one, the fur at its neck soggy and matted around a small spot of blood. Most likely, Sandy thinks, the hapless skunk had been rummaging around her trash can by the back door when Stink stalked out of his tractor tire and struck. The banging on the screen door would have been the skunk's body, slamming against the aluminum frame when Stink snapped his neck.

Sandy stuffs a trash bag from beneath the kitchen sink into her back pocket, presses a dish towel over her nose, and steps out the door, carefully stepping over the motionless, acrid body on the stoop. Stink looks up to her, panting, his tail beginning to wag. He had killed innumerable skunks, his constant rank odor the proof of his passion.

161

Their carcasses lay scattered throughout the pine trees surrounding Sandy's house, and he even ate them on occasion, though not so often since Sandy had begun feeding him tastier fare. But this is the first time he has brought his prey to her, the first time he has offered it up to her in tribute.

"I suppose I should be honored, right?" she says to the dog and lightly scratches behind one ear, leaning back from the overpowering smell rising from his fur.

Sandy walks to her truck and removes one of her work gloves from behind the front seat. Holding her breath and using her gloved hand, she lifts the dead skunk by the tail and, hoping the tail doesn't snap free, drops the body into the trash bag. She ties the bag shut and places it in the trash can. Stink's eyes follow each of Sandy's motions, and he stares at the closed trash can while Sandy tosses her glove into her truck and walks back to the stoop.

"You're really proud of yourself, aren't you?" she says to Stink, petting him lightly again, trying not to get much of the scent on her fingertips. "Well, you know what this means? Now you get another bath, smart boy."

It had only been a week since Sandy and Stink had felt secure enough in their new bond for her to give him a bath. She knew it would take more than soap and water to cut through the residue of years' worth of ticks and skunks on his skin and fur. Sandy had heard people talk about tomato juice as the tried and true antidote for skunk stink on a dog, but she had heard as often that it just didn't really do that much good. She called a local veterinarian's office for suggestions.

"Douche," the veterinarian's assistant had said.

"I beg your pardon?"

"Yeah, I know it sounds weird, but douche the critter. It's the only thing that really works at all."

"Douche. Really?"

"Yeah, really. I swear, I'm not kidding you. And none of that frilly, scented crap either. Just plain Massengill douche."

"Okay. Thank you," Sandy had said. Soon she would have to take Stink to the vet's office for shots and a check-up, she had told herself as she hung up the phone.

And damned if the douche hadn't worked pretty well. By no means did it completely eliminate Stink's embedded rankness. But at least she could sit by him, pet him without holding her nose.

She pushes the broken screen door aside, and opens her back door. Stepping over the threshold, she pauses and glances back at Stink, who has risen from his sitting position and is now sniffing around the lid of the trash can.

"Let's see if we have enough of your douche left," Sandy says, walking into her kitchen. Margie had said she wouldn't get there until later that morning. Sandy calculates she has enough time to have a little breakfast, bathe Stink, make another run up to Keefe's cabin to check on him, and be home again before Margie arrives with the letters. She'd have to forget her plan to clean the bathroom in honor of Margie's visit. She leans her head back out the door, looking down at Stink, who turns his face away from the trash can and up to her.

"How do you like your eggs?" Sandy asks.

* * *

Sandy ties a length of rope to his new collar and secures the other end to one of the porch posts while Stink slurps raw eggs from the bowl she set on the ground before him. She had done the same when she first bathed him a week ago, but she wonders if the rope is actually necessary. He hadn't resisted her then, and he seems relaxed and accepting of the impending douching now as well. In fact, as far as Sandy can tell, most of Stink's previous hostility and suspicion evaporated when she refused Tommy Akers the last tractor tire, and whatever distrust remained after that vanished when she freed him of his colony of ticks. He still refused to venture very far from his tire, limiting his territory to the clearing around Sandy's house and the occasional foray into the surrounding pine trees. As long as he could keep his tire within easy reach, he seemed satisfied. He had declined one invitation from Sandy to take a ride in the truck, and she hadn't asked him again. He wouldn't come in the house either, and Sandy hadn't pushed it, given that despite the bath, a definite odor still clung to his skin and fur.

When she first bathed him, rather than fighting her, rather than resisting what she thought must be a strange experience for a dog who had led a life such as his, he had acquiesced, sitting placidly as she soaked him in the douche solution, calm under her touch. He had closed his eyes and luxuriated in the feel of her firm hands soaping his bristly fur, massaging his irritated skin, and scratching his mass of scabs and scars. That evening, after Stink's bath, Sandy was sitting on her back stoop, sipping tea from her green mug. He waddled around the corner of the house, sat beside her, and rested his damp head in her lap. Sandy scratched his snout and behind his wet ears, and they sat together that way for an hour, watching the light disappear behind the ridge.

By all readable signs, as far as Stink was concerned, he was her dog now. The rest would be up to Sandy.

She pours the douche solution over his head and along his backbone in small dribbles, cupping her free hand on his flanks to catch the rivulets flowing off. Across the river, the gray sky above the ridge blues into morning as she works the solution into his skin and fur, watching how the moisture darkens his mottled brown-orange-yellow coat. The same way Keefe's white hair had darkened to a dull gray from a night in rain and river water, from fever sweats.

* * *

Sandy had closed the door on the rain falling outside Keefe's cabin and returned to the bedroom. Keefe remained unconscious. She lifted a stray strand of damp, gray hair from his forehead, resting the backs of her chilled fingers on his brow to test his fever. She held them there a moment longer, compensating for the cold in her own fingers to get a better sense of his temperature. The fever was worse, but his breathing remained steady enough, though a bit raspy now. Her fingers still touching his forehead, Sandy leaned down to Keefe's face and brought her lips to his ear.

"I'm sorry," she whispered, and returned to the cluttered living room.

She hung the worn brown fedora from one point of the set of antlers mounted on the wall. The old wicker creel hung from another point. Weathered, its leather strap cracked, Sandy wondered how long it had been since Keefe had actually used the creel. He didn't strike her as a man who would hang such an antique in his home simply as decoration, to evoke a woodsy, angling motif. Everything she saw in the mass of stuff that clogged the room looked to have had a definite use at some point in time. A wooden wading staff hung by a leather thong from another antler tip.

She left the broken binoculars on the coffee table, amid the books, ashtray and cigarettes, squirrel tails, feathers, and fly boxes. They looked as if they might have belonged there as well as any place else. Setting Keefe's hip boots upright in the corner behind the sofa, she looked around the room for a better place to hide the shock pack. Wherever Keefe normally stored the pack, it was certainly not here in the room packed with the other material of his life. The only unoccupied space in the room was the path through all the mess, big enough for little more than the passage of a single person. Sandy opened a small broom closet in Keefe's tiny kitchen. It contained what it was intended for: a broom, dustpan, bucket, and old mop. Sandy pushed these things into the back of the cabinet and jammed the shock pack in, barely able to latch the cabinet door. The pack was evidence and had to be hidden. Someone might come by. After all, she had. The broom closet would have to do until Keefe could tell her otherwise.

Her skin was tender under the rough wool as Sandy returned to the living room, inhaling its disarray. She felt again the sensation that there was a distinct order to the chaos surrounding her, felt again that this room was both an arena and a sanctuary. Around the vise and lamp on it, the surface of Keefe's tying bench was littered with feathers and fur, scissors, thread, brass beads, glue, and other implements, ones unknown to Sandy. A small hook was clamped in the vise, its shank partially wrapped with brown thread. Sandy looked at it briefly, tallying in her mind a half dozen or so fly patterns it might be built into. She ran her fingertip along a shimmering piece of peacock hurl, aquamarine and iridescent, and continued trailing her finger from the feather onto the bench top, leaving a meandering track through the dust, weaving around spools and scissors, rising over dried globules of spilled epoxy.

She had never learned to tie her own flies, had never tried. Though she had become an expert knot tier, as all fly fishers must be, she had not taken the next logical step. Perhaps it had seemed to her a bit like sewing, a domestic skill she had never acquired. She was fortunate if she could sew on a button, and she remembered that on more than one occasion Vernon had growled about having to stitch up tears in his own work clothes. Perhaps she lacked the patience for fly tying, but as she traced loops in the dust around Keefe's tying tools, she thought she might like to try now. Maybe when he was better he might show her a pattern or two. Maybe.

Sandy looked up from the work surface of the bench to the shelf above it, and noticed again the contrast between the dusty clutter of the tying area and the immaculate cleanliness of the upper shelf and the crystal lamp and silver canister on it. She reached tentatively for the canister, then withdrew her hand and walked around the coffee table, along the bookshelves, sweeping her fingertips over the spines as she went, and sat on the leather sofa. Leaning forward, she peered through the open fireplace to check Keefe's breathing in the bedroom.

So many books. More books than she'd ever been in the same room with if she excluded those occasional trips into the library of the community college. Had he actually read them all? Could one person have read all these books, and if he had, how in the hell could he possibly remember everything he had read? Did he need to remember everything he had read, or was that the point of having all the books around him? Not to remember but to remind him of all he had forgotten or might forget if the books weren't close at hand? Sandy thought of the tiny library in her little vinyl-sided house. Three small shelves, two of them containing old textbooks from nursing school, the third stacked with back issues of fishing magazines. And that "one book."

A couple years after she started fishing, once it became evident that fly fishing mattered more to her than pretty much everything else in the world, Margie had bought her a copy of *A River Runs Through It* for a birthday present. The clerk at the fly shop up in Roanoke had told Margie that if you could only read "one book" about fly fishing, that was the "one book" to read. Sandy still hadn't finished it, and it sat, half-read, beside the latest issue of *Fly Fisherman* and the mahogany fly box on her own coffee table at home. She'd stopped at the part where the author had paused to whine about what inferior game fish eastern brook trout were. The book was, to Sandy, a bothersome trout river with long stretches of dry shoals over which she had to hike and stumble until she came to the next deep, trout-rich pool. She had seen the movie with Vernon before she took up a fly rod, and thought she liked it better, though she remembered little of it. Mostly she remembered the fishing scenes, and chuckled to herself when she recalled how beautiful she thought they were when she first saw it, Brad Pitt standing mid-river flourishing his wildly flamboyant casts in the midst of the extravagant scenery. She nearly laughed out loud when she thought how ridiculous that casting was in reality and how utterly absurd it would be on an Appalachian mountain trout stream like the upper Ripshin now absorbing rainwater outside Keefe's cabin.

Sandy touched her torn earlobe delicately and poked among the books piled on Keefe's coffee table, expecting to find a well-thumbed copy of the "one book," but as far as she could tell from the covers, most of the paperbacks there were mysteries and crime novels. One very thick cloth-bound book lay open beside the ashtray and a half-pack of non-filter cigarettes. Sandy hadn't smoked a cigarette since the one Margie had given her in the hospital parking lot after her farewell party. She tapped one of Keefe's cigarettes from the pack, spilling flecks of tobacco on the table. Rolling the cigarette between her fingers she thought how oddly thick and squat it looked in compared to the long, slender filter cigarettes Margie smoked. She snapped open the lighter lying beside the ashtray and lit Keefe's cigarette, coughing slightly when the smoke hit her raw, rain-chilled lungs.

Sandy looked at the open book on the table through the wisps of smoke curling up from the cigarette lodged between her fingers. It appeared to be something like poetry, and she turned the book over to check the cover, which was black with an old photo of a bearded man in a broad-brimmed hat. *Whitman: Poetry and Prose*. She recalled her dinner with J.D. at the Damascus Diner, his remark that Keefe had "a real thing" for this Whitman. Her eyes fell on a line at the top of one of the open pages. "Undrape! You are not guilty to me, nor stale nor discarded . . ."

She tapped ash from the end of the burning cigarette, inhaled another lungful of smoke, and followed her own gaze up to the silver canister as she exhaled without coughing. What was it and why was it maintained so in the only meticulously clean spot in the entire room? She thought she might know, might have a hunch, but stopped herself before the thought could form further, stopped herself before she walked through the clutter and yanked the lid from the silver canister. She came to apologize for an intrusion and she was intruding again.

"For god's sake, what the hell are you doing?" she scolded herself. "What are you thinking anyway?"

She stubbed out the cigarette, mashing the burning ember down sharply, and spraying ash in a ring around the ashtray and onto the squirrel tail lying nearby on the table. A faint sound came from the bedroom, the sound of Keefe groaning softly and stirring under the blankets. Sandy rose from the sofa and strode to the bedroom to check on him. He was fitful, still unconscious but not for long. His skin burned her fingers with fever, and she realized that she must take him to the hospital over in Sherwood. He was unconscious, had a severe ankle sprain, probably a concussion, and a raging fever. Pneumonia was likely to set in. She was a nurse. She knew these things, and yet she had dawdled in his home because she was drawn into the close warmth of the cabin's exquisite mess, was reluctant to leave this place she had dreamed of since she had seen it that one other time, this arena that echoed with the battles and the life that lured and enticed her. Wrapped in the coarse wool of Keefe's sweater, surrounded by the detritus of his life, she had felt a peace and security she couldn't define. And she hadn't wanted to leave his cabin until that definition took shape.

Her torn earlobe was probably going to need a couple of stitches, too.

"Idiot. Idiot," she reprimanded herself, as she began to search the cabin for Keefe's keys.

Keefe's pants still lay crumpled on the floor, and she plunged her hands into the damp pockets, knowing as she did so that she wouldn't find the keys there. The door had been unlocked when she carried him in. While searching the mess on Keefe's coffee table, she spotted the keys, lying beside a wallet on the kitchen counter. She leapt from the porch into the rain, climbed into Keefe's truck, fired it up and swung it around so the passenger door was parallel to the front steps.

Keefe appeared to be on the brink of regaining full consciousness, mumbling low and actually limping and shuffling on his own as Sandy led him to the door, his arm draped over her shoulder, her arm wrapped tightly around his waist to support him. She lifted him down the steps, his feet barely touching the planks, and drew him through the sliver of rain slicing between the eaves over the porch and the truck cab. After strapping Keefe into the passenger seat, his chin bouncing on his chest, Sandy ran back into the cabin to grab a blanket and returned, stopping to lock the door. It took only a moment to find the house key. There were only four keys on his key chain, and she already knew which was the truck key. She wrapped the blanket around Keefe's torso and legs and tucked it over his shoulders and under his bobbing chin. He looked to Sandy like a gray-haired version of dozens of sick and injured children she'd seen swaddled in the front seats of cars by frantic mothers screeching to a stop at hospital emergency room entrances. Only as she stepped back into the driver's side of the truck cab did she notice that she still wore her waders.

Gravel and mud sprayed from under the tires as Sandy spun out of the clearing, the windshield wipers clicking, and headed down the rutted fire road. She kept one hand firmly pressed to Keefe's chest to hold him in place against the bouncing of the truck. She assumed that one of the other two keys on his chain would open the lock on the fire road gate. Halfway down the road to the gate, Keefe's chin rose feebly and his eyes fluttered partially open and he turned to Sandy.

"Sorry for what?" he said, and his chin slumped back onto his chest and his eyes closed.

At the gate Sandy shut off the truck, jerked the keys from the ignition, and trotted around the truck to the rusted padlock at the end of the gate. Her own truck was parked several yards away, off to the side of the fire road, on the other side of the gate. The first of the two other keys did not fit into the lock at all. She tried the other key. It slid easily into the lock, but wouldn't turn. She jiggled it and wiggled it and strained against it, leaving little dents in her thumb and index finger from the pressure, but it refused to budge. Sandy set her teeth and tried again. Nothing.

"There's a trick to it. You have to pull it back out just a hair before it'll catch."

The voice was faint, muffled, and Sandy barely heard it. Keefe sat upright in the cab, trussed up in the blanket, his eyes open, his head leaned back against the rear window.

"Just a hair," he said again.

Sandy did so, and the old padlock popped open with a metallic squeak.

Keefe's head jerked back and forth with the movement of the truck, but he remained upright and conscious. Sandy turned from the fire road onto the pavement of the county road and accelerated, placing her hand again on Keefe's chest to steady him. Keefe looked down at it curiously, and she removed it once she reached cruising speed.

"I fell, didn't I?" Keefe said, his voice weak and garbled.

"Yes," Sandy said.

"And the shock pack?"

"I got it. I put it in the broom closet in your kitchen."

Keefe's head still jerked and rolled against the rear window as a slight grin crawled across his lips.

"The broom closet," he said.

"I didn't know where else to hide it for now," Sandy said. "I can move it later."

"It's fine. At least it wasn't poor J.D. who found me."

"Mr. Keefe, you need to be quiet and calm. You've injured yourself."

"Yes, it feels that way. My ankle?"

"Yes, and you have fever and may have a concussion."

"Taking me to the hospital, aren't you?"

"Yes."

"Don't suppose I could convince you otherwise?"

"No. You could be seriously hurt."

"Doesn't appear I could stop you, so . . ."

Keefe's eyes drifted in their sockets, flat and dull, and they fell upon the wet, glistening hillside passing the truck window.

"Please just rest there and try not to talk or move," she said. "We'll be at the hospital in just a little while."

"That sweater you're wearing. Looks familiar."

"I'll explain later."

Keefe shivered. His eyelids fluttered again and closed.

Sandy left the blanket on the seat of the truck, found an abandoned wheelchair, and rolled Keefe, barefoot and slumped, into the emergency room. He was weak but fully conscious by then.

"Is there anyone I should call, Mr. Keefe?" she asked.

"No," he answered.

"No one?"

"No one."

Keefe lifted his eyes up to Sandy.

"I'm afraid I've forgotten your first name, Ms. Holston," he said. "I remember that casting of yours but I've forgotten the name."

"Sandy. Sandy Holston."

"Nice to meet you again, Sandy. Seems I was quite fortunate to meet you again."

"It was nothing, Mr. Keefe."

"Given the circumstances, I think you should call me James, don't you?"

"Okay. James."

At the nurses' station, Sandy explained the situation, omitting any reference to the shock pack and what led Keefe to the middle of the upper Ripshin the previous night. She had taken Keefe's wallet from his kitchen counter along with his keys and held it clutched in her hand along with his keys. Keefe looked up at her again and grinned as she handed it to him, so he could give the nurse his identification.

"Thank you," he said to Sandy. "You seem to have taken care of everything."

A nurse rolled Keefe away to an examining room, and Sandy called after him.

"I'll wait for you." Keefe's head nodded in affirmation as he disappeared into a room.

Sandy told the resident attending her that the torn earlobe probably wasn't as bad as the blood made it appear. Since the torn halves of the lobe had already adhered, he instructed a nurse to clean the lobe and apply a butterfly bandage. He wrote her a prescription for antibiotics and explained to her curtly how to care for her ear. That she worked as an LPN at the nursing home in Damascus was clearly marked on her chart, but the young doctor appeared to ignore that, and Sandy kept quiet while he talked, waiting for him to leave so the nurse could finish up. The knowing look that Sandy had seen before came over the nurses' face as she swabbed Sandy's ear.

"Doctors. The little snot," said the nurse, tearing the wrapping from the bandage. "Sure do feel a lot more secure now that he told you how to take care of a boo-boo, eh?"

"Yeah. Much more secure."

"So, you're over at the nursing home in Damascus?"

"Yes."

"Been there long?"

"A few months."

"A girlfriend of mine works over there. Liz Martin. Know her?"

"No, I don't think so," Sandy said.

"Now what in the world kind of pants are those you're wearing?"

"Waders."

She gave them her name as the contact for Keefe and left, while Keefe stayed behind reluctantly after the attending physician insisted he remain overnight for observation. She returned to his cabin, parked his truck and locked it. Inside, she made up his bed and hung his wet clothes up in the bathroom. As she felt the cabin's lure beginning to draw her in again, she checked once to see that the shock pack remained in the broom closet, scooped up her own wet clothes and gear, and left, locking the door behind her. Her fly rod still leaned against the wall on the porch. She bent down and lifted her rod by the worn cork grip. The ant pattern she had caught the big brook trout on earlier was still hooked into the fly keep. The rainfall had decreased to a light drizzle and beaded into a shimmering coat of moisture on Keefe's sweater as she walked the fire road back to her truck.

Sandy drove her own truck back to Sherwood to pick up Keefe after she got off work the next day. The ankle was badly sprained, requiring Keefe to stay off it for at least a week and to walk with a crutch or cane for another week after that. Luckily, there was no concussion, only a contusion.

"Just a hard-headed old codger, I guess," Keefe had said about the diagnosis.

There was, however, a mild case of bacterial pneumonia setting in, which could worsen without proper care, the physician said, and Keefe was signed out into Sandy's hands.

"It appears I'm at your mercy," Keefe said, as Sandy rolled him out to her truck and helped him into the passenger seat. The old sweater lay folded in the center of the seat beside a brown grocery bag.

"Don't worry. I'll be easy on you." She turned the key in the ignition, shifted into gear, and turned out of the hospital exit.

"So, you never answered my question," Keefe said.

"What?"

"Sorry for what? Why did you tell me you were sorry?" Keefe coughed, deep and phlegmy.

"Later. Rest now."

"You appear to be in charge at the moment, so I'll relent."

"Yes."

"But I'll expect an answer at some point," Keefe said and coughed again.

"Yes. At some point. Later. Now rest. We'll be back to your cabin in no time."

"Cabin? It's more of a bungalow, don't you think? Perhaps a cottage. Too many modern conveniences to call it a cabin."

On the ride out to his bungalow, Keefe was as pleasant and personable as might be expected of someone in his condition. Quiet, for the most part. But once Sandy got him home, helped him inside, and began her attempts to care for him, he grew sullen, petulant, and cranky. Injured and unconscious, he had been helpless and in dire need of her assistance. And he was grateful for it. However, now that he was safely back home, in control of his senses, and with relatively minor medical consequences, Sandy felt he no longer saw her as his rescuer. As she unpacked a bag of supplies she had brought for him and set a pot of chicken broth on the stove to heat, she sensed his gray eyes boring through her back, marking her as nothing more than an intruder again.

He flatly refused to take to his bed, insisting that he take up his convalescence on the cracked old sofa in his crowded living room.

"Fall asleep here most nights anyway," he grumbled.

His complaints were silent but undeniable as she tucked a blanket around him and propped up both his injured head and wrapped foot on pillows. On the coffee table beside him, she set two large glasses of water and one of orange juice, a small brown plastic bottle containing his antibiotics, a thermos of the hot chicken broth, and a cracked, white coffee mug with an Adams fly pattern painted on it that she had found in his kitchen. From the bag of supplies she removed a box of tissues, opened it, and set it down with the other provisions, along with a thermometer. The look on Keefe's face was that of a trapped and wounded animal.

"None of this, for the time being," Sandy said, as she scooped his cigarettes and ashtray from the table.

"I don't smoke but two or three a day," he said, and broke into a raw, rattling cough.

"You smoke none a day for now," Sandy said.

Sandy could find no trash receptacle other than a large, galvanized trash can in the kitchen, so she folded down the grocery bag and set it on the floor by Keefe for his refuse.

"Thank you, Sandy. Now, I think all this will be more than adequate," Keefe said.

"I need to take your temperature and listen to your lungs," Sandy said, ignoring Keefe's comments and producing a stethoscope from her back pocket.

"Really now, young lady, that will be . . ."

"Hush," Sandy said. She inserted the thermometer under Keefe's tongue, pulled down the blanket, lifted Keefe's sweatshirt, and slid the head of her stethoscope into the thin tufts of gray hair on his chest.

Keefe lay quiet, chastised, his lips clamped around the thermometer, his rib cage rising and falling as Sandy moved the head of her stethoscope to various spots on his chest. She clipped the earpieces of the scope around her neck, checked the reading on the thermometer, and reached for the bottle of antibiotics.

"Not too bad," she said. "Fever has come down a bit. Just a little fluid in your right lung. Here. Take this."

She tapped a blue pill from the bottle, handed it to Keefe, lifted his head from the pillow, and held a glass of water to his lips. Keefe coughed slightly as the pill washed down his throat. Sandy reached to the bruise on the side of his head and touched it gently.

"How's this feel?" she asked. Keefe winced and shrugged.

"There's no chance you're going to leave me alone, is there?" he said, as she laid his head back on the pillow.

"Someone's got to care for you. At least for a little while. And unless you've got someone else in mind . . ."

Sandy's stethoscope swung from her neck as she walked to the door and took the carved wading staff down from the hook and leaned it against the arm of the sofa behind Keefe's head.

"For the next week, you don't get up, except to go to the bathroom, and you use this when you do, if I'm not around. Okay?"

"It appears you're going to be around, whether I like it or not."

"Could be."

"I must owe you some money for all this," Keefe said, nodding to the items Sandy had arranged on the table.

"Later," she said.

"Is that your response to all questions?"

"Could be."

Sandy stepped into the kitchen to put away the remaining supplies she had brought. Several more cans of chicken broth and two more boxes of tissues went into a cupboard. Three more cartons of orange juice went into Keefe's refrigerator. Checking to see that Keefe was not watching her at the moment, Sandy slipped one of Keefe's cigarettes from the pack and laid it by her keys and stethoscope on the counter before stashing the pack at the back of a cupboard above the stove.

"Is it later yet?" Keefe asked as Sandy walked back into the little living room and sat down in the arm chair.

"Excuse me?" Sandy said.

"Is it later yet? You insist on saying 'later' in response to my questions. I think it's time for an answer. You've got me all strapped in here, unable to escape. I'm resting, as instructed. Maybe I could have one answer now. Why did you tell me you were sorry?"

"I didn't think you were conscious then."

"Well, I heard it, nonetheless, and you must have said it for a reason. Don't you think I should know what you were apologizing for? Doesn't seem your apology would make much sense otherwise."

Sandy leaned back in the armchair, dropped her hands into her lap, and sighed.

"Can't be that bad if I have no idea what sin you have committed against me," Keefe said. His chest arched and collapsed as he was convulsed by a coughing fit. Sandy leaned forward and held her hand lightly behind his shoulders until the fit subsided.

"Go ahead," Keefe said, clearing his throat.

"For the other day," Sandy said. "You know. The other day. A couple of weeks or so ago."

Keefe's brow wrinkled and pinched into a clump of furrows.

"I'm afraid I don't know what you're talking about."

Sandy inhaled deeply, realizing she had one final task yet to complete her penance.

"I intruded on you when you were, you know," she said, and her eyes went up to the silver canister atop the tying bench and Keefe's eyes followed. "I intruded on you then, and then . . . after . . . when . . . you know. I just sat there and watched when I should have left you in private. It was rude, and I'm sorry for it. I don't know why I just sat there. I'm sorry."

A grin spread over Keefe's face until it was broken by a short cough.

"Oh, that," Keefe said. "Don't give it a second thought. It's the price I pay for my propensity for unusual ritual. Not the first time I've been exposed in my eccentricities, so to speak."

"Well, I'm still sorry."

"Apology accepted."

Sandy's eyes returned to the canister above Keefe's tying bench, and he saw the chastened but unfulfilled curiosity in them.

"Is it . . . ?"

"My wife," Keefe said.

"I thought maybe," Sandy said quietly, almost reverent.

"Twice a year, on the anniversary of her birth and her death, I place just a pinch of her in the waters out there. In remembrance."

Sandy's eyebrows knit together tightly for a moment, involuntarily revealing a hint of uneasiness in response to the explanation of Keefe's rituals. Keefe closed his eyes and cleared his throat.

"It's my way," he said.

"And the other?" Sandy asked hesitantly. "The . . ."

"Just good for the soul to fish naked every once in a while," Keefe said.

Keefe tugged the blanket from himself and struggled to sit up.

"What are you doing?" Sandy said. "Do you need something?"

"You said 'except to go to the bathroom,'" Keefe said, reaching for his wading staff. "Well, I should like to go to the bathroom now."

Leaning on his staff, with Sandy's arm supporting him, Keefe hobbled through the mess of his room to the bathroom, stopping at the doorway.

"What?" Sandy said.

"I don't wish to seem totally ungrateful, Sandy, but I do think I'd like to tend to this business on my own, if I may."

Sandy relented and stood back, releasing him.

"Okay, but be careful."

"I have been doing this on my own for some time now." He limped into the bathroom and closed the door.

Sandy recognized the look on Keefe's face as she led him from the bathroom back to the sofa. Resistance and resignation. She'd seen it on the faces of patients before, usually those with illnesses and injuries that were temporarily debilitating, maybe painful and enduring, but not permanent or life-threatening. Usually men. Resistance to a condition that challenged their firm belief that they were resilient, strong, capable, independent, and self-sustained. Resignation to the realization that, for the time being, they were not. She gave little thought to the emotional struggle of this resistance and resignation. These people, these men, needed help, needed care, and it was simply her assigned job to give that care. Nothing more, nothing less. As she expertly settled Keefe back onto his sofa, she tried not to think too much about why she felt responsible for this injured man, why she so wanted to care for him, so needed to care for him. She tried not to feel overly pleased that she could tell by the look on the face of this very private man that, in the time he had been in the bathroom, he had accepted his temporary need for the help of this young, determined woman who had pulled his twisted body from the river and forced her attentions upon him. Sandy hoped it didn't show on her face how glad she was to have gained access to Keefe's cabin. She had gotten in.

Sandy lifted the shock pack out of the broom closet, carried it into the living room, and leaned it against the side of the arm chair. Keefe followed her movements, his eyes fixing on the pack when Sandy set it down.

"Now, I suppose you're the one with the question," he said. "Want to know why?"

"Not really. Think I've got a pretty good idea why," she said. "You sure have pissed off J.D. though. I saw him early yesterday morning, before I found you."

"Ah, you know him then. Poor J.D. Seems he takes my little slaughters personally. He's a good fellow. Was a good student, too. I used to be his teacher before I retired."

"Yes, he told me once."

"A good fellow, but never much one for the subtler variations in life. Likes things clear-cut and definite. Likes for there to be just one way to do things. Once he gets his teeth into a way of doing things, well then, that's the way it's going to be, come hell or high water."

Keefe doubled up into a wracking cough. Sandy came to the side of the sofa, held a tissue to his mouth, then handed him a glass of water when the coughing subsided.

"Thank you," he said.

"Do you think what you're doing will work?" Sandy asked.

"Don't know. Seems to have worked so far. That hatchery is the main source of stocked trout for this area. And I know, because J.D. has told me, poor fellow, that he has authority to extend the stocking up this way as long as he can meet the needs of the main recreational areas first."

"The reservoir and the tailwater," Sandy said.

"Correct. A few slip upstream from the reservoir from time to time as it is now. So I've been trying to keep him at bay, kill just enough so he doesn't have any extra stockers to spread around. And about the only spot they could get their stocking truck in up here is right out there, in that pool."

Keefe tilted his head toward his front door, indicating the wide pool down from the front of his bungalow. His lips grew tight for a moment, and his eyes closed.

"And that just can't be. I can't allow that," he said. "They don't belong here."

Sandy nodded, but Keefe continued.

"The upper Ripshin here and its tributaries are the only waters left on this side of the ridge that have never been stocked. The only place left where the native brook trout exist as they have for centuries. The only waters that haven't been colonized by alien trout. And those brook trout are our barometer. Their well-being is a gauge for the well-being of the entire watershed."

Sandy looked back to Keefe's face at the mention of that word and stifled a laugh, recalling Margie's misspoken mention of it as the "water bed."

"That's got to be worth something in this world," Keefe continued. "That's got to be saved somehow."

"Makes sense to me," Sandy said, and placed her hand on the pack frame beside the chair. "It does. Maybe I don't really understand why it's so important for something to belong in a place, but I can feel that it is."

Sandy turned her gaze back to the door and over to the window, looking out through the darkening day to the upper Ripshin and knew, for the first time, that she had run *to* this place as much as she had run *away* from Vernon.

"Can't say that I'm sure either," Keefe said. "The whole country is colonized, just like those stocked waters. And we know that. We have to know that. Maybe that's why something native, something that truly and undeniably belongs here is so valuable. Because we know that we can never truly belong here. We're aliens, all of us, unless you have a great-great grandmother who was a Cherokee princess or some such. Lot of fools around here claim nonsense like that. No, we're from someplace else originally. We don't belong here, so we value all the more fervently that which does. We're desperate for it. Make any sense?"

"Maybe."

"Of course, it all may be moot. It appears I'm out of commission for the time being. Maybe for good," Keefe said, surveying his reclined and incapacitated body.

"I wouldn't worry too much. You'll be up and killing little alien trout again in no time."

Keefe grinned.

"So, can I assume you're not going to turn me into the authorities?"

"Not anytime soon."

"My capture would certainly put you into good standing with J.D."

"I'm in plenty good standing with J.D. as it is. Too good."

Keefe reached to the thermos, unscrewed the stopper, and poured himself a mug of chicken broth. Sandy gripped the pack frame more firmly and tilted it away from the chair.

"Where does this go?" she asked.

Keefe explained how to find the little cave up the hillside behind his bungalow where she would find the over-sized duffle bag in which he stored his device for slaughter and preservation.

"There's a flashlight in that drawer by the sink. It's getting dark out," he said, as he leaned forward and sipped at the broth in the cracked mug.

Over the following few days, Sandy kept a close watch on Keefe, driving the fire road up to his bungalow twice a day, before and after work. He couldn't hide his discomfort with the idea but had relented when she asked for his key to the fire road gate.

"It's official, then," he had said. "I'm your prisoner."

"Looks like it."

She checked his vital signs, the yellowing bruise on the side of his head, and cleaned and rewrapped his ankle. She emptied his refuse, washed his dirty glasses and thermos, and replenished his supply of water, juice, and chicken broth. She refused to allow him a cup of coffee. Keefe had little appetite, but one day she cooked him a massive plate of mashed potatoes when he admitted to a craving for that one thing. Sandy tended to his needs with her usual precision, but carried out her actions with more attention to the little details than she ever would in her professional life. When she stopped by after work, she lingered longer than necessary.

Keefe's appetite improved but remained limited almost exclusively to chicken broth and mashed potatoes. His fever had dissipated by the third night of his convalescence and his lungs were beginning to clear, but he was still weak, sleeping a lot.

A half-eaten bowl of stiff, cold mashed potatoes sat on the coffee table. Sandy leaned forward in the arm chair and scooped a fingerful into her mouth as Keefe slept. He'd been out for over an hour, while Sandy reorganized his sick-bed accoutrements and sat in the arm chair, listening to his breathing and thumbing aimlessly through a few of the books on the table. Keefe had read little since his injury, though Sandy had asked if he wanted any books that were not within arm's reach, anything from the shelves of volumes surrounding him.

Reclined in the arm chair, her eyes periodically fell upon the gleaming silver canister, solitary on the shelf above the tying bench. Again she thought how oddly the canister stood out in the only clean, orderly spot in the room. As she stared at it, she realized that her ministrations to Keefe should include keeping the remains of his dead wife in their usual condition. She took a towel from the kitchen and wiped the shelf and lamp clean of dust, and ran the cloth around the simple, shining curves of the urn, careful not to nudge the lid loose. Setting it back in place, she stood with her hand resting on the shelf, her gaze locked on the canister. She found Keefe's altar to be a troubling mixture of touching devotion and excessive grief. The woman was dead, for god's sake. People died sometimes and there was nothing to be done about it. Put her to rest, she was thinking, and the corners of her mouth tightened into a grimace at the moment Keefe's voice rose behind her.

"She died in a car accident. A few months after we moved up here. Fifteen years ago. Hardly had a chance to get to know the place."

"I'm sorry," Sandy said. She wondered if her voice sounded cold and unfeeling, showing her discomfort with his maudlin practice.

Keefe's eyes were distant, staring across the room, past Sandy, to the isolate urn, and on through it.

"Her hands were beautiful. Strong but delicate. Perfectly shaped."

Sandy removed her hand from the shelf and returned to the arm chair. The leather-covered cushion hissed as she sat.

"When they brought me in to identify her body, her hand fell out from under the sheet. The attendant stumbled against the gurney. That's all I saw, but I knew it was her. All I needed to see. All I could bear to see. Her hand. Her beautiful hands. I think sometimes I knew so little about her, but I knew her hands."

Sandy wondered if she should say something, ask the dead woman's name or something.

"She never really wanted to come here. Said it was a place for me. Said there was no real place for her here. But she came anyway, because I wanted to. Gave up her house, her life, to come out here with me."

"She must have loved you very much," Sandy said, straining to make her voice kind and sympathetic, as she had tried to learn to do in hospitals and nursing homes.

"Yes. Almost as much as I loved her. And that love killed her. Coming to this place, only to die a few months later, it was the worst thing that ever happened. Only one thing could have been worse."

"What?"

"Not coming to this place." He coughed and reached for a glass of water.

Sandy rose and scanned the room, making certain Keefe was adequately equipped for the night, and prepared to leave.

"So, Nurse Holston. What's your history?" Keefe said, looking up from beneath his blanket on the sofa. "What brought you out here to the heart of our little watershed?"

"Moved here from Dalton's Ferry. I took a job at the nursing home in Damascus last spring."

"Well, then, perhaps this little convalescence of mine is a rehearsal for the inevitable."

"Could be."

"But why here?"

"The fishing's good here."

"It is that, we know. But something tells my old wits that there's a bit more of a story to it than just a job and some good trout waters. Young woman such as yourself. I appear to have plenty of time to listen."

"Later."

"Ah, yes. Later. Nurse Holston's standard response. I'll hold you to that. If you're going to insist on hanging about here, fussing over me, at least you might tell me your story. Amuse an old man. I have nothing else to do at the moment."

"Another time," Sandy said, tucking the blanket up to Keefe's chin and walking to the door. Her eyes ran over the room once more, checking, before she stepped out into the night.

Later that same night, Sandy sat on her stoop, with Stink at her feet. She sipped wine from her green mug and thought about her "story." She thought about Vernon, when he was part of a roofing crew, scooting around the roof of the hospital—the first time she saw him. She thought about Vernon mashing the red-haired man's head on the bar top—the last time she saw him as a free man. She thought of Vernon, alone and abandoned in the middle of the stream. She thought of the box of letters, faithfully written, unanswered, and jammed into a trash can full of fast-food wrappers. She thought of herself, alone on the bank of a river, a fly rod in her hand. She thought of herself here on this stoop in the insect-loud night with a tick-scarred dog at her feet.

What part of her life was her "story"? What portion of her thirty-two years merited the telling of it now? Should she tell it to Keefe? Why, because he had spilled his guts, was she obliged to do the same? Did she want to tell him, of all people, the story she had never told fully to anyone? She had told Margie, but she had told her only the outside of the story. The inside of her story remained solely in her custody. Did she want to tell her story now, need to tell it now? Need to speak it out, once, fully and finally? Was Keefe the audience she had been waiting for?

When Sandy arrived at Keefe's bungalow the next afternoon, the old man was not on the sofa. He sat hunched over his tying bench, peering through the magnifying loop at the fly-in-progress in the vise. His wading staff leaned against the edge of the bench within easy arm's reach. He barely grunted a greeting when Sandy knocked lightly and entered. He was sullen today, no longer loquacious and curious as he had been the night before. Sandy was merely an intruder again. She would have to give him something, make an offering, in exchange for her persistent presence here. Keefe scowled and continued his work as she felt his forehead for any remnants of fever, fingered the bruise on his temple, and slipped the tip of her stethoscope under his shirt to listen to his lungs. The wrap on his ankle was fraying and dirty. She would have to change it before she left tonight.

She pulled the stethoscope from her neck and watched over Keefe's shoulder as he wrapped brown thread meticulously around a bare hook shank. Keefe seemed to ignore her, intent on the fly beginning to form under the lighted magnifier, but Sandy could feel his back tense, a stiff barricade to her hovering presence behind him. It was time to talk. She laid her stethoscope on the coffee table and sank into the arm chair. She ran her eyes over the sick-bed items on the table. The water glasses were half-full and covered with smeared fingerprints. A half-eaten plate of mashed potatoes sat cold and crusted beside the cracked white mug. Sandy leaned forward and looked into it. Keefe had made himself a cup of coffee, but she said nothing. Leaning back into the chair, she looked at Keefe's rigid back and spoke.

"My ex-husband's been in prison for the last seven years, but he's getting out in a couple weeks. I guess that's a lot of why I'm here now."

Keefe looked up from his work, turned to Sandy and met her eyes. They held each other's gaze for a moment, then Keefe turned back to the fly in his vise. Keefe worked and listened as Sandy spoke, and her story took a shape for him beyond her words, shimmered and swelled to life before his eyes alongside the fly taking shape under the touch of his nimble fingers. Slowly, imperceptibly, Keefe's back relaxed and his fingers grew more supple as he wound thread into place around the hook shank in rhythm with the pace of Sandy's voice. She led him through the slaughter at the bar, the blood, the icy mist in the air that night. She omitted the lingerie. Keefe shifted to a different color thread, and Sandy turned to what she could recall of the trial, the temporary vacuum in the little house in Dalton's Ferry, the first prison visits, the mountains surrounding the prison, the tackle box, her earring. She slowed, lingered over the parts that still puzzled her—the absence of Vernon's scent in the house, the tingle in her fingers when she touched the fly rod, the name of Dismal Creek, the sensation of having returned home when she first stepped into a trout stream with a fly rod in her hand—and Keefe's hands fluttered over his vise as she scratched out a form for these parts. Keefe laid two pieces of iridescent feather to the hook shank, pinched them into position, and began to wind thread around them as Sandy rose into the escape plan, the Mondays waiting, the fishing, the big brook trout, Vernon exploding from the brush into the creek. Delicately placing the tips of his scissors to the thread securing the feathers in place, Keefe clipped the thread from the completed fly as Sandy's narrative closed around the image of the abandoned, frantic convict clambering out of the creek and her absolute certainty that the split-second decision she made that day was no choice at all but, in fact, her only viable option at the time.

Keefe lifted his eyes from the magnifying loop and sat upright at the tying bench. He laid down the tiny scissors and turned to Sandy when she stopped talking. His eyes followed her as she stood from the chair and walked into his kitchen and drew a glass of water from the tap.

"What happened then?" he asked.

Sandy slumped back in the arm chair, exhausted, drained by the telling so long in coming. She raised the glass to her lips and drank steadily, swallowing half of it, then rested the glass in her lap, cradled loosely in both hands. Depleted, she surrendered the rest of her story in brief. In a few sentences, she brought Keefe up to the present. The ease of divorcing a man in prison. The letters, both plaintive and threatening, arriving

with regularity. Vernon's impending release. The move to the little house
outside Damascus on Willard Road, the new job at the nursing home,
and inheriting a towering pile of tires and an angry, heartbroken dog.
Her acceptance of the fact that she had merely delayed the inevitable.

Sandy finished the glass of water and turned her face to the dark
window behind the sofa.

"I just couldn't think to do anything else. I thought I was waiting
for him to escape, but by the time he got there, he was just a dangerous
man, coming in between me and a good fish."

Keefe leaned back in his chair and looked at the urn above his bench.

"You found a new way to live, a new life," Keefe said, "and he would
have dragged you back into his. You didn't have any other choice."

"You don't think I'm the worst bitch who ever lived?" Sandy said.

Keefe pushed himself up from the tying bench, clutched his wading
staff, and hobbled to the side of the arm chair, resting his free hand on
its back behind Sandy's head.

"I think it's an honor to know you, Sandy Holston." Bracing himself
on the staff and the back of the chair, Keefe leaned down. Sandy watched
his face descend to hers, then closed her eyes as he kissed her lightly on
the forehead.

Keefe pushed his wobbling body upright again and shuffled around
the table and lowered himself onto the sofa.

"So, what happened?" he said.

Sandy opened her eyes and pinched her eyebrows together in response
to Keefe's question.

"What happened?" he said again. "Did you ever get back there and
get that big brook trout?"

At the sound of Keefe's voice, Sandy felt her body relax, clean and
replenished.

"Yes," she said. "The next week."

"What did you take it on?"

"Yellow stonefly."

"Ah, that'll do it, most times."

Keefe settled back on the sofa, nodding in confirmation. Their eyes met and held one another in mutual understanding.

"How's your ear?" Keefe asked.

"It's fine," Sandy said, tapping the scabbed lobe with her middle finger.

"I'd like a cigarette now, please," Keefe said. "Just one?"

"Later," Sandy said. "I need to change that ankle wrap now."

* * *

Stink rolls on the grass. Twisting and writhing happily, he grinds his backbone into the ground, pumping his crooked hind legs, then pulls himself to his feet, grunting, and shakes. Sheets of water fly in a circular arc from his lopsided body, along his quivering flanks, sousing the ground around him.

"Maybe you could take it easy on the skunks for a while," Sandy says, stepping back to avoid the spray. "I'd take it as a personal favor."

Sandy's skin still glows pink from her shower as she walks into the kitchen, pulling her ponytail tight. She lays her breakfast dishes in the sink, picks up her keys from the counter, and checks her watch. Plenty of time yet.

After locking the kitchen door, she turns toward her truck and stops. Stink sits beside the truck, his tail brushing over the dry dirt as it wags. Sandy tilts her head, a look of curiosity on her face, as she walks to the truck and opens the door. Stink tries to leap in, but his bowed hind legs fall short. Clawing the seat with his front paws, his back paws search out a footing on the running board, and he hauls himself up into the cab.

"Well, it seems we've passed another milestone," Sandy says, climbing in beside him.

She starts the truck and closes the door. Reaching to Stink, she scratches lightly behind his ears, then slips her fingers under his chin and scratches him again.

"Good boy," she says.

Stink takes one faltering step toward her, his tail thumping against the back of the seat, and drags his speckled tongue over her cheek. Sandy smiles, wipes the wet cheek on her sleeve, and pushes him back to the passenger side.

"Stay over there. You're wet and you still don't smell all that pretty."

* * *

Sandy calls his name when she enters the bungalow and checks both the bedroom and the bathroom anyway, but she knows as soon as she opens the door that Keefe is not there. He has been limping about fairly capably since the ankle wrap came off a week ago. He could be almost anywhere within walking distance. His truck, the fenders splattered with dried mud, sits in the same spot Sandy parked it in three weeks ago.

She could cover the ground more quickly if she drove the fire road upstream from the bungalow, but the road narrowed above Keefe's place and turning the truck around to come back would be difficult. Stink has waddled off to the riverbank for a drink, and without much thought about it, she calls to him as she starts up the fire road on foot.

"Stink. Come on, boy."

To Sandy's surprise, he toddles across the clearing, river water dripping from his jowls, and falls into his wobbly gait at her side.

"Good boy," Sandy says. "Let's see if we can find the old coot. See what kind of mischief he's gotten himself into this time."

She assumes that Keefe will be by the water. She hopes he's just sitting on a rock, watching the current, waiting for sight of the ring of a rising trout. She hopes he's not fishing, fearful of his weak ankle slipping again. She prays he's not in his wet suit, belly down in a pool, breathing through his snorkel, keeping an eye on things when his pneumonia is barely gone. Her pace quickens, and Stink keeps up with her. She scans the upper Ripshin from the fire road above as she walks, searching for Keefe along its banks. She jumps, startled, and Stink releases a single, sharp bark when Keefe calls to her from the opposite side of the road, from a small clearing up the hillside.

"Looking for someone?"

"Yes. A stubborn old man who should still be recuperating from a sprained ankle and bacterial pneumonia. Seen anyone like that around here?"

"Not lately. Come on up."

A gentle incline leads Sandy and Stink up into the clearing where Keefe sits on a stump. His wading staff leans against the edge of the stump. The clearing is ringed by oak, hemlock, and maple trees. A few wild rhododendron spread in tangles along the edge of the clearing closest to the fire road. Patches of yellow and red speckle the green maple leaves, the first hints of colors that will explode from these trees over the next couple of weeks. Within the clearing, set out to its farther edges, sit three old, dilapidated chimneys of stacked fieldstone, the free-standing remains of structures long since carted off, demolished, or decayed.

Stink waddles up to Keefe, sniffs his pant leg, and walks clockwise halfway around the stump. He lifts his leg against the stump behind Keefe, then completes his circuit and settles to the ground at Keefe's side. His tongue lolls from the side of his mouth.

"Sorry about that," Sandy says, referring to Stink's marking of Keefe's stump.

"Nothing to be sorry about. It's what they do. Suppose I should be honored in a way."

Keefe reaches down and vigorously pets and scratches the scruff of Stink's neck. He holds his hand out to the side, motioning Sandy to a stump adjacent to his own.

"Have a seat," he says.

Sandy sits down and reaches with her fingers to the faint spot of yellow and purple fading from Keefe's temple, tilting her head to the side as she examines the last vestiges of his bruise.

"I'm fine," he says. "Stop fretting over me."

"It's what I do," Sandy says, a grin creeping across her lips.

"When you're not fishing, right?"

"Right."

Keefe pets Stink again, and the dog looks up at him.

"I assume this is the tire-crazed dog in question?" Keefe says.

"That's him. His name's Stink," Sandy says. "He came with the name, but it fits, I guess."

"Yes, I can sense that," Keefe says, his nose twitching. "He's an odd-looking old cuss, but he doesn't seem so irascible as you made him out to be."

"We've worked out our differences."

Keefe smiles, his hand still resting on Stink's head, and looks up. His gaze sweeps the clearing.

"Cenotaphs to those who came before." Keefe points with his chin toward the three chimneys.

"Cenotaphs?" Sandy says.

"Cenotaphs. Monuments to the dead—without the bodies. A few of the old-timers around here still call it the Rasnake Homestead."

"How old are they? The chimneys?"

"I don't really know much about it. Probably settled around the 1840s or so. That would be about right. People came in here and settled in spots like this after they ran the last of the Indians out. Might even have been Indian cabins first, and then settlers took them over. That happened a lot."

Sandy drops her elbows to her knees and looks from chimney to chimney. The Rasnake Homestead, she wonders. Were they all members of the same family, or strangers who threw in together for one reason or another? Did the game tracking the woods and the native trout finning the waters below provide them adequate sustenance? Did they plant gardens? Cook up moonshine? Did they pass freely in and out of each other's cabins, set so close together in this clearing? Or did they keep to themselves, recognizing each other's desire for privacy and isolation? Could they do such a thing in such a place? Did they have shelves of books within their little cabins?

"Do you think they ever got lonely?" Sandy says.

"I should think so. From time to time, at least."

Keefe reaches down for his wading staff, runs his hand over Stink's back, and lifts the staff. He sets the point to the ground and pushes himself up.

"See. Fit as a fiddle. Fully independent, once again."

Sandy smiles as she stands along with Keefe, and Stink rises after her, his tail wagging.

"Thanks to you," Keefe says. "Thank you, Sandy."

"It's nothing. It's what I do."

"That's a lie, but I'll accept it if you will. So, are you going to do a little fishing, or did you just come up here to check on your invalid."

"Wanted to make sure you weren't lying in some pool in your frog-man suit, scaring away the trout and aggravating your pneumonia."

"I'm fully recovered, I assure you."

Sandy and Keefe walk down to the fire road from the clearing. Stink sniffs among the rhododendron, lifts his leg, and follows. Sandy can see that Keefe is much improved, but she watches his stride closely, noting the degree of his lingering limp as they walk the road back to his bungalow.

"In fact, I feel so much better, I'm thinking of doing a little fishing myself," Keefe says. "Imagine, not having fished at all in three weeks. Unthinkable. Yes, I'm going to fish today."

"Later," Sandy says.

Keefe digs the point of his staff into the gravel and stops, turning sharply to Sandy.

"I've had quite enough of this 'later' business, Nurse Holston. I'm fine, and I'm going fishing today, whether you like it or not."

"No, I meant later," Sandy says, smiling up at Keefe's stern face. "Wait till later this afternoon. Usually a pretty good Caddis hatch around two or three o'clock."

* * *

Margie is sitting on the front deck when Sandy and Stink pull up the gravel driveway in the truck and stop behind Margie's minivan. Margie leans back in one of two plastic lawn chairs on Sandy's porch, her feet propped up on the rail. The backs of her dimpled thighs are visible beneath the hem of her shorts. She wears sunglasses and her head tilts back, resting on the back of the chair. Her arms hang loose at her sides, a cigarette burning in her right hand. A blue nylon overnight bag sits behind the chair. Stink toddles off to the water bowl by his tire when Sandy opens the truck door, and Margie raises her arms up and out and holds them there. Her gesture could be one of greeting to Sandy or reaching out to embrace the early autumn sun blazing down on her.

"Welcome to paradise," Margie says as Sandy walks across the yard to her porch.

"Paradise? Hardly."

"Honey, I ain't been anywhere without my two screaming kids in more years than I can remember, so anyplace I am and they ain't is paradise to me, girl. I'm a terrible mother."

"You're a good mother," Sandy says, coming up the steps.

Margie hops up from the chair, her arms still spread wide, and draws Sandy into a deep, consuming embrace.

"Oh, I've missed you honey," she says.

Sandy sinks into Margie's embrace, surrendering to it, swallowed in its lushness. When Margie begins to pull back, Sandy clings tighter to her, reluctant to leave the circle of her friend's arms.

"Damned if you haven't gotten downright affectionate since I've seen you, girl," Margie says.

"I've missed you, too," Sandy says, and pulls back, releasing Margie.

The two women look at each other, smiling. Margie tilts her head to the side and examines Sandy's ear, releasing her friend's hand and running her finger over the fading pink ridge of scar tissue.

"What happened?"

"Earring got snagged and tore out. It's healed up fine though."

"We'll have to pierce it again while I'm here."

Stink trots around the corner of the house and up the steps, thrusting his snout directly into Margie's crotch, sniffing.

"Hey, there, don't you think you should at least buy me dinner first," Margie says, squatting, stroking the top of Stink's head with her hand. "So this is the ferocious beast you inherited?"

"Stink."

Margie's nose wrinkles as she continues to pet the dog.

"Good name for him. I thought I detected a hint of skunk in the air when I pulled in."

"We had a little incident earlier this morning."

"Well, this is truly one ugly dog, but he doesn't seem so mean as you described him. He's sweet."

"Yes. We've turned over a new leaf. Seems I've been accepted now."

"Good boy," Margie says, standing up and leaning down into Stink's face. "Keep it up. This woman needs all the sweetness she can get. She's really not as tough as she tries to be once you get to know her, right?"

Stink's tail thumps on the deck planks as he thrusts his head toward Margie and licks his tongue over her lips and nose.

"That was lovely," Margie says, wiping her face with her palm. "Thank you so much."

"Sorry," Sandy says.

"Sorry what?" Margie says. "That little lick is nothing. A piece of cake compared to the slime two human boys can produce, trust me."

Margie takes a last pull from her cigarette and turns to Sandy.

"You got an ashtray in this place?"

Sandy sets Margie's overnight bag on the floor by the sofa and turns on the flame under the tea kettle. While the kettle heats, Sandy gives Margie the nickel tour of the little, sparsely-furnished house where she has lived since spring, leaving Margie to freshen up in the bathroom. Pouring their tea in the kitchen, Sandy fills in a few blanks about the people and places around her new home, raising her voice so Margie can hear her in the bathroom. When Margie emerges, Sandy hands her a mug of tea and an orange plastic ashtray she found in one of her cupboards when she moved into the house. Margie runs her hand gently down Sandy's spine as the two women walk back out to the deck. Margie's cigarettes and lighter lie on the porch rail. She lights one and drops into the plastic chair beside Sandy's.

"I don't get the thing with the pile of tires," Margie says.

"Me either," Sandy says. "But they're gone now, except for Stink's."

"Must have been a lot of work, getting rid of those."

"Not too bad."

"That was sweet of you to leave Stink his tire. He does seem attached to it."

Sandy smiles and sips her tea. Margie exhales a long plume of smoke, sets her mug on the porch rail, and reaches into one of the loose pockets of her shorts, producing two crumpled envelopes.

"Here they are," she says, passing the envelopes to Sandy. "Like I said, he claims he's a Jesus freak now. Or some such nonsense."

Sandy shifts her mug to her other hand and takes the envelopes from Margie. She sets her tea on the deck beside her chair and examines her wayward mail. One worn envelope is inscribed with her former address, stamped, postmarked, and bearing a returned stamp. The other envelope, never mailed, bears only two words, a name, on the front. *Sandy Adams.* Margie leans over and looks at the front of the unmailed envelope.

"I guess you never told him you changed your name back," she says.

"Never told him anything," Sandy says. "Wouldn't have mattered anyway."

Sandy tears open the postmarked letter first and begins to read. Her face is stony, cold, registering nothing but the flitting movement of her eyes across the page. *I have much to atone for. So do you.* The orange plastic ashtray rattles on the porch rail as Margie stubs out her cigarette. *. . . my one true wife, as intended. Be ready.*

"More of that blood-of-christ crap?" Margie asks, and lights another cigarette.

"Let me have one of those," Sandy says, nodding. Margie passes her the cigarette she has just lit and taps another from the pack for herself.

Tim Poland

Sandy crosses her legs and opens the envelope with her old name written on it, holding the long, white cigarette out between her fingers. A thin strand of smoke shimmies up into the late morning air.

Dear Sandy,

If you're reading this, then I guess Margie was good enough to forward these letters on to you. If you didn't already, read the other letter first. It will tell you of the new man Vernon Adams has become.

Have you read it? Then you know now that you have nothing to fear from me, that I bring only love and devotion to you, to us. You didn't need to hide from me. I would have probably found you sooner or later. Actually, by the time you get this, if you do get this, I'll probably have already found you. Unless you're living in a cave in a desert somewhere.

It's impossible to hide from the sight of God. And it's pretty hard to hide anywhere in the world these days. The world doesn't work like that anymore. Prison taught me that. We have computers here, and they taught us how to use them. Rehabilitating us, you know. And I have been rehabilitated, in all ways, Praise Jesus. The last couple of years I've been out of the fields, for the most part, and working in the prison computer lab, taking orders for catalog companies. I've learned to use these computers pretty good. And I've learned that with a computer and a social security number, I can find most anyone. And what I can't figure out on my own, another con in here for identity theft will show me. He's one of our Christian brethren in here, the one who led me to Christ. Do you think I'd forget your social security number? Do you think I'd forget anything about you?

I am a man who keeps his promises, a man who honors his commitments. Now more than ever. When I said till death do us part, I meant it. Such is God's command. You're my wife. Always will be, no matter what. And the first thing I'll do when I get out of here is to find my wife. I promise you that. You have nothing to fear from me. I want only your forgiveness and to love you and bring you to the blessed salvation I have found and that we can share.

Your loving husband, in Christ

Vernon

"It appears I'm off the hook," Sandy says, handing the letters to Margie. "Saved."

As Margie reads, Sandy rises from her chair and finishes her cigarette standing at the porch rail, her eyes following the line of the ridge rising from the far side of the river. Here and there along the ridge, maple leaves are flaring into their fall colors.

"Oh, Jesus. He sounds crazier than ever," Margie says, as Sandy mashes her cigarette in the ashtray. "*God's command?* What is that shit? You're not falling for this, are you?"

"Why not?" Sandy says. "Whatever Vernon is, he's always been honest. Someone who liked to follow a simple, orderly plan. Makes sense for him, I guess."

"Come on, honey. Look at this shit . . . *ordained that we be together . . . blood of his salvation . . .* and my personal favorite, that old standard . . . *till death do us part.* Damn, it's creepy, creepier than the I'm-going-to-kill-you-bitch letters."

"Margie, he was hurting. Now he's found something to make the hurt go away."

"Uh, girl," Margie says, and pushes herself out of her chair and clasps Sandy's shoulders. "Girl, do I have to remind you that he's a killer. He killed that guy."

"I was there, remember."

"Exactly. So you should know better than anyone what he's capable of."

"He's changed now. You read the letter."

"I don't care how much fucking redemption he claims he's wallowing in. I'm not buying it. As far as I'm concerned, he's still a killer and still someone to be worried about."

Sandy sighs and walks a few steps to the end of the porch. She leans forward over the rail and looks around the end of her house. Stink is curled up in his tire, sleeping.

"Nothing to worry about anymore," Sandy says.

"One thing's for sure," Margie says. "It sure makes all this, this moving here to get away from him kind of ironic, don't you think?"

"I don't know. He'd never live anywhere but Dalton's Ferry. You know that."

"Fucking momma's boy is what he is," Margie says.

"Yeah, and either way, I guess I'd still want to put a little distance between us. I don't know."

"Well, I don't care how much God he's got in his gut now, as far as I'm concerned, he's still a dangerous man. And so you're just going to sit here and wait for him to show up?"

"Something like that. I can handle Vernon. Don't worry about me."

"I'll decide who and what I worry about," Margie says. She walks to the end of the deck and slides her arm across Sandy's shoulder, drawing their heads together and holding them there. "And I worry about you, honey."

"When I moved down here," Sandy says, "I thought I was moving away from Vernon, away from Dalton's Ferry. But the longer I've been here, well . . ." Sandy draws her head away from Margie's and looks off along the ridge, her eyes following it upstream.

"What?"

"I don't know. The longer I've been here, I don't think it was about Vernon at all. I didn't move away from him. I moved to this place. I feel like I belong here somehow. I feel at home for the first time in my life. This is my home."

"Something tells me you're not just talking about this house, right?"

"Right," Sandy says, and her eyes sweep the ridge again, following a line in the direction of the headwaters above the dam and reservoir.

"Your water bed," Margie says, holding up her hand to stop Sandy before she can correct her again. "I know, I know. *Watershed*. Just kidding, honey."

"Yes. The watershed. It's my home."

"I do believe you're just a little bit crazy, girl," Margie says, and kisses Sandy on the cheek. "And I love you for it."

Margie steps away and takes another cigarette from her pack on the porch rail.

"Well," she says, "are we going to sit here all day yacking and worrying, or are you going to show me this watershed of yours?"

Sandy walks to Margie's chair and picks up Vernon's letters, folding them back into the envelopes. The letters still in her hand, she waves it in an arc toward the ridge.

"You're in it. It's all around you," Sandy says.

"Well, how about we go see some of your watershed that's actually got some water in it. Let's go fishing."

"You want to go fishing?" Sandy's eyes open wider and her eyebrows arch.

"Why not? If this fly fishing business is what gets you all hot and bothered, well, I thought I'd like to see what all the fuss is about. I could do with being a little hot and bothered myself. You got an extra pair of those rubber pants around here that I could fit this ass into?"

"I think I can come up with something," Sandy says, a smile running freely across her face. "And maybe a rod for you, too."

The patched old neoprene waders Sandy dug out of a gear bag in the bottom of her closet cling ferociously to Margie's ample rear as they walk the path across the road from Sandy's driveway down to the riverbank.

"I ought to be able to sweat a few pounds off this thing, just walking," Margie says to the back of Sandy's head as they near the river. "Damn, girl. These things are hot."

"You'll cool off once you get in the water," Sandy says.

"Ah, words of assurance from the lady with the tight little ass. I feel cooler already."

Sandy thought it best to guide Margie, step by step, through the sum of her knowledge and skill—rod weight and flexibility, line and leader size, the basic knots and how to tie them, an inventory of her fly boxes from dry fly patterns to wet flies to nymphs and streamers and how each was fished, strategies for reading the water, a brief natural history of trout and other members of the *salmonidae* family. After running through the various weights and lengths and composite materials of modern fly rods, Sandy unwinds a length of fine tippet and begins to explain its purpose and size before she catches a glimpse of Margie's face, her forehead tilted forward, her eyes looking up at Sandy past arched brows, like an exasperated librarian peering over the tops of the sunglasses slipped down on her nose.

"Are fish and water ever actually involved in any of this, sweetie?" Margie says.

Sandy ends her streamside seminar, grins, and promptly ties a Royal Wulff pattern onto each of their lines.

"It's pretty," Margie says, squinting at the tiny fly. "The red around the middle and the white fluffies sticking up there."

"They're called hackles," Sandy says, and leads Margie into the cool, glassy waters of the lower Ripshin.

At first, Sandy just fishes. She keeps things simple, precise, limiting her casts to the crisp, sharp strokes of the traditional ten o'clock-two o'clock motion, avoiding her tendency to slip into a trickier sidearm delivery. Margie stands off to the side behind her, watching, thigh-deep in the Ripshin and happy to have the heat of heavy neoprene waders diminished by cool river water. Sandy drifts her fly easily along the seams of currents, occasionally tossing back to Margie bits of information about the basic logic of the fly cast, about where a trout is likely to be, how and why that trout is likely to be holding in water like that, and how her cast is intended to play on the trout's habits. Margie seems more than willing to listen, now that a demonstration accompanies Sandy's instruction and that she is no longer boiling in the neoprene.

Sandy takes a couple of modest rainbows, stocked trout for which she has little regard, but which seem to please Margie enormously.

"Oh. Oh, you caught one," she says. "You actually caught a fish."

"Well, yeah," Sandy says, speaking to Margie over her shoulder as she draws the rainbow to hand. "That's kind of the point of all this."

"Yeah, I know, but I just didn't, well, you know."

"Yeah, I know," Sandy says, cupping the trout, pinching out the fly, and sliding the fish back into the water.

Sandy moves Margie into position and guides her through her first fly fishing lesson. She instructs with a light touch, tightening the angle of her elbow here, adjusting her line hand there. Margie's first casts roll out as expected, tumbling in tangled piles before her or thrashing the water behind her when she brings her rod forward too late. Once the fly catches on the shoulder of her shirt as she brings the rod forward.

"Hang on. I'll get it," Sandy says, wading to her, resting her hand on Margie's shoulder as she works the hook free of the fabric.

"At least I caught something," Margie says.

After a half-hour of hammered water and tangled tippet, Margie begins to get the hang of it, to fall into a rhythm. Her casts are crude, charting a simple arc of line over her head, but she begins to put the fly on the water in the general vicinity of trout. Sandy watches her friend and realizes why it is working for Margie so quickly. Margie doesn't care. She is unconcerned with acquiring prowess, expertise, or precision. She is unconcerned with mastering this method of angling. She couldn't give two shits whether or not she catches a good fish. Margie's having fun. She's knee-deep in cold, flowing water, having fun with her friend in the clear light of an early autumn day. Sandy smiles and wraps her arms around herself just before the rainbow hits Margie's fly.

"Oh. Oh. Shit, I got one," Margie says. "What the hell do I do now?"

"Hold your rod up," Sandy says, wading to Margie's side. "That's it. Now, retrieve your line and pull him in."

Sandy sets her hand on Margie's line hand, leads her through one retrieve, then steps back, leaving Margie to bring the fish in on her own.

The rainbow is small but scrappy and squirms from Margie's grip twice before she can secure it and remove the fly. Sandy holds the rod for her while she wiggles the hook from the trout's lip. Its back shows only a hint of the green that will darken if the fish survives into next year. The sides are the dull silver of a hatchery raised rainbow, infused with a faint pink glow.

"Nice little fish," Sandy says.

Margie's eyes are fastened to the little trout cradled in her hand. She runs the index finger of her other hand gingerly along the green spine and looks up at Sandy.

"It's beautiful," she says, and the fish squirts from her hand and disappears.

Margie rises, shaking the water from her hands. A smile slices madly across her face.

"Oh, honey. That was so beautiful," she says, reaching out to Sandy's hand and squeezing it. "Think that calls for a cigarette."

Margie fishes the long pack out of her shirt pocket and shakes a cigarette out far enough to wrap her lips around the filter tip and draw it out.

"Want one?" she asks Sandy, holding the pack out.

"Maybe later," Sandy says.

Margie's lighter makes a thin, brittle sound as she snaps it and dips the tip of her cigarette into the flame. She tilts her head back and exhales, her eyes bright with the shine of unexpected joy. The narrow line of smoke is still dissipating into the air when they hear it. A loud splash. They both turn their eyes downstream in time to see the widening rings of a trout rise spread over the surface of the water and settle. Sandy knows immediately. The resonance of the splash, the breadth of the rippling rings. The sign of a big brown trout, roiling at the surface.

"What was that?" Margie says.

Sandy has already dropped into a half-crouch, moving toward the bank, her eyes riveted on the fading spot of the downstream rise.

"This way," she whispers to Margie. "Come on."

Margie stoops her shoulders and ducks her head in imitation of Sandy's stalking crouch as she follows Sandy up the bank and through the streamside brush. Sandy stops and squats in a patch of long, matted grass, her eyes fixed on the spot of the rise. Margie trudges up behind her and drops to her knees.

"Where is it?"

Sandy raises her hand and points across the river, over a deep depression worn in the riverbed to the far side of a massive rock protruding above the surface of the water.

"There," she says, as the trout rises again, rolling in the film of the surface, sending out a huge rippling ring.

Sandy begins to creep to the river's edge. Margie begins to follow, but Sandy holds her back with a raised hand.

"Wait here. It's too deep to wade all the way over there."

"How you going to get to it?"

"Cast across the rock. It's probably holding under the edge of it."

Margie waits and watches in the long grasses as Sandy checks her watch and moves out into the shallows. Her line feeds out into a series of long, false casts, parallel to the bank until she has enough line in play to reach across the rock to the rising trout. She swings her rod tip toward the middle of the river and shoots a long, tight loop, her arm reaching out with the rod, and drops the fly over the rock in the trout's feeding lane. The fly drifts slowly over the deep pool with no response, and Sandy flips her loose line off the rock as the fly floats out of the trout's range. She repeats her cast once, again with no result. On her third cast, a mirror-image of the previous two, the fish strikes.

Knee-deep at the edge of the deep pool, Sandy sets the hook, plants her feet, and arches her back against the weight of the fish. The big brown first thrashes at the surface, allowing Sandy to catch him off guard and lead him out into the water on her side of the rock before he dives. Her rod quivers, bowed nearly in half from the weight of the fish. Her elbow is locked at her side, and she leans onto it, playing the big trout back and forth through the pool, beginning her slow retrieve as the fish begins to slow down.

"Come on," Sandy calls over her shoulder to Margie.

Margie's eyes are wide and awe-struck as she pushes herself up from the long grass and stumbles into the shallows.

"Net him," Sandy says.

"What?" Margie says, sloshing up behind Sandy.

"Net him. I could use some help with this one."

Sandy jerks her head backward, indicating the net clipped to the back of her vest. Margie releases the net and grips it so tightly in her fist that her knuckles go white. She steps up to Sandy's side, but seems confused as to what to do next.

"Go on a little ways upstream there and I'll guide him over to you," Sandy says, as she dips down, leaning into the force of a fresh run by the trout.

Ten yards upstream from Sandy, clutches the net in front of her and sets herself in a crouch, posed like a rubber-clad base runner, set to steal second.

"Oh my god, it's huge," she says, as Sandy leads the brown trout toward her in the shallows. "Almost. Almost. There."

Gliding into the shallows near her legs, the trout makes a sudden lurch and thrashes as Margie takes a wild swipe at him, misses, and loses her footing, dropping with a grand splash onto her rear.

"Son of a bitch," she says, thrusting herself back up and shaking water from her hands and arms. "Get him back. Get him back."

"Relax. I've got him," Sandy says. "Just dip the net under him."

Margie's chest is heaving noticeably, and Sandy can't restrain a grin that sneaks onto her face as she leads the fish back into Margie's reach. The net is deep and full, the trout's tail rising and twitching a full six inches above the loop as Margie lifts it from the water.

"Holy shit," she says. Sandy wades up to her side, reeling in line as she comes.

"Holy shit," Margie says again. "My god, it's enormous."

"Yeah. A nice fish," Sandy says. She lodges her rod under her arm and hefts the big trout from the net, cupping its fat belly, which glows iridescent yellow in its fall spawning colors. She removes the fly from the trout's lips and holds it gently but firmly down into the surface of the current.

"Oh, let me?" Margie says.

Sandy proffers the big fish, inching it closer to Margie, who tosses the net to the bank and reaches her hands into the water, under the trout's belly.

"One hand there, and hold its tail with your other hand," Sandy says.

"My god, it's beautiful," Margie says.

"Yeah. Nice fish," Sandy ways.

"So beautiful. Should I let it go now?"

"Let it get a little more oxygen. It's had a pretty tough fight. It'll pretty much let you know when it's ready to go."

"Beautiful," Margie says, just as the huge trout snaps its tail, splashing both women in the face, and flashes off into the depths of the pool.

Margie stands up in the shallows, wipes drops of Ripshin river water from her face and turns to Sandy, beaming.

"I get it now."

"Hunh?" Sandy says.

"I get it now. I understand why you're so nuts about this. I haven't touched anything so beautiful since Luke was born. So beautiful, honey."

Sandy smiles and slides her arm over Margie's damp shoulders.

"Yes, it is. Come on, we better get out of here."

"Why?" Margie asks, just as the sound of the siren blasting at the dam a half mile up stream makes its way down the river to their ears.

"Because of that," Sandy says, nodding upstream. "They're starting to release now. The dam upstream."

Margie's eyebrows pinch together.

"The siren means they're starting to generate power, and to do that, they release more water through the turbines in the dam."

"So?"

"So, that means that in about ten minutes, a three-foot wall of water is going to make it down here, and this river is going to be a deep, churning flood. And unless you want to drown or spend the next six hours sitting back there on the bank, we need to get going."

"Well, if you put it that way, let's get the hell out of here."

They wade upstream and cross over to the path leading back to Sandy's house. Sandy breaks down their rods while Margie tries to smoke a damp cigarette, waiting to see the rise in the water. Margie drapes her arm around Sandy's shoulder, her fingers playing in Sandy's ponytail.

"You know, while I'm here, I ought to cut your hair. You'd look so cute with it short."

"You think?" Sandy says. She hooks the flies to her drying patch and pats carelessly at the strands of hair stringing out from under her cap.

"Oh yeah, we'll do it tonight. Get a pizza, drink some wine, and give you a makeover. We'll do that ear again, too. A real girl's night. What do you say?"

"I'll think about it," Sandy says. "Here it comes."

They turn back to the stream, Margie's arm still around Sandy's shoulder, as the surge of released water begins to reach them. The two women stand side by side, quiet for a moment, watching the placid surface of the slow current boil up into a raging torrent.

"My god," Margie says. "Beautiful. I'll never make fun of your *watershed* again. Will you take me fishing again? Teach me more of this fly fishing stuff?"

"I'd love to," Sandy says, her hand reaching up to Margie's hand on her shoulder.

"One thing, though," Margie says. "Maybe I could get some of these wading pants here that aren't so goddamn tight and hot? Stop cramming myself into your hand-me-downs and get something made for my ass instead of that little bitty thing of yours, okay?"

Sandy smiles down from the bank into the rushing deluge and tightens her grip on Margie's hand.

* * *

"Mind if we stop by the nursing home for a minute?" Sandy's right hand is hooked loosely on the steering wheel. Her left arm rests on the open truck window. "I need to pick up my paycheck."

"Sure. I can see where you work," Margie says. "Make sure you haven't completely wrecked your career by moving down here."

A brown paper grocery bag sits on the seat between them. The red and green edges of two flat boxes, each containing a frozen pizza, are visible at the opening of the bag. Plastic produce bags of lettuce, tomatoes, cucumbers, and red peppers rest against the pizza boxes. The three bottles of red wine at the bottom of the grocery bag clink together from the vibrations of the truck rolling over the road through Damascus. On her lap, Margie holds a large cardboard box containing her new waders. At the fly shop in Sherwood, she had, at first, railed at the cost of the gear Sandy suggested as most appropriate for her needs.

"Are you kidding? For that much money, they ought to be covered with lace and pearls and come with a guarantee to get me laid." She relented when Sandy told her she could get something much cheaper in rubber or vinyl at the local K-Mart's going-out-of-business sale and be even more uncomfortable than she was earlier in Sandy's old neoprenes.

"Looks like J.D.'s here," Sandy says, as they pull into the parking lot of the nursing home. His green government SUV is parked carelessly at an angle across the two handicapped parking spaces to the left of the front entrance.

"J.D.? Oh, the fish warden with the crush on you, right?" Margie says. "How's that going? He still sweet on you?" Margie needles Sandy in the ribs with her finger.

"Stop it," Sandy says, flinching. "No, I think he's finally given up on me."

"Poor bastard. If he only knew you like I know you."

Sandy walks down the hallway from the main office, folding her paycheck into her pocket. Margie is leaning over the counter of the nurses' station, looking at the computer and racks of files. The station is unattended.

"You usually work this wing?" Margie asks.

"Mostly," Sandy says. She looks around the lounge area and nods to a couple of the residents sitting there. "Let's go."

"What's the rush? Don't I at least get to meet this J.D. guy? I want to see what kind of men you're throwing away these days."

The face Sandy turns to Margie struggles between a grin and a scowl.

"Sorry," Margie says.

"Forget it."

Margie wraps her hand around Sandy's arm and squeezes gently as three members of the nursing staff emerge from a room down the hall and walk toward them, speaking softly among themselves. Sandy recognizes them, two nurses' aides and one of the other LPNs. The two aides veer off and walk down another hallway. The LPN spots Sandy and walks up to her.

"Hey," she says. "I know you're off today, but could you help me a minute? I need someone to pronounce with me, and no one else is around. Ada Callander died."

Sandy recalls the careless placement of J.D.'s SUV in the handicapped slots. He'd been called. There wasn't much time left.

"Sure," Sandy says, and she and Margie follow the other LPN back down the hall.

Ada Callander lies in a lump. Thin wisps of white hair fall over a face still bent from the thrust of the stroke. Her lower lip droops under the weight of a swollen, distended tongue. J.D. sits slumped on the edge of a chair beside her bed, one leg extended, the knee on the floor. He holds one of his mother's limp hands and pats gingerly at her swollen face, trying to push up the drooping lip.

"Mama? Mama?" he says. "Mama, wake up. I'm here. It's J.D."

Sandy steps to J.D.'s side and the other LPN walks around to the other side of the bed, clamping her stethoscope into her ears and leaning over Ada Callander.

"I'm sorry J.D." Sandy says. Her voice is flat, clinical. J.D. looks up at her, his eyes red and dry, and tries to speak.

"But she's . . . she was . . . "

"She's dead, J.D.," Sandy says. Her hands hang at her side.

Margie has positioned herself behind J.D. and fires an angry scowl in response to Sandy's cold diagnosis.

"I'm very sorry," Sandy says, flinching under Margie's scowl.

Margie's hands rest on J.D.'s shoulder, smoothing, rubbing gently, running up and down the top half of his spine, petting him. Sandy sees what she had seen before and always been mystified by—Margie's seemingly infinite capacity to console. Despite years of professional detachment and decaying bodies, Margie actually cared. She felt the loss her patients and their families felt. No matter how many times she had been in these situations, she could reach deep into a storehouse of compassion and produce exactly the feeling that was needed at the moment. And she meant it. She cared.

"J.D., I'm Margie. I'm so sorry for your loss. She's at peace now. No more pain. Why don't you come over here with me and let them do what they have to do. Come with me."

Margie guides J.D. up from the chair and over to the wall across from the bed holding his mother's body. He stares down at her, his eyes growing redder, one clenched hand held to his mouth as if stifling a belch.

"Mama. Mama. I'm sorry, Mama. I should have . . . should have . . ."

"There, there now," Margie says. She continues to pet his back and shoulders. One hand rests on his arms. "There's nothing you should have done. It was time for her to go. Go ahead. Let her go."

Moisture finally begins to collect in J.D.'s eyes, and he collapses onto Margie.

"There now," she says, holding the heaving body of the man down onto her shoulders and breasts. "There now."

Sandy removes the stethoscope from her ears, hands it back to the other LPN, and looks at her watch.

"Time of death, 4:43," she says.

Sandy and the other LPN arrange the body, lay it flat, and manage to push the tongue and drooping lips partially back into place.

"Thanks," the LPN says to Sandy.

"No problem," Sandy says, and turns to Margie, who still pets the sobbing J.D.

"We'll be finished in a bit."

"I'll stay here with him for a while," Margie says, leading J.D. back to the chair at his mother's bedside. "Come on, sweetie. Sit down by your mother."

Sandy smiles at Margie and lays her hand hesitantly on J.D.'s shoulder.

"I'm so sorry, J.D.," she says and follows the other LPN out of the room.

Sandy glances through the doorway into Edith Moser's room as she passes down the hall. The old woman has rolled her chair to the window and is struggling, almost frantically, to reach the cord to open her window blinds.

"I'll be right there," Sandy calls to the LPN and enters Edith's room. "Can I help you, Edith?"

"Out. Out. I need to see out. I can't—"

"I'll get it." Sandy reaches over the woman's head and pulls the cord. Late afternoon light floods the room, and Sandy squints in the brightness. "How's that?"

"Thank you," Edith says. "I need to see out."

"Anything else I can do for you?"

"It was Ada Callander, wasn't it?" Edith Moser's face settles into a calm gaze through her window.

"Yes," Sandy says. "She had a stroke."

"I knew her when we were younger. Woman had such a thing for hats."

"Were you good friends?"

"Me and Ada? Lord, no. Never could stand the woman. Not many people could. Not likely to be many folks at that funeral. She did love that boy of hers, though."

"If there's nothing else . . ."

Edith Moser turns from the window to Sandy.

"What are you wearing, child?"

Sandy looks down at herself and realizes for the first time since she and Margie left her house earlier that she is still wearing her vest.

"Oh. It's my fishing vest. Forgot I still had it on."

"I used to fish. Loved just sitting on the bank, watching my bobber, listening to the water. Never even cared that much if I even caught a fish."

"I know the feeling," Sandy says.

"Sure wish I could go to Ada's funeral. Be a shame for that boy to be alone there. Wish I could go. Wish I could go anywhere. Funeral. Fishing. Anywhere."

Sandy lays a hand on Edith's shoulder.

"See you later, Edith," she says and walks out.

* * *

Later that evening Sandy sits on a chair in her little kitchen. Her hair is wet and lies in thick strands on the sheet wrapped around her shoulders as Margie begins to snip away at it with a small pair of scissors. A straight pin sticks through the scarred lobe of Sandy's ear, and she holds it in place, turning it slowly as Margie cuts her hair. The remains of pizza and salad are scattered on the kitchen table around a half-full wine bottle and two wine glasses, covered with the smudged prints of fingers and lips. One empty wine bottle sits beside an unopened one on the counter by the sink.

"Poor J.D.," Margie says. "I may be a sap, but I think a sad man crying is a goddamn sexy thing."

"Margie," Sandy scolds. "His mother just died today."

"So? Woman like me, I got to take 'em where I find 'em. If that makes me a desperate slut, so be it. I think he's sweet."

"He's a good man, Margie."

"Hey, waders or men, I don't mind taking your hand-me-downs."

"You're awful," Sandy says, smiling as a long lock of hair falls into her lap.

"Honey, you are going to look so cute with short hair."

Sandy never really gave much thought to her hair, kept it long and straight, trimming off the ends herself from time to time, pulling it back into a ponytail. Just another way she was different, apart from other women, she thinks. She realizes she had kept it long because Vernon liked it that way, and after he got sent up and she started fishing, she rarely considered it. Just a part of her body to be tended to when necessary, nothing more. As Margie cuts and clips, runs the comb through her wet hair, Sandy thinks that it will be nice to have her hair short. One less thing to fuss with.

"How's the ear?" Margie asks.

"Fine," Sandy says. She takes her fingers away from the pin in her ear lobe and reaches to the table, picking up the two wine glasses and passing one over her shoulder to Margie.

"Ah, yes. That's what we need. More wine. Much more wine," Margie says. "So, how's that old coot, the one with the cabin? Have you passed him on to someone else or is he still interesting to you?"

Sandy is quiet. She looks down at her hands in her lap. One hand holds the glass of wine. In the other she twirls a thick chunk of damp hair. Margie sets her wine glass down on the counter, places her hands on Sandy's shoulders and leans down to fix her friend with a stare.

"Hmmm?"

"I see him around some. He's fine, I guess," Sandy says.

Margie draws out a strand of Sandy's wet hair between her fingers and sets the scissors to it, eyeing where to make her cut.

"That's nice," she says. "Now tell me the real story."

* * *

Autumn creeps further across the Rogers Ridge watershed. The days remain warm but the evenings take on more of a chill. Green drains from trees, each day leaving more of a mottled wash of red, yellow, orange, and brown. A gentle wind sweeps up the hillside, shaking the drier brown leaves into a crisp rattle. Sandy feels a tingle as that wind tousles the loose strands of hair around her face and wafts across her bare neck. The hem of her dress flutters just below her knees, and a single strand of imitation pearls hanging from her neck glistens silver-white in the blazing afternoon light. She stands behind Edith Moser's wheelchair, her hands resting on the handles.

The turnout for Ada Callander's funeral is slight, but not quite as bad as Edith had predicted. There are enough people seated around J.D. on metal folding chairs at the little hillside cemetery, just barely enough, to give the impression that the deceased's life had not gone completely unnoticed in the world. Two cousins, with their spouses and a portion of their children, a couple of J.D.'s coworkers from the district office of the game and fisheries department, the hatchery manager, and his son, whose tinted, spiky hair seems to change colors every time he shifts and slumps in his seat. From time to time, the hatchery manager elbows his son into an upright position, only to have the boy slouch again. Sandy stands behind Edith Moser's wheelchair. James Keefe's empty chair sits beside them.

Keefe stands beside the minister, before Ada Callander's coffin, facing the small group of people. Strands of his silver hair twitch in the breeze. The thick black volume of Whitman—from which J.D. asked if he would be good enough to read "a little something"—lies open in his hands, his thumbs tightly holding the fluttering pages down in the breeze. Keefe's voice is soft but strong enough to be heard on the breeze. Sandy detects a hint of that rhythm of the river in his voice as Keefe reads.

I bequeath myself to the dirt to grow from the grass I love,
If you want me again look for me under your boot-soles.

Failing to fetch me at first keep encouraged,
Missing me one place search another,
I stop somewhere waiting for you.

Keefe closes the book and takes J.D.'s hand, pressing it and nodding to him, then walks back to his seat, his lingering limp imperceptible to all eyes except Sandy's. The breeze plays in the leaves and flowers of a spray of gladiolus resting on top of the coffin. Three other floral arrangements sit on the ground around the grave. Sandy looks at the one Margie sent. A grin almost escapes into view on her face as the minister steps forward to complete the ceremony.

I am the resurrection and the life: he that believeth in me, though he were dead, yet shall he live . . .

Two men with shovels lean against a backhoe, waiting as the tiny group of people disperses following the funeral. Keefe walks behind Sandy as she rolls Edith to where J.D. stands speaking with the hatchery manager.

"Just so's you know that whatever my son did, he didn't do the other," the hatchery manager says.

Sandy and Keefe trade a quick furtive glance as they walk up to J.D.

"I know," J.D. says to the hatchery manager. "I know that."

"Sorry for your loss," the hatchery manager says, and walks away to where his son sits slumped in the front seat of their car.

"Young man, I knew your mother," Edith says to J.D., reaching her veined hand up to his. "She was a loving mother, and you have my deepest sympathies."

"Thank you, ma'am."

"I'm so sorry, J.D." Sandy says. She begins to reach for his hand, but pauses and puts one arm around his shoulder in a partial embrace.

"Thank you," J.D. says. "Thank you for coming. And thank your friend, Margie, for the flowers. That was mighty nice of her."

"She's a good person. I'll tell her."

Sandy begins to turn away and push Edith forward, then stops and turns back to J.D.

"Or, you could call her yourself."

"You think that would be okay?"

"I think she'd like that."

"Your hair looks nice."

"Thanks," Sandy says, raising her hand to her hair involuntarily.

Sandy recites Margie's phone number to J.D., and he scribbles it onto a scrap of paper and stuffs it back into his jacket pocket as Keefe extends his hand.

"My condolences to you, J.D."

"Thanks, professor. And thanks for reading that. I still don't know that I get it all, but it always sounds nice when you read it."

"Glad to do it, son."

Keefe helps Sandy settle Edith into the cab of Sandy's truck and stash her wheelchair in the back beside Sandy's fishing gear.

"How's the ankle?" Sandy says, as she closes the tailgate.

"Just fine, thanks to you. Don't even need my staff anymore."

He looks down at the healed ankle and gives it a little shake.

"Until later," Keefe says, walking to his own truck. "Come up some time. Fishing's good right now. I'll show you some pools farther up, up where some of the big old hogs still are. Maybe make you some dinner. Pay you back for all those mashed potatoes. Of course, I'm not much of a cook."

Sandy had spent days, weeks in and around Keefe and his cabin. She'd pulled him from the river, touched and soothed his naked, injured body, nursed and maintained him and his cabin until he recovered. But he had never *invited* her to his upstream world. She wonders if he can sense the shiver that his casual invitation sends up her spine to the wispy hairs on her neck. Her hand gropes at the skirt of her dress, holding it in place in the breeze.

"Maybe I should do the cooking," Sandy says. "I'm not much of a cook either, but I can come up with a little more than mashed potatoes if I really apply myself."

Sandy walks to the cab of her truck and climbs in, tucking her dress under her as she slides into the seat. Edith is looking at her with a knowing grin carved through the wrinkles on her face. She leans forward and looks at Keefe's receding figure through Sandy's open door, then turns her face back to Sandy.

"What?" Sandy says.

"You know, you really do look so young and sweet with your hair short," Edith says, and looks again toward Keefe, the grin broadening into a full smile.

"Thanks for bringing me, dear," Edith says to Sandy as she starts the truck. "Oh, it feels so good to be out, out in the light, even for a funeral."

"I was happy to, Edith."

"Could I ask just one more favor, dear?"

"What?"

"Could we drive back along the old river road? I'd so love to see the water. If it's not too much trouble."

"No trouble at all. I was thinking of going that way myself."

Miles downstream from the dam and her little vinyl-sided house, Sandy steers her truck slowly along the stream-hugging curves of the old river road, keeping the truck steady, so Edith will not be bounced around the cab. They drive through a green landscape, shaded from brazen autumn by the hemlocks and pines flanking the road. Sandy leans into another curve, and Edith holds up her hand, pointing.

"Could we stop up here, just for a minute?"

Sandy eases her truck softly onto the gravel in the turn-out and stops. Edith Moser is still and small on the seat of the truck, gazing out the window at the river, her hands folded in her lap. Both women are silent for several seconds, soaking in the sound of rushing water, until Edith breaks the silence.

"Used to live just up the road a piece. Sometimes, when things got too mean at home, I'd get my pole and walk on down here, sit right down there on that big rock."

"Edith," Sandy says, "would you like to get out for a while?"

"Oh, could I?"

Edith Moser is light, feathery, and Sandy lifts her directly from the cab into the seat of her wheelchair and pushes her to the edge of the turn-out, stopping only a few inches before the ground breaks down to the riverbank. She locks the wheelchair's brakes tight and wedges a stone under the front of each wheel, just to be on the safe side.

"There. How's that?"

"Oh, it's just so lovely. I do think it's the most lovely thing I've seen in years, bless your heart."

Sandy tugs her dress down and squats by the old woman's chair, one hand gripping one of the armrests.

"Do you hear it?" Edith says. "The sound of the water. It's a living sound, like blood pumping through a heart."

Sandy rubs the shiny stud in her scarred ear lobe and tilts the ear to the stream. She slides her hand over the exposed nape of her neck, then over the band of fake pearls around her throat.

"Yes," she says.

"I think it was the sound of the water, more than anything else, that I loved. Seemed to just wash out all the yelling and meanness in the world. Sometimes I'd sit down there so long, I plum forget about the time. Be late getting home, and then there'd be hell to pay. But I do think it was worth it, as long as the water was here. As long as the sound of the water was here."

Sandy lifts her hand from the armrest and lays it on Edith's arm, squeezing gently.

"Time to time, I'd catch a catfish or two, or some bluegills. They went a lot easier on me when I got home if I brought some dinner with me."

"No catfish in here anymore," Sandy says. "Just trout, mostly."

"Don't make no difference to me," Edith says. "As long as the river's here and there's something alive in it, well, it's just fine by me."

A trout flashes in the deep pool below, and both women turn their eyes immediately to the ring of the rise. Sandy feels her legs lock into a crouch beneath the folds of her dress. The fine hairs on her neck bristle. The old woman turns her gaze from the water to the young woman's face beside her.

"Go ahead, dear. We got time," she says.

"Oh no," Sandy says. "That's okay. Not now. Besides, I can't. I'm wearing a dress."

"Why in the world should that stop you? Some of my best times down here was in a dress. Sneak out of the house after Sunday morning meeting, still wearing my go-to-meeting dress. Head right on down here, dress, pole, and all. Felt better than the kind of praying they did in church. Go on. I'm fine right here."

Sandy turns to the sound of another rise in the pool, then back to Edith Moser.

"Are you sure?"

"Never more sure of anything. Go on."

Sandy gets what gear she'll need from the back of her truck. She rigs her rod with a Black Caddis pattern, and pulls her waders up over her bare legs, tucking the skirt of her dress inside them and snapping the buckle.

"I'll only be a minute," she says to Edith, who waves at her as Sandy drops down the embankment to the stream. Her pearls bounce on her chest as she angles down the slope to the tail of the pool and wades in.

She takes the trout on her second cast and plays it quickly and easily to hand. Not much of a fish. A reasonable rainbow, its flanks silvery and mottled, a band of bright pink washed over the speckled silver. A stocker, but Sandy feels no disgust in it. She removes the fly, clamps her rod under her arm, and holds the fish up and out for Edith to see. The old woman looks down from her chair on the precipice above, smiles her face into a maze of crevices, and clasps her hands together, shaking them like a champion celebrating a victory. Sandy sets the trout into the current, holds it there for a moment, then releases it.

"You do that so beautifully, dear," Edith says. "Can I see that there pole of yours?"

Sandy steps up from the embankment. Water drips down the legs of her waders, and scraps of dead leaves and mud cling to her boots. She lays the fly rod across the armrests of the wheelchair. Edith runs her frail fingers up and down the cool, green graphite and taps at the cork grip above the reel.

"Mighty fancy stuff," Edith says. "Good deal fancier than my old cane pole. But it does seem to work pretty much the same way as my old pole. Just fancier, don't you think?"

"Yes, I suppose so."

Sandy drops her rod into the truck bed, sits on the tailgate, and peels off her wet waders. She runs her hands down her abdomen and thighs, smoothing at her hopelessly wrinkled dress. She shrugs as she closes the tailgate and walks back to Edith, who reaches out and takes one of

Sandy's hands into her own, patting it with the other. Her eyes are fixed on the river below.

"Thank you, dear. Thank you so much for stopping here. For letting me be here one more time." Edith turns her face up to Sandy, still patting her hand. The old woman's eyes glisten amid the wrinkles.

"It was my pleasure," Sandy says, tightening her hand into Edith's. "Are you ready to go now?"

"Oh yes. I'm ready now. We better get back to that old place before they start to think I hopped on into that hole with Ada Callander, just to save you another trip to the cemetery."

* * *

Stink lies stretched out on his side in the middle of the kitchen floor, snoring, his front paws twitching, and Sandy steps over him on her way to answer the phone. For the last week or so, Stink has been coming in the house with Sandy, their bond finally complete. He still spends much of his time in his tire, but more and more he chooses to be where Sandy is. And since he hasn't killed a skunk since that last one two weeks ago, his odor has grown tolerable enough for her to let him in. She now keeps food and water for him both inside the house and out by his tire. Sandy thought about removing the broken screen door completely and installing a pet door, so he could pass in and out of the house as he wished, but she felt the risk of him dragging a skunk inside her little house remained too high. Maybe later, during the winter when the skunks were hibernating. Late afternoon light tumbles through the kitchen window. She walks through the light and pulls the top of her scrubs over her head and combs her fingers through her short hair as she stops at the ringing telephone. Looking down at the phone, she lets it ring another time, and takes a deep breath. As she reaches for the receiver, she knows it can only be one of two people on the other end of the line. It's the middle of October, and Rogers Ridge is pocked with the audacious colors of autumn. Margie is coming for another visit tomorrow. Vernon was released from prison this morning.

"Hello," Sandy says, and releases the air from her lungs when Margie's voice crackles through the receiver.

"Honey? I just saw him. He pulled up in front of my house just as I was leaving. And he's coming down there tomorrow."

"Are you all right?"

"Sure. I'm fine. I'm fine."

Margie's voice comes through distant and tinny, wrapped in a vague rumbling sound.

"Are you calling from your van?" Sandy asks.

"Yeah. I'm on my cell. It was strange, honey. Very strange."

"Tell me."

Sandy listens and Margie talks. She tells her how she had just tossed her bag into the back of her minivan and backed out of her driveway when Vernon's white van pulled up in front of her. When he stepped out of the van, she hardly recognized him at first. He looked older, worn, and something else.

"What?" Sandy asks.

"I don't know. He looked . . . rough. Roughed up. Make any sense?"

"Yes, it does."

Margie tells her how he held his hands up, motioning her to stop, and walked up to her minivan, saying he just wanted to talk to her a minute. She snapped her door locks, rolled her window up, and told Vernon to watch himself because she had a gun.

"Sure I do," Margie says to Sandy. "I always have it. Right here in my purse. Damn thing's loaded, too. I make sure of that."

"What did he do?"

"Stopped right where he was and held his hands up even higher. It was really kind of funny, now that I think about. Anyway, he swore he just wanted to talk for a second."

"And?"

"So I let him talk. Turns out, he really did just want to talk. And it was the damnedest thing."

"What did he say?"

"He said he was sorry. Can you believe that?"

"Yes, I can," Sandy says, squatting down to scratch Stink on his belly. The dog rolls belly up as she scratches, and one of his hind legs begins to quiver and kick.

"You know, he sounded like he meant it, too. Said he was sorry about all the things he said in those letters. Said he was sorry about everything."

Margie's voice breaks up, her signal fading.

"Margie? Margie, are you still there?" Sandy speaks loudly into the phone.

"Yeah, yeah. I'm here."

"He say anything else?"

"Uh-hunh. Said he needed to tell you he was sorry. To see you again. That, and that he'd be praying for both of us. For all of us. Sheesh."

Sandy nods, says nothing, and drops from her squat to sits cross-legged on the floor, still scratching Stink's belly.

"Sandy? Honey? You still there?"

"I'm here."

"Well, you don't believe all that Jesus shit of his, do you?"

"I don't know. I think so."

"Don't kid yourself, girl. What about all those mean-ass letters? Threatening letters. Whatever was in him before that made him write those letters is still in there somewhere. He's a killer, honey. A killer."

"Not anymore, Margie. He's a sad man who lost his wife. Lost his life. I think maybe he just wants to clean the slate and try to start over again."

"Jesus, Sandy. You got a hell of a lot more faith in mankind than me."

"It's not faith."

"Faith or not, he's coming to your house tomorrow. I told him I wasn't going to tell him where you lived, and he said he already knew you were down there outside Damascus. Had your address. How the hell did he know that?"

"The internet. My social security number. You read the letter. There are ways to do that."

"Yeah, but so quickly? Goddamn. Of all the skills for that bastard to learn in prison. Anyway, he asked me to tell you he was coming, since he still didn't have your phone number. Said he wanted me to tell you he was coming so you wouldn't be caught off guard. So what do you think? What are you going to do?"

"I already told you. Nothing. I'm not running. This is my home. No need to run now anyway. Relax, Margie. He's not going to hurt me. I believe him. Just wants to set things straight and then go on, and I'll let him. I owe him at least that much."

"You don't owe him shit. But one thing's for sure. You're not going to face him alone, and that's that. Whether you like it or not."

Sandy smiles and pushes herself up from the floor. Stink grunts and rolls back down on his side.

"I'm on my way right now. I'll be down there in an hour or so," Margie says.

"Now? I thought you weren't coming until tomorrow morning." Sandy says.

"No, I'm driving as we speak."

"I'll leave the house open for you. I have to go back in to work now. One of the other nurses is sick, and I told her I'd cover the night shift for her."

"You leave nothing open. Lock your goddamn house. I'll be fine. What time do you get off in the morning?"

"Seven, but . . ."

"But nothing. J.D. and I will meet you at the nursing home when you get off."

Sandy leans her elbows on the kitchen counter, and a grin twitches at the corners of her mouth.

"J.D.?"

For a moment there is no response, and Sandy wonders if the signal has faded again.

"Margie? You still there?"

"Yeah, I'm here."

"Uh, you and J.D.?"

"Well, he called me. After his mother's funeral, to thank me for the flowers and all. You know."

"And?"

"Well, we talked, and, as they say, one thing led to another. He's sweet. He came up here a couple of times. We had dinner. The boys really like him. You don't mind, do you? Taking your hand-me-downs, and all, you know?"

"He's not a pair of old waders, Margie. He's a good man. And so, you were going to come down here tonight all along. You just weren't coming to my house until tomorrow, eh?"

"Well, since you ask, yes. Taking it to the next level and all. And don't you say a thing about me being fast, girl. At my age, you got to work fast. And why not, if two people like each other? Hell, life is short."

"Margie, who are you trying to convince? I'm happy for you. Really I am."

"He really is a good man, Sandy. But you had your chance."

Sandy smiles and wraps her free arm around herself.

"I hope it works out for the both of you."

"Me, too. Hell, I'm as excited as a high school virgin. If it wasn't for this Vernon shit, I think I'd be wetting my pants about now. Do you have any idea how long it's been since I've been laid, girl?"

"I might make a guess."

"A long goddamn time, that's for sure."

"Are the boys with your mom?"

"Yeah, she loves having them. Gives her a chance to show off, to show Matthew and Luke how a real mother does it, homemade cookies and all that shit, instead of the slacker they're stuck with."

"You're not a slacker. You're a good mother," Sandy says, pausing before she continues. "You're a good friend, too."

"And you're getting sentimental now. I better hang up before you embarrass yourself. I'll see you in the morning, honey. Okay?"

"Okay."

"Oh, by the way," Margie says. "It's Jerome David."

"What?"

"Jerome David. That's what J.D. stands for."

Sandy leans at the kitchen sink and looks out the window. She breathes deeply, slowly, to settle the conflation of emotions throbbing in her chest. Margie and J.D., together. Vernon, finally coming.

"Come on, Stink," she says, opening the kitchen door. "Time to go to work. Get on out to your tire."

Stink groans as he rises, stretches himself, and waddles out the back door. He stops at the trash can, sniffs it for a moment, lifts his leg against it, and walks up the slope to his tractor tire. Sandy locks her back door, and swings the broken screen door closed in front of it.

"Got to replace that damn thing," she says as he walks to her truck, stopping at Stink's tire on the way. She leans over him, brings her face close to his, and scratches behind his ears.

"Be a good boy while I'm gone. Stay here. Keep an eye on things. And no skunks, okay?"

Stink yawns widely, licks Sandy's hand, and drops into his tire, grunting again as he curls up to sleep.

"Going to be interesting around here tomorrow. Get some sleep. You'll need it. God knows, I won't be getting any."

The sun dropping behind the hill in back of Sandy's house lights the top of the ridge across the river. Sandy shifts into gear and turns her truck toward the maniacal blaze of color scorching the top half of the hill on the far side of the Ripshin River.

* * *

The mornings are cooler now, and Sandy's bare skin bristles into goose bumps from her shoulders to her ankles as she peeks through the blinds of her bathroom window, watching Margie and J.D. sipping coffee together on the front deck. Margie reaches her hand to J.D.'s face, strokes his cheek with her fingertips, and kisses him. A brief, familiar kiss. The kind of kiss shared by two people at home with one another, Sandy thinks. She finishes toweling off from her shower, shakes out her short hair, and slips into her bedroom to get dressed, recalling how she had found Margie and J.D. cuddled together in the front seat of his

SUV this morning, necking like school kids while they waited in the nursing home parking lot for Sandy to get off work.

On her way out, Sandy had stopped in Edith Moser's room, helped her with the last buttons on her blouse, brushed her hair, opened the blinds, and pushed Edith to the window, so she could see out into the early morning light more easily.

"Thank you, dear. Bless your heart," Edith had said, patting Sandy's hand as she left.

Outside the front entrance, Sandy had done something she had never done before. She stopped and scanned the parking lot, reading the terrain before her. Vernon's white van was nowhere to be seen, and she scolded herself for being fearful and skittish. There was no reason for it. She knew he was coming, and he knew where she lived now. He had even sent word to prepare her. He wasn't going to lie in wait for her. He would walk right up to her, and she would meet him there, face to face.

Sandy turned her eyes from all the other vehicles in the parking lot to J.D.'s government SUV, parked beside her truck. The soles of her work shoes made no noise as she walked through the gray light across the parking lot to J.D.'s truck, taking him and Margie by surprise.

"Do your parents know what you two kids are up to out here?" Sandy said, smiling and leaning against the door.

Margie and J.D. jumped in the seat and broke apart. J.D. fumbled with his cap, pulling it off as if he was actually caught in the act by a stern parent. His face flushed red from his chin to the bald spot on top of his head.

"You sneaky bitch," Margie said, laughing and reaching over J.D. to take a playful poke at Sandy.

"Uh, sorry. Uh, excuse me," J.D. muttered, looking down into his lap.

"Relax, J.D.," Sandy said.

"Look," Margie said, taking J.D.'s face into her hand. "Look. It's so cute. He blushes. Can you believe it? He actually blushes."

"Cute as a button," Sandy said, and even surprised herself when she reached through the open window and pinched J.D.'s cheek.

"Stop it you two," he said, and his face flushed crimson.

By the time Sandy is dressed and emerges from her front door, a small party is underway on her front deck, and Margie is the hostess. She holds a large thermos in her hand and peers into the cups of the group of men standing around her, checking to see if they need more coffee.

"Thank you, ma'am," says the deputy sheriff as Margie tops off his mug.

Stink is on the porch, keeping quiet and close to Margie, but the hackles on his back are up, his eyes locked on the deputy. The officer stands a few steps away from the others, young and ruddy, crew-cut and stolid, the morning light glinting on the black patent leather of his gun belt. When he turned his cruiser up Sandy's driveway a few minutes earlier, Tommy Akers had been coming down the road in his pickup. He had followed the cruiser up the driveway to see what all the fuss was about and now stands with his own cup of coffee, talking with J.D. Tommy has pushed his binoculars to the side, so he can rest his coffee cup on the great hump of his belly. He leans over the railing and spits a brown gob to the ground before turning back to J.D.

"So, word is someone's been knocking off your little trout up at the hatchery," Tommy says. "Catch 'em yet?"

"Not yet," J.D. says, raising his cup to his lips. "But I will."

"Well, can't say as I blame 'em. Never could get partial to them damn trout of yours."

"Not mine. They're state property, and someone's been destroying that state property, for some reason."

"And I can't say as I don't hope they destroy a little more of it."

"Let it go, Tommy. There haven't been any catfish in the Ripshin for fifty years now. Don't you think enough is enough?"

Margie has the coffee thermos in one hand and hooks Sandy's arm with the other and pulls her into the group.

"Why don't the two of you put a sock in it and stop the pissing contest," Margie says. "Nobody gives a shit about your little fish fight. We're here for Sandy. Remember? Her ex-husband? Ex-convict? Religious fanatic? Killer? Coming here this morning? Any of this ring a bell?"

"It's okay, Margie," Sandy says.

J.D. and Tommy both nod to Sandy and look down into their cups.

Margie releases her grip on Sandy's arm. She sets the thermos on the railing and takes Sandy's green mug, which is sitting there as well.

"Here, sweetie. I know you're not much for coffee, so I made you a cup of that herb tea of yours."

"Thanks," Sandy says, and lowers her lips to the mug. Her damp hair falls around the sides of her face as she sips her tea. Stink positions himself between Sandy and Margie, and Sandy reaches down and rests her hand on his head, her fingers scratching the side of his face.

Margie sees that Sandy is looking at the deputy sheriff, off to the side of the deck. She slips her hand through Sandy's arm again and leads her to him.

"This is . . . oh, I'm sorry. I forgot your name, deputy," Margie says.

"Lambert, ma'am," he says.

"Deputy Lambert. This is Sandy Holston. It's her ex-husband that's coming."

Sandy extends her hand and tries to smile.

"Hello," she says. "Uh, why are you here, if you don't mind me asking?"

"I had J.D. call and ask him to come out," Margie says. "Just to be on the safe side."

"Thank you," Sandy says to the deputy, "but it really isn't necessary. You needn't have bothered."

"I'll be the judge of that," Margie says. "Hell, if we left it up to you . . . well, you think you can take the world on single-handedly. And you can't, girl. You need help from time to time. Everyone does."

"No trouble, ma'am," the deputy says. "I owe J.D. more than one favor, though I will have to leave if a call comes in."

"Of course. Thanks again," Sandy says. Margie leads her back to J.D. and Tommy, who have begun to argue again.

"Will you two cut it out and make yourselves useful," Margie says. "Like, for example, why don't you tell Sandy how cute she looks with her hair short."

"Stop it, Margie," Sandy says.

"Looks very nice," J.D. says, fumbling with the bill of his cap.

"Nice?" Margie says. "Oh, we're going to have to work on you if that's all you can come up with."

"Looks right pretty," Tommy says, and lifts his cup from his belly to his brown-stained lips.

"Well, at least that's better than 'nice,'" Margie says. "Her hair's adorable, and you both know it. Some of my better work, if I do say so myself."

Sandy grins, squeezes Margie's arm, and squats beside Stink, who is eyeing the deputy again.

"It's alright, boy. It's alright," she says, wrapping her arm around the dog and stroking his chin. "Margie's decided we need him here, okay?"

"You do, and that's that," Margie says. She reaches down to Sandy's face and flicks a wayward bang from her forehead as everyone on the porch hears the crunch of gravel under tires and turns to see Vernon's white van pull up the driveway into the clearing in front of Sandy's house. The van crawls past Tommy's pickup and the deputy's cruiser, veers around J.D.'s dark green SUV, and rocks to a stop down the grade from Sandy's truck. The blue lettering on the side of the van—Adams Home Construction—now faded and weathered.

Sandy's thigh muscles tighten in her crouch, and her fingers clutch the folds of skin on Stink's neck. The wispy hairs on her neck stiffen. She runs her hand over Stink's back, smoothing his raised hackles, soothing him as a low growl erupts into a single, sharp bark.

"It's okay, baby," she says. "It's okay."

Sandy's line of sight is obscured. The others on the porch have pushed forward into an informal line of defense between Sandy and the white van, leaving Sandy crouching behind them. Margie's thick thighs to her left, the deputy's creased brown uniform slacks to her right, Sandy stares through their legs and across her yard, through the dusty glass of the van's window at the face of the ex-husband she has not seen since he last emerged from trees seven years ago to discover a wife who had become something different from what he imagined her to be. She takes her hand from Stink's neck, and he bolts through their legs, down the steps, and lopes to the van, circling it frantically, barking. Sandy stands and steps through the line of people before her.

"Let me through," Sandy says. "I'm going to talk to him."

"Not alone, you're not," Margie says.

"That's exactly what I'm going to do."

"Honey, we're all here to . . ."

Sandy cuts Margie off with a brusque wave of her hand, then brings the hand down gently on her friend's shoulder.

"Margie. I'm going to talk to him. That's all he came here for, and I owe him that. Please. This one's my job. Alone."

"Well . . . we're all staying right here, and the son of a bitch better not try anything or there'll be hell to pay, right deputy?"

The deputy nods and J.D. sets his coffee cup on the railing. Tommy Akers spits over the side of the deck. All three of them stare at the white van.

"It'll be fine, Margie," Sandy says. She walks down from the deck, calling to Stink as she approaches the van.

"Stink. Stink. Stop it. Go on up to your tire. Go on. That's a good boy."

She watches as Stink retreats up the slope to his tractor tire, slinks inside it, and sits, his eyes riveted on Sandy and the van. Turning to the van, Sandy withdraws a couple of steps, and nods to the man looking at her through the windshield. The door of the van opens, and Vernon steps out. He closes the door slowly, softly, his eyes flitting back and forth between Sandy and the people on her porch. Sandy looks at the face she last saw caught in the crosshairs, trapped and abandoned, confused and outraged in the middle of Dismal Creek. A few new furrows cut across his forehead and along his cheeks. Sandy notices a tiny scar transecting one of his eyebrows. Flecks of gray are just visible in the short hair at his temples. The hard, furtive visage his face acquired in prison is there, but it has lost the reptilian cast it took on during the time leading up to the escape attempt. It is the face she has expected.

"Hello, Vernon," Sandy says. She slides her hands into the back pockets of her jeans.

"Hello, Sandy." Vernon appears unsure of what to do with his own hands. In a seeming imitation of Sandy, he slips one into his pocket. The other flutters about uncertain until he lays it on the sill of the open van window.

"Looks like you've called up the cavalry," he says. "You needn't have."

238

Sandy glances up at the people gathered on her porch. Both the deputy and J.D. are wearing their side arms, as usual. Sandy realizes that if she includes the shotgun resting in the rack inside Tommy Akers's truck and the little .25 in Margie's purse, everyone there with her to meet Vernon is armed.

"Margie's idea. Don't hold it against her. She means well."

"You cut your hair. Looks nice."

"Thanks. Margie did it."

"Seems Margie does a lot around here."

Sandy says nothing. Her eyes stay locked on Vernon, showing no response.

"Well, I'm out. But, uh, guess you can see that, right?"

"Yes. What do you want, Vernon?"

"Not sure. Just to see you, I guess."

"How'd you find me?"

"Pretty easy, really. With a computer and a social security number, sooner or later, you can find most anybody. Had a little trouble at first. Kept looking for Sandy Adams. Then I tried Sandy Holston, and found you in no time. So, you took back your maiden name?"

"Nothing to take back. It was there all the time."

Vernon looks down at his feet and toes the gravel.

"Did you get any of my letters?" he asks.

"Every one of them."

"Don't suppose you read them, did you?"

"Every word."

"Why didn't you ever answer any of them?"

"Didn't know what to say. Didn't think there was anything I could say at that point."

"Sorry about some of the things I said in them."

"Did you mean what you said?"

"I suppose, at the time. I was real angry."

Vernon looks up from his feet and shifts the hand resting on the sill of the van window to his free pocket. Sandy takes her hands from her pockets and folds her arms in front of her.

"Sorry," Vernon says. "I was angry. Hated you, I guess. Wanted to hurt you, but I don't feel that way now. I've been saved now, Sandy. The love of Jesus has washed the anger from me. I'm a new man now."

Sandy looks at the hardened face, searching for a sadness behind the rough features.

"I'm glad you feel that way now, Vernon."

"Guess all along I loved you more than I ever hated you. Expect that sounds kind of crazy."

"Doesn't sound crazy at all."

Vernon's hands visibly clench inside his pants pockets. He looks past Sandy, up the slope to Stink's tire.

"See you got yourself a watch dog. Funny looking old mutt."

"He came with the place."

"Looks like a nice little house. Someone did a good job putting up that deck on the front."

Sandy glances up at the house, but says nothing.

"And you're right here by the river. That's nice if you fish. Do you? Fish? Seems the last time I saw you, that's what you were doing."

Vernon's voice stiffens around these last words, and Sandy tenses at the shift in his tone, seeing the scene at Dismal Creek and searching Vernon's face for traces of his departed anger and bitterness resurfacing.

"Yes. I fish," she says.

"Why?" Vernon asks.

"Why do I fish?" Sandy says, and realizes as soon as she says it that that is not Vernon's question.

"No. Why, Sandy?" he says. "Why'd you leave me there? I guess that's the one thing I just never could understand. Guess that's why I came here today. Thought maybe you could at least tell me that. Can you at least tell me that now?"

Sandy presses her arms tight around herself. Her eyes run past Vernon, through the trees, across the river, and up the side of the ridge. The sun has not yet topped the ridge, and she thinks that in about another hour or so there should be a fairly decent hatch from the smooth current of the river. Should be able to take a few of the bigger brown trout on the surface.

"I'm sorry, Vernon. I don't know if I can explain it. Not sure I understand myself. I suppose, well . . . I was just someone else by then. I'd found another way to live. By the time you got there, I wasn't waiting for you anymore. I was waiting for something else. Something like that. I'm sorry I can't give you a better answer."

"Waiting for something else," he says. "That seems like an answer to me."

"I'm sorry, Vernon. For everything."

Vernon looks up at the people on the porch again. Tommy has stepped to the side of the deputy. The deputy watches Sandy and Vernon, his hand resting on the butt of his pistol, and Tommy spits over the porch rail. Margie is leaning into J.D., her arms wrapped around his waist.

"Looks like Margie got herself a boyfriend," Vernon says.

"Yes. Seems like it."

"I suppose you got a new boyfriend, too."

Sandy tries to push back the image of Keefe that rises in her mind.

"No. Just me. And Stink."

"You and Stink," Vernon says, a nervous chuckle gurgling in his throat. "Could there be any chance for you and me again? Try to start over?"

"No, Vernon. I'm sorry."

"Like I said, I'm a new man now, Sandy. With God's guidance and the love of Jesus in our hearts, I know we could make it right this time. In my heart, I know it's what God intends."

"It's not what I intend."

"You're waiting for something else, right?"

"Don't, Vernon."

"I thought it wouldn't hurt to ask. Just to let you know that I'll always be your husband. Always be waiting for you."

"You should leave now," Sandy says.

She takes a tentative step toward Vernon, unfolds her arms, and extends a hand. He takes his hands from his pockets, wipes one along his pant leg, and takes the offered hand in his. Sandy feels that the hand, already rough and strong from a working life, has grown rougher, brittle, from the prison years.

"Good-bye, Vernon. I hope your life works out. I really do."

"Thanks. God willing, I hope so, too."

Vernon opens the van door and climbs into the seat. He starts the engine, then pauses, turning again to Sandy.

"I'll always love you," he says. "Can't change that. And to me, you'll always be my wife."

"No, Vernon. I'm not. Good-bye."

The white van backs slowly around J.D.'s SUV and, shifting into gear, rolls down the driveway, turns up Willard Road, and disappears behind the trees.

Sandy stands alone in her driveway, watching where Vernon's van vanished. Margie trots down the steps and walks briskly to Sandy, enfolding her friend's stiff body in her warm arms.

"Well?" Margie asks. "What did he say? What did you say? What? We couldn't hear shit from up there."

"Later," Sandy says. "Later. Need to fish now."

"Don't you want to get some sleep? You've been up all night."

"No. Need to fish now."

"Okay, sweetie. Whatever you say."

Sandy remains quiet and rigid and Margie takes over again. She thanks the deputy for coming by and waves to him as the cruiser departs. She tells Tommy Akers it was nice meeting him as he stuffs himself into the cab of his truck and drives off. She kisses J.D. on the cheek, smiles up into his face, then grows stern.

"And remember," Margie tells him. "Be back here by six. The girls here are actually going to make you dinner, and this Keefe guy is coming for dinner, too. Finally get to meet this mysterious old geezer."

"Professor Keefe," J.D. says. "And he's not that old."

"Whatever," Margie says. "Just be here, okay?"

"Are you sure you'll be alright?" J.D. asks.

Margie looks quickly at Sandy, who nods slowly.

"We'll be fine," Margie says. "He's gone now. Besides, I've got my gun."

"Not sure but that doesn't worry me more," J.D. says.

"Go on. Get," Margie says, smiling and stroking his cheek. "And be back here at six."

Margie drapes her arm over Sandy's shoulders and waves to J.D. as his SUV pulls away.

"What would you think," Margie says, "if I moved down here. They're hiring over at Sherwood Regional Hospital. Thought I might apply. Be closer to my loved ones and all. What do you think?"

Sandy's tight body loosens and her arm comes up around Margie's shoulder.

"I think I'd like that. I'd like that a lot," she says.

"Thought you might. Now, I may not be the expert fisherwoman that you are, but I'm guessing those trout won't catch themselves. Let's go fishing."

"Yes," Sandy says. "Fishing. Yes, let's go. While we still have time. Should be a good hatch pretty soon."

"Think I might be able to get one of those big ones this time?"

"Maybe."

"And you promise me you'll tell me what went on with Vernon? All of it?"

"Later. I promise."

Arms around each other, the two women walk up the steps to Sandy's house to get their gear. As they open the front door, Margie stops, grasps Sandy's shoulders, and holds her at arm's length.

"Oh, I just can't get over how good your hair looks short. So cute," she says.

"Come on," Sandy says. "Those trout won't catch themselves."

* * *

The hatch is heavy for this time of year on the lower Ripshin. Above the silky water, the air is thick with flurries of caddis and midges. All around Sandy and Margie, the glassy surface explodes as delirious trout slaughter insects that float in the film, waiting for their new wings to dry enough that they may escape into the air, out of the range of the jaws of raging trout. Sandy's line is taut, and her reel sings as she plays another fish through the deep pool, leading it flawlessly through the water toward her waiting hands.

"My god," Margie says. "Another one. Starting to feel a little greedy, girl."

"A feeding frenzy like this doesn't happen often around here," Sandy retrieves the brown trout. "You don't question it. You just fish it."

In the short while they had been fishing, they had already caught over a dozen fish. Even Margie had taken several, though not as many as Sandy.

"This must be the part of the river where all the dumb ones live," Margie had called across the water, "if I'm catching this many."

When it became clear that the hatch had unleashed such a furious response from the trout here in the stretch of the Ripshin at the end of the path leading down from Sandy's house, they had decided to keep a few of the better fish for dinner that night.

"Hell with that chicken in the fridge," Margie had said. "We'll show those guys that women can bring home meat for their men, too."

Sandy had shot Margie a scowl at the implication that Keefe was her *man*, but Margie had laughed it off.

"Lighten up, girl. You're not fooling me for a minute," Margie had said.

Margie had one good fish in the pouch of her new vest, and Sandy had two in her pouch. Margie had flinched at first when Sandy inserted her thumb into the mouth of the first fish they decided to keep and jerked upward, snapping the fish's spine.

"Ew, cold-blooded, honey," she had said.

"Better than letting them flop to death. If you're going to kill a fish, then kill it, quick and clean. You owe the fish that much, at least."

Sandy brings the brown trout to hand. Its belly is fat and full, and the carcasses of a couple of naturals cling to its lip around Sandy's fly.

"I think this ought to be enough for dinner," Sandy says. She breaks the trout's spine and slides it on top of the other two fish in her pouch as Margie's line is hit hard.

Margie shrieks and raises her rod high, holding it with both hands.

"Maybe just one more, eh?" Margie says, as she feeds out line to her running fish. "In case anyone's really hungry, okay?"

Intent on the fish Margie is bringing in, the two women do not notice any of the occasional traffic on Willard Road, from which they are periodically visible through breaks in the trees on the bank. They pay no attention to Stink's faint barking in the distance.

"Whew," Margie says. "That was amazing. So, that enough fishing for today?"

"They're still rising pretty steady," Sandy says. "No reason to stop fishing. We've got a little more time."

"Well, I need a cigarette and a rest. I'm tired."

They had played Margie's fish back upstream a bit and end up near the mouth of the path from Sandy's house. Margie wades to the far side of the river and sits down heavily in the matted grass on the bank. Her lighter clicks a flame to the end of her cigarette. Sandy peels line from her reel, preparing to cast to another rising trout. In the moment of calm, both women hear Stink's barking growing louder, closer, and they turn in the direction of the sound as Vernon steps sideways into view on the bank. He holds a thick branch in his hands, jabbing it at Stink, trying to fend off the advance.

When Vernon reaches the edge of the riverbank, he stops and cocks his arms. The fallen oak branch in his hands is thick, heavy, and he wields it like a baseball bat, swinging it quickly and fiercely, striking Stink squarely in the side of his skull. The dog emits a curt yelp and drops from view in the long grass on the bank.

"Stink. No," Sandy shouts.

"Shit. Oh, shit," Margie says, fumbling at a pocket of her vest, as she wades back out to Sandy's side.

Sandy freezes in a half-crouch, stock still except for her hand, which reels in her loose line. In the distance, the siren at the dam upstream sounds, registering in Sandy's ears as she keeps her eyes locked on Vernon.

Vernon flings the branch up the bank and splashes ankle-deep into the water.

"Is that something else you were waiting for?" he screams. "Is it? Well, so much for your damn mutt, you lying bitch."

"Vernon, no," Sandy says. "No, Vernon."

"You bastard, I'll shoot you," Margie says. "I swear, I'll do it, you son of bitch."

Sandy turns to Margie, who has managed to fish the little .25 from her vest pocket. Sandy had forgotten about the gun.

"Stay where you are, or I'll do it. I will."

Margie clutches the pistol in both hands. They shake visibly, and Sandy reaches to them, gripping Margie's quaking hands and pushing the gun down sharply.

"No, Margie. No," Sandy says.

"Are you crazy?" Margie jerks her hands free of Sandy's grip and points the gun at Vernon again. "Look. Look what he did."

"Go ahead and shoot, you fat bitch," Vernon says as he begins to wade with faltering steps toward the two women. "God stands with me and guides my hand."

"Fine," Margie says, and pulls the trigger.

The gun fails to fire.

"Shit. Damn safety," Margie says. She turns the gun over in her hands, switches off the safety, and trains the gun once more on Vernon's approach.

"No, Margie," Sandy says.

"Like hell," Margie says, and fires. The report of the gun is a sharp pock and the sound lingers over the surface of the river with the acrid scent of gunpowder. The shot hits the water a foot to the left and ten yards behind Vernon. The pace of his clumsy wading is not altered.

"God guides my hand," he shouts.

Sandy reaches again to Margie's hands and pushes the gun down.

"No, Margie," Sandy says. "No. Get back. Get back."

Sandy pushes Margie toward the bank.

"But . . ." Sandy cuts her off.

"No. Go. Get up the bank. This is my job."

Margie moves cautiously toward the bank, momentarily transfixed by the stern look in her friend's eyes.

Vernon begins to struggle through the deepening water and slips on a moss-covered rock, his slick-soled shoes giving no footing on the slippery riverbed. He sinks to his chest and comes up slapping at the surface of the water, his clothes soaked and heavy. Margie backs up the bank, the pistol still in her hands, aimed again at Vernon. Sandy hooks her loose fly on the catch on her rod and begins to move downstream, wading backwards with careful but certain steps, keeping Vernon squarely in her sights.

"Vernon, don't. Go back," Sandy says.

"No going back now, babe. Not now," he says. "Not for me or you. Our path is ordained."

Sandy glances downstream and continues backing away with the current as Vernon advances.

"Seven years. Seven years for you," Vernon says, punching at the water that reaches to his thighs as he wades awkwardly toward Sandy.

"I'm sorry, Vernon. I am," Sandy says.

"Fuck him, honey," Margie says from the bank, keeping abreast of Sandy. "If he gets close to you, I'm going to shoot him. I am."

"Margie, no," Sandy says.

The muzzle of Margie's gun follows Vernon's slow progress.

"Seven years because of you," Vernon says. "Seven years and all you can come up with is 'I was waiting for something else'? Damn you to hell."

"I'm sorry."

"Your 'sorry' will rot in hell along with you."

Vernon slips again, slashing at the surface as he tries to right himself.

Sandy stops. She looks quickly behind her, then darts her eyes back to Vernon, who is up and again approaching. Her knees bend and she sets her feet. She frees her fly and begins to peel line from her reel, resuming her downstream retreat, raising her rod and beginning to cast out line. As she casts, she veers gradually toward the center of the river, and Vernon, thirty yards upstream, matches her course. Keeping her false casts to the right of Vernon, she gauges the distance of her line and listens for the current breaking around the huge rock in the center of the deep hole behind her. She feels the heel of her boot slide onto the ledge at the edge of the pool and stops, setting herself, feeling the weight of the trout in the pouch on her back. Vernon advances down the middle of the stream, his clothing clinging and sodden with river water, and Sandy cocks her arm into her back cast, waits a second, then shoots her line forward in a tight loop. Her fly has just hissed past Vernon's ear when she stops her cast with a jerk and yanks back, raking the hook of the fly through the scalp on Vernon's left temple.

"Damn you," he screams, flinching and pressing his hand onto the wound on the side of his head.

"Holy shit," Margie says from the bank.

Sandy does not hear Margie's voice. She says nothing. She is focused on her target as she continues her backward course, following the perimeter of the hole, moving almost imperceptibly toward the far bank where Margie watches, her pistol still tracking Vernon. The ledge around the hole curves back toward the center of the river, and Sandy follows it, working her way to the tail of the hole, feeding her line out in another series of casts as Vernon nears the head of the deep pool. Sandy shoots another cast, dead on target for Vernon's nose, and he ducks, evading her fly and slipping from the ledge into the hole.

Vernon drops from sight, completely submerged in the pool, then shoots through the surface, gasping, cursing, flapping desperately under the weight of his water-logged clothing. His arms flailing, he beats his way upstream through the slow current far enough to regain his footing in the shallower water above the hole.

"I'm going to kill you," he says through clenched teeth.

Along the bank, Margie matches Sandy's downstream progress and shouts.

"Vernon, I'll shoot. I swear I will."

"No, Margie," Sandy says, and moves further around the edge of the pool. When Vernon begins to follow, matching at the head of the pool her movements at the tail of the pool, she draws him into a cat-and-mouse game, reversing her course, back and forth, keeping the deep pool between them, keeping Vernon near the head of the pool in the center of the stream. When she sees the wall of water begin to rise around the bend upstream from the end of the path where Stink lies in the long grass, she begins to send her line out again. Her casts are long and loose, sailing over the pool, keeping Vernon on guard, all his attention on the encroaching hook on the end of her line. Sandy times the approaching torrent and shoots a final cast at Vernon, clipping his ear as she jerks her line back; Vernon loses his footing again. Smacking angrily at the water, Vernon struggles to regain his footing, as Sandy skirts the edge of the deep pool and wades rapidly toward Margie on the far bank, reeling in her line as she moves.

Vernon regains his feet, clenches his fists, twists his mouth into a tortured snarl, just as the rising flood hits his back and washes him face first into the deepening hole before him. Two steps from Margie and the bank, the surging water hits Sandy and knocks her forward. One hand clutches a fistful of the long grass that is now sinking beneath the swollen current, the other holds tightly to her rod. Margie sloshes into the rising water, grabbing the arm that holds the rod, and tugs Sandy up to the bank above the current. The moment Sandy is secure, they both turn back to the churning river as Vernon surfaces. His arms appear first, flapping frantically, followed by his face, visible only from the nose up. His hair is plastered to his forehead. Bobbing in the enraged current like a plastic bottle, he thrusts his head out of the rushing water, and inhales a single, desperate gasp of air before the torrent slams his head against the craggy surface of the boulder at the center of the deep hole.

Sandy lies on her side, rigid, barely breathing, watching the river, the fringe of the current slapping at the toes of her boots. Margie sinks to her knees, and exhales slow and long.

"Holy shit."

Flopping at the end of a limp neck, Vernon's head bounces across the craggy surface of the exposed rock, as the current twists and rolls his body over the submerged edges of stone and shoots it face down into the main current, drifting toward the next bend on the roiling skin of the rolling flood.

Margie jams her pistol into her vest pocket and pulls Sandy to her feet. Her rod is still clutched in her hand, her body still rigid, her breath coming in short, shallow bursts. Margie holds her upright, an arm around her waist, as they watch Vernon's body float away.

"Holy shit," Margie says and turns her face to Sandy's stony visage. "Girl, I always loved you. But now, I goddamn respect you."

Margie's words are punctuated by a short bark from the opposite side of the surging river. Stink is sitting up in the long grass. A smear of blood is visible along his jaw line and down his neck.

"Stink," Sandy says, barely able to gasp out the syllable.

He barks once more, turns, and waddles slowly up the path toward their house.

A shiver runs up the length of Sandy's body. She drops her rod onto the grassy bank. A wrenching, rasping groan shakes her torso, and she sinks against Margie, collapsing both women onto the bank. The hard parts inside Sandy crack open, and she breaks into convulsed, unrestrained weeping, gasping for breath as her lungs suck desperately for the air to feed her crying. Margie gathers Sandy onto her damp breast, pulling her close, enclosing her friend's wet, shuddering body in her thick, sturdy arms.

"There now," she says, petting Sandy's head and back. "There now, baby. There now. Tell Margie everything. Let it out. Tell me everything."

The October sun rides above the gorge of the lower Ripshin, flaming the face of Rogers Ridge in garish autumn brilliance. And as the sun moves the day from morning to midday and on into afternoon, the two women sit, one exhausted, emptied and crumbled in the strong arms of the other, waiting for the raging waters to recede. Sandy cries and talks and cries and tells Margie everything, dumping the pent-up weight of all that the last seven years had left piled in her like a truckload of old tractor tires. She tells Margie everything, scraping clean the encrusted interior of her trout-fired heart. And Margie holds her, rocks her, through the afternoon until, as the sun begins to dip into the ridge behind Sandy's house, J.D. and Keefe appear at the end of the path. And Margie still holds Sandy close, not releasing her for a moment, as she calls across the river, telling J.D. and Keefe what they need to know in order to do what they must do. She keeps Sandy pressed tight to her while the two men listen, then walk back up the path to call the authorities and check on Stink, as the siren at the dam upstream signals that the turbines are being shut down and the flood choked back behind the dam for the night. By the time other sirens can be heard shrieking down Willard Road, Sandy sits with her head on Margie's shoulder, each of them smoking a soggy cigarette, but Margie keeps one arm firmly around Sandy. Across the river, Keefe appears again at the end of the path and begins to rock on his feet under his brown fedora, watching and smoking a cigarette in the fading light, while J.D. waits for the approaching sirens out on the road. Through the trees the sirens shut off and the vehicles screech to a halt as the torrent dissipates, and the surface of the Ripshin River settles back into its more tranquil flow. Margie lifts Sandy to her feet, picks up their rods and places Sandy's in her hand. With vest pouches heavy with fish, Margie locks her arm around Sandy's waist and leads her through the quiet water toward the far bank and Keefe and J.D. and Stink and home.

And Become
Undisguised and Naked

Sandy stands concealed at the edge of the trees. The night is unusually mild and warm for the end of October. A thin film of perspiration coats the skin on her bare neck, the feather hanging from her ear brushing over it. She raises binoculars with one cracked lens to her eyes and watches J.D.'s government SUV bounce on its springs in the distance.

Word of what had happened at the end of the path from Sandy's house had spread rapidly around Damascus, the Ripshin Valley, and most of the Rogers Ridge watershed. A man had died in the raging waters of the Ripshin River, his death witnessed by two women, that nurse who had moved into Calvin Linkous's house on Willard Road at the end of the spring and a friend of hers who was visiting from out of town. The dead man, who had been released from prison just the day before after serving time for a violent crime and who was the ex-husband of that nurse, had gone for the two women, tried to attack them, apparently, but had been caught unaware by the rising waters of the lower Ripshin when the hydroelectric dam had begun to generate power and release water. The man had been drowned and washed downstream. The two women survived. The story made sense. There were no serious questions or doubts about the course of the events. There was no mention of a gun.

As Sandy and Margie stood wrapped in blankets, describing what had occurred and answering questions in the strobing flash of the lights on the cruisers and ambulances, Sandy felt the presence of Keefe's eyes on her. He stood to the side of the crowd, under his fedora, beside J.D. Callander and Tommy Akers, who had stopped again to see what all the fuss was about, and Sandy knew that Keefe knew. The authorities could interpret the evidence at the scene. It was immediately clear to them. The two women, through quick thinking and good fortune, had eluded their assailant. It was obvious. Keefe's eyes peered from under his fedora, calm and kind. He knew. He understood. Sandy had killed Vernon. She had played him like a trout, lured him into position to receive the full force of the oncoming wall of water. Vernon had come for her, as he said he would, and she had met him face to face, as she said she would. And she had killed him intentionally, with calculation, precision, and skill. She had killed him even more deliberately than Vernon had the red-haired man in the bar seven years ago. She was a killer, and Keefe knew it. And he understood it. He accepted it. He admired her for it. Killer to killer. He might even have loved her for it.

Vernon's white van was found sitting in Sandy's driveway, and his body was found the next morning, a mile downstream, bobbing face down in the current. His feet were snagged in the massive roots of a fallen sycamore, his legs snapped at the knees, his clothing saturated and torn. A small clot of men, gathered at the gas pumps at the Citgo in Damascus, listened as one man told that he had heard one of the murderer's eyes was missing, had been eaten right out of his face. A man with a shaved head and a camouflage cap stood nearby, pumping gas into his orange Camaro and listening, his face tight-lipped and grim.

When he heard the stories going around about what had occurred, a young man wearing an Atlanta Braves cap muttered, "Humph. Women fishing. Figures."

Stink had been found bloody and whimpering inside his tractor tire. He'd been stunned and his jaw broken when Vernon clubbed him. The veterinarian who set and wired Stink's jaw back into place assured Sandy that he'd recover completely, that dogs were remarkably resilient. He'd need to be put on soft food during his recovery and would hurt and move a bit slower for a while, but he'd be fine in no time.

The other nurses and nurses' aides at work still viewed Sandy from a distance, as they always had. But now, they no longer thought of her with disdain as the aloof, "cold fish." Once the history of the events got around, they gazed at her with awe, a woman for whom two men had died. They feared her and admired her. Some of them wished that they were a woman for whom a man would kill, for whom a man would die.

The day before Vernon's body was buried in a small ceremony in Dalton's Ferry, his mother had called Sandy at work. Sandy had stood calmly at the nurses' station and listened silently to her former mother-in-law's voice crack in the phone, screaming, calling her a whore, blaming her for her innocent son's demise, and summoning down the wrath of God on Sandy and all who came within her orbit. Sandy said nothing. She let the woman wail uninterrupted for two minutes, then hung up. But before she left work that day, Sandy sat by the window with Edith Moser, watching the sun set as the old woman patted her hand and stroked her short hair.

A few days after Vernon's body was recovered, Keefe had insisted that Sandy come to his cabin along the headwaters of the upper Ripshin. They ate a simple lunch Keefe had prepared for them and shared a cigarette.

After lunch, Keefe reached into a box behind the cracked leather sofa, produced his wet suit, and told her to change in the bathroom. He sat on a rock overlooking the wide pool in front of his bungalow, following the course of fallen leaves on the surface of the current and watching Sandy, lying belly-down in the pool, breathing through Keefe's long snorkel. She sank for an hour into the dense, subsurface silence of the flow of the upper Ripshin, gazed into the depths of the pool and waited for the frightened brook trout to begin to stir from their hiding places, their ivory-tipped, orange-bellied bodies flickering at the edges of the pool, accepting her odd presence as a threat no longer, simply an alteration in the streambed to which they apparently must adjust. As the current pushed against her, she felt her guilt lift from her submerged body and rise to the surface, collecting like an eddy of stagnant film to be washed down the slope, broken apart and shredded on the rocks of the riverbed, flushed away and useless. She breathed a long, rattling column of air through the snorkel and let it go, casting it off as a foolish indulgence to feel guilty for doing one thing when there was absolutely no other thing she could have done. She rose out of the water and waded to Keefe on the rock. Keefe dipped his fingers into his shirt pocket and pulled out what looked like a more colorful and delicate version of a Gray Ghost streamer, long, feathery, and delicate. The hook had been cut off, and a thin, gold jewelry hook dangled from the eye of the fly.

"I tied this for you," Keefe had said, handing it to her. "Thought maybe you might need something to replace the one you lost that night."

Sandy removed the stud from her scarred left ear lobe, handed it to Keefe, and hung the new earring from the new hole in her ear.

"Thank you, James," she had said, and leaned over and kissed him lightly on his stubbled cheek.

Soon after Vernon had washed down the lower Ripshin, Margie had decided to take the job at Sherwood Regional, move down here with her boys, and push ahead full steam with J.D. He liked her and she liked him and the boys liked him and life was "just too goddamn short to fuck around and waste time." Over the last two days, she and Sandy had looked for a place and found a decent duplex, just the other side of Damascus, that would work just fine for her and the boys until she and J.D. thought it would be all right with the boys if they moved in together. She'd spent the days house hunting with Sandy, keeping an eye on her friend to be sure she was holding up. She spent the nights with J.D. She'd laughed when she told Sandy that they'd driven out to the hatchery because J.D. was anxious and wanted to stake out the place, make sure his killer didn't return and foul up his plans for the last scheduled stocking of the season. Margie had laughed harder when she told Sandy how his stake out ended up having more to do with sex than surveillance.

"What the hell," Margie had said. "If we're going to sit out there half the night, watching for his little fish killer, might as well have some fun, right? You know, I never did it in a car when I was in high school. Did it most everyplace else, but never in a car. Always felt like I missed out on something."

J.D.'s SUV settles down. The windows are steamed over. A door opens and Margie steps down from the vehicle. Her blouse disheveled, her slacks already undone, she walks behind it, squats, and pees. J.D. sits in the front seat and wipes the condensation from the inside of the windshield. When Margie returns to the SUV, she leans over to J.D., kisses him, and says something to him. He nods, turns the ignition key, and Margie closes her door. The headlights of the dark green SUV slash into the darkness, illuminating for a moment six pens of hatchling trout, before the car turns out onto the gravel lane and rolls away from the dark, abandoned hatchery.

Sandy brings the broken binoculars down from her eyes and smiles as she watches J.D. and Margie disappear down the road. She reaches

258

behind her and flips the ignition switch on the shock pack, feeling the whirring of the motor through her back.

Glancing quickly toward the hatchery manager's house to be sure no lights have come on, she grips the cathode wand, holding it out before her like a fly rod, and advances on the pens of trough-bred trout.

*　*　*

After she has secured the shock pack in its bag in the cave on the hillside behind the bungalow, Sandy walks up the steps of the porch, enters Keefe's cabin, and drops her waders behind the sofa. He is standing at the fireplace, barefoot, stirring the last faltering flames, letting the fire burn down for the night. He turns to her, the look on his face a question waiting to be answered. Stink is curled up on one end of the sofa, snoring. He looks up for a moment through half-opened eyes when Sandy enters, then drops back off to sleep.

"It went fine," Sandy said. "Worked just like you said it would. Had to wait for J.D. and Margie to leave. They were there again."

"Poor J.D.," Keefe says. "Maybe we should stop this. I'm beginning to feel a little guilty. I hate putting the boy through this."

"If something's got to be done, then it's got to be done," Sandy says.

She reaches over the back of the sofa and scratches Stink gently behind his ears. Her fingertips pat lightly over the shaved, rough skin of his jowls where the wires that secured his jaw had protruded. Satisfied that her dog continues to heal properly, she walks through the cabin to the bedroom. Keefe leans against the mantle over the fireplace, his eyes following her. In a minute Sandy reappears. She has removed her socks, and the top three buttons of her shirt are undone.

"I'm tired," she says. "It's been a long night. Let's go to bed."

Keefe stands away from the mantle and turns slowly to Sandy.

"I'm easily old enough to be your father," he says.

Tim Poland

Sandy undoes the remaining buttons on her shirt and lets it fall open. Her skin flickers in the firelight.

"Yes, and that would make me young enough to be your daughter," she says. "What's your point?"

* * *

Sandy Holston and James Keefe stand together on the riverbank. The waters of the upper Ripshin are low, clearer than crystal and dotted with fallen leaves, glimmering faintly in the autumn light as they spread smoothly over the deeper pools and churn through the chutes and over the rocks, carving their course down the slope. The maples have given up their leaves and stand bare, naked branches clicking in the breeze. The oaks and ashes and alders still hold tightly to their final flashes of fading red and dull brown. Stink lifts his leg over a scrawny rhododendron, looks briefly at Sandy and Keefe, then waddles across the clearing, up the steps of the cabin, and through the open door.

Keefe lodges the urn securely in the crook of his arm and opens his book. Sandy rests her rod on her shoulder, glances across the open pages in Keefe's hand, then raises her eyes to the flowing water as Keefe reads.

They are alive and well somewhere,
The smallest sprout shows there is really no death,
And if ever there was it led forward life, and does not wait
    at the end to arrest it,
And ceas'd the moment life appear'd.

All goes onward and outward, nothing collapses,
And to die is different from what any one supposed,
    and luckier.

Keefe closes his book and hands it to Sandy. He steps from the bank into the cool current and wades to the center of the pool. Opening the urn, Keefe retrieves a pinch of his wife's remains and sprinkles the ash onto the surface of the stream, adding the final, crucial spice in a delicate and complicated recipe. The pinch of ash swirls and spreads around Keefe's legs and washes past him. Sandy remains on the bank, calm and still, holding her rod and the book, watching him, feeling the dense fiber of his stubborn grief shoot across the pool and split into thousands of strands, encircling for one taut moment the clearing, the cabin, the river, Sandy, and the entire watershed in the web of his old and fading pain. For that one moment the web quivers in the morning breeze before the strands snap into a million tiny specks and wash down the river like scattered ash. Keefe bows his head, holds his chin pressed to his chest, breathes deeply, and upends the urn, pouring out a smoky stream of ash into the waiting waters of the upper Ripshin.

Sandy picks up Keefe's rod from the ground beside her and exchanges it for the empty urn when Keefe wades to the bank. He returns to the center of the pool, lifts his rod, and slices the autumn morning with his elegant, simple casts. The second cast brings a brook trout to his fly, and Keefe draws the fish to hand. He kneels in the stream, frees the trout from his hook, and holds the small fish lovingly in the cupped palm of his hand. He runs a finger once over the blue-green back and once along the blazing orange belly, pushes a long, deep breath from his lungs, and releases the brook trout back into the pool.

Keefe holds his rod at his side and wades out of the pool. Sandy takes his hand in hers and draws him from the water onto the bank. His hand stays in hers for a moment, and they stand together, listening to the rush of the flowing waters.

"What about the next part?" Sandy asks, handing him the book.

Keefe takes the book, looks at it, and turns his face to Sandy, a gentle grin cutting across his craggy face.

"Of course. Why not?" he says, and opens the book.

It is for my mouth forever, I am in love with it,
I will go to the bank by the wood and become undisguised
*   and naked,*
I am mad for it to be in contact with me.

Sandy hears the rhythm of the river, unbroken, in his voice.

Sunlight shaves the top of the ridge above the river gorge. A kingfisher clacks as it alights in the branches of a sycamore, and Sandy Holston and James Keefe drop their clothes in a heap on the river bank. The crisp autumn air licks their bodies to life, thrusting its tongue beneath their skin, lapping at their tingling blood and flesh, lifting them from the bank to the flowing, trout-lush water. Sandy fingers her earring, takes Keefe's hand and presses it in her own. His hand returns the pressure.

"It'll be cold," Keefe says.

"Yes, it will be," Sandy says.

Naked, but for Sandy's feathery earring and Keefe's brown fedora, they wade together into the pool. Stink lumbers from the cabin, hobbles across the clearing, and sits watching from the bank beside the pile of clothes, the book, and the empty urn. At the middle of the stream, Sandy and Keefe release each other's hands and move apart into casting position. Their rods rise in an easy, shared rhythm. Their casts are precise and deft, knowing. On a common beat pulsing between two bodies, their lines loop through the air, hover a moment, and fall gently into place on the seams of the fanning current, a lure and an offering to the trout rising through the waters rippling around them.

The Safety of Deeper Water

Tim Poland grew up in Ohio and now lives and works in the New River Valley near the Blue Ridge Mountains in southwestern Virginia. He is the author of *Escapee* (America House, 2001), a collection of short fiction, and *Other Stones, Kinder Temples* (Pudding House, 2008), a chapbook of poems. His fiction, poetry, and essays have appeared widely in various literary journals. He is the recipient of a Plattner/ *Appalachian Heritage* Award (2002). His work has been included in the *Best of the Net* anthology (2007) and has also been nominated for a Pushcart Prize. He is a professor of English at Radford University in Radford, Virginia.